ROGUE
TROOPER
the quartz massacre

Rogue Trooper is a Genetic Infantryman, or GI, bred to fight in the galaxy's deadliest war zones. When Rogue's brothers-in-arms are ambushed at the Quartz Zone Massacre, he vows to get revenge on the traitor general who sold them out. With three of his comrades stored as sentient life-chips in his rifle, helmet and backpack, Rogue must go through hell if he is to avenge his fallen comrades.

Experience the battlefield at first-hand in this action-packed novelization of the hot new Eidos game.

More Rogue Trooper from Black Flame

CRUCIBLE
Gordon Rennie

BLOOD RELATIVE
James Swallow

More 2000 AD action from Black Flame

ABC Warriors

THE MEDUSA WAR
Pat Mills & Alan Mitchell

RAGE AGAINST THE
MACHINES
Mike Wild

Durham Red

THE UNQUIET GRAVE
Peter J Evans

THE OMEGA SOLUTION
Peter J Evans

THE ENCODED HEART
Peter J Evans

MANTICORE REBORN
Peter J Evans

Fiends of the Eastern Front

OPERATION VAMPYR
David Bishop

Nikolai Dante

THE STRANGELOVE GAMBIT
David Bishop

IMPERIAL BLACK
David Bishop

HONOUR BE DAMNED!
David Bishop

Strontium Dog

BAD TIMING
Rebecca Levene

PROPHET MARGIN
Simon Spurrier

RUTHLESS
Jonathan Clements

DAY OF THE DOGS
Andrew Cartmel

A FISTFUL OF STRONTIUM
Jaspre Bark & Steve Lyons

Rogue Trooper created by **Gerry Finley-Day**
and **Dave Gibbons**.

ROGUE TROOPER

THE QUARTZ MASSACRE

the quartz massacre

Rebecca Levene

BLACK FLAME

To Alan Trewartha for the help and Magnus Anderson for the enthusiasm – thanks!

A Black Flame Publication
www.blackflame.com

First published in 2006 by BL Publishing, Games Workshop Ltd., Willow Road, Nottingham NG7 2WS, UK.

Distributed in the US by Simon & Schuster, 1230 Avenue of the Americas, New York, NY 10020, USA.

10 9 8 7 6 5 4 3 2 1

Cover illustration by Ben Flynn and Mark Harrison.

ISBN 13: 978 1 84416 269-7
ISBN 10: 1-84416-269-9

A CIP record for this book is available from the British Library.

Printed in the UK by Bookmarque, Surrey, UK.

THE LEGEND OF THE ROGUE TROOPER

Nu Earth is a hellish, nightmare planet ravaged by war. The planet's atmosphere is devoid of life, poisoned by repeated chemical attacks and deadly to inhale. But the planet is close to a vital wormhole in space, a fact which has dragged its two rival factions - the Norts and the Southers - into a never-ending war. Now Nu Earth is a toxic, hell-blasted rock, where millions of soldiers in bio-suits wage bloody battles and die in their millions. Nu Earth is too important to lose. Not an inch of ground can be lost!

Here is where the legend of Rogue Trooper was born. Created by Souther forces, Rogue Trooper is the sole surviving example of the Genetic Infantrymen: a regiment of soldiers grown in vats and bio-engineered to be the perfect killing machine. Complete with protective blue skin and the ability to breathe the venomous atmosphere, the Genetic Infantrymen became renowned figures on both sides of the conflict. Moreover, the mind and soul of the GI could be downloaded onto a silicon chip in case of a mortal wound on the battlefield. Once downloaded, the dog-chip could then be slotted into special equipment and preserved until the soldier could grace a newly grown body.

Betrayed by a general in their own high command, almost the entire regiment of GIs were wiped out in the Quartz Zone Massacre. The sole survivor managed to save just three chips from his former comrades and slot them into his gun, helmet and backpack. Now he is a loner, with just the disembodied personalities of his comrades for company, roaming the chemical wasteland in search of revenge: the Rogue Trooper.

PROLOGUE

Rogue's first memory was of battle. The combatants were only two weeks out of the artificial wombs, barely five years old by normal standards, but they fought with all the ferocity and relentless will to win of real soldiers.

The Gene Genies, the genetic engineers who were the only parents Rogue had ever known, had divided the batch of children into two. They'd given Rogue's group red bands to wear around their heads, and the other group was given green. Then the little boys received sticks and were told that if any of the other group was left standing at the end of the game, they'd be going without supper that evening. "Pretend they're Norts," the Gene Genies said.

Standing at the side of the limb-flailing, squealing free-for-all that followed, one of the nutritionists assigned to the youngsters by Souther High Command said, "Oh, they're so cute, aren't they?"

Beside her, the Gene Genie in charge of training frowned and tugged at the hem of his long white coat. "We didn't design them to be cute. We designed them to kill."

Rogue didn't know what he was called back then, or what made him and his brothers so special, but he knew that the Gene Genie was right. He'd been born to fight.

By the time Rogue's body resembled that of a twelve year-old human – apart from the blue skin, which marked him out forever as something else – Rogue knew exactly what he was. He was a Genetic Infantryman, a GI, and he'd been designed as a secret weapon by the South Side, the good side, in their ongoing war against the evil, untrustworthy, cruel and cowardly Norts.

Rogue leaned against the cold metal of the bulwark and stared at the blue-green mass of the planet below. This space station, Milli-Com, was the only world he'd ever known. He'd never known what it was like to feel real earth beneath his feet, or real grass; he'd never basked in the sun under a wide blue sky, or listened to the cheeps and rustles and roars of a land filled with life. And he never would. When his training was complete, he wouldn't be sent down to the world below. He'd be sent to Nu Earth, the most important theatre of the whole vast war, the world guarding the black hole which was the central nexus of the subspace shipping routes.

He had never set foot on Nu Earth, either, but he knew that there was no grass there. The sky wasn't blue. It roiled yellow with the chem clouds that killed anyone who breathed them; anyone besides him and his fellow GIs. That was one of the many things that made them so special. Rogue peered down at the jewel-like planet one last time and wished for a moment that he was less special and more normal.

"You're supposed to be at weapons practice," a voice interrupted his thoughts. It was the trainee that the Gene Genies called Trooper B12, and whom Rogue and his fellow GIs had nicknamed Bagman.

"So should you," Rogue said.

Bagman grinned. "Old Kinsey's running the session. He never takes roll call. And it's not like he can tell us apart. Advantage of being clones."

"So what are you sneaking off for?" Rogue asked. "Need some extra time to pack your kit?"

Bagman rolled his eyes at a joke he'd heard many times before. It was how he'd got his nickname: his disproportionate attachment to the semi-automated kitbag that all the GIs had been issued when they were ten. The rest of them hated the things, the extra weight they had to carry from then on through every training drill. But Bagman spent endless hours sorting through his, making sure everything was there in the right order, that the auto-dispensing arm was oiled and fully functioning, the nano-manufacturer fully charged. "These things are great," he would say. "They don't just carry equipment, they make it. Feed 'em battlefield scrap and they can make you a micro-mine or a med kit or even a Sammie out of it." The others always sighed – they knew this already – and rolled their eyes whenever Bagman finished, as he always did, "A GI's best friend is his bag."

"It'll be your only friend if you carry on that way," Gunnar usually muttered, but Bagman didn't mind.

Bagman looked at Rogue, as if wondering whether he could be trusted, then seemed to decide that he could. He lowered his voice to a soft hiss which drifted sibilantly down the echoing metal corridors of the station. "It's that door."

Rogue frowned. "The emergency airlock?"

Bagman lowered his voice even further, leaning right in until his mouth was nearly against Rogue's ear, his eyes darting nervously to left and right. "They say it's an airlock. But if it's just an airlock, why won't they let us anywhere near it?"

Rogue said loud enough to make Bagman wince, "Because if we go outside it we'll be in a vacuum, and even we can't survive that."

Bagman smiled pityingly at him. "You go on believing that, Rogue, if it makes you happy."

• • •

Training carried on.

They'd started guns at year ten, and now they were on to heavy armaments, the Sammies, which could take out a Nort Hoppa from a hundred yards (if the Hoppa hadn't taken you out first). Gunnar found his name, and a place right at the peak of the GIs hierarchy, when he proved to be an almost preternaturally accurate marksman.

Trooper H14 excelled at hacking, infiltration, all the skills the others disdained. "A trooper's most important asset is under his helmet," he told them when they laughed at him for sitting hunched for hours over his terminal during downtime, learning the intricacies of Nort technical specs. They started calling him Helm, of course.

Rogue wasn't a specialist like Gunnar or Bagman, but as a tactician he was second to none, the trooper who could lead a battle simulation and win it every time. Bagman went on polishing his kit, and staring at the emergency airlock door, wondering.

The Gene Genies began to mutter, when they thought the GIs couldn't hear, that something must have gone wrong with the cloning programme, that some element of individuality had crept in that was never meant to be there. They refused to use the names the troopers had given themselves, sticking resolutely to G12, or I04, or R13, and punishing any GI who was caught calling themselves anything else. The GIs didn't care. They carried on using their names anyway, when they were on their own. And they continued to grow more different, more individual, as if nature's evolutionary urge was working with all its might against the homogenising force of the cloning programme.

Only Rogue felt like he didn't have an identity yet. He had a name, but he was never quite sure why the others had given it to him. He felt like he still had to grow into it, to earn it – just as Gunnar had striven ever harder to master his weapons training once that was what he was known for, the one thing which made him unique.

Then one night, long after curfew, Rogue heard one of the other GIs stirring in his sleep, twisting round in his steel bunk bed, then climbing out and creeping out of the sleeping chamber. On an impulse he couldn't quite explain, he chose not to report him to the Gene Genies as he should have, nor to ignore him and go back to sleep, as any of the other GIs would have, but to get up and follow.

Rogue paused a minute at the door to look back at the others, checking that they hadn't been disturbed, and for a moment he was struck by how orderly they looked, row after row on top of each other in their metal beds like pupae in a honeycomb.

Outside the room, the corridor was deserted, the dark form of the GI Rogue was following only visible as a black blot in the dim red nighttime lighting. Rogue didn't have any trouble recognising him. The slight swagger in his shoulder, the looseness with which he swung his legs, told Rogue that it was Bagman.

So he wasn't surprised when the other GI stopped in front of the emergency airlock door. Nor was he surprised when Bagman turned around and said, "You can stop creeping, Rogue. I know you're there."

"What are you doing, Bagman?" Rogue asked, drawing level with the other GI at the airlock.

Bagman folded his arms over his chest, stubbornly, as if he expected resistance. "I'm going in," he said.

"You know that's a bad idea, right?" Rogue asked, glancing into the darkness at the ends of the corridor, seeking any sign that they'd been observed. He didn't find any. Something about the quality of the air, the gentle hum of machinery idling in neutral, told him that they were the only beings awake on the station.

Bagman shrugged. "What's the worst they can do?" Before Rogue could tell him that they could throw them both in the brig, maybe even flunk them out of the whole GI programme, Bagman twisted the big metal wheel on the front of the door and flung it open.

It wasn't an airlock. Bagman had been right about that. For a moment, they couldn't see exactly what it was, their view of the room behind the door obscured by the thick green-yellow fog which filled it from floor to ceiling. Rogue hesitated, reluctant to walk on blindly, but Bagman strode straight into the fog as if finding this strange hidden chamber was the most normal thing in the world. Rogue walked after him. His eyes squinted into the fog, but the swirling mass of it deceived him, making him see solid shapes where there was nothing but air.

Except, he realised, some of the shapes were solid. And they were moving closer.

It's just the Gene Genies, Rogue told himself. This is probably some sort of test, and we've just failed it.

But whatever the figures were, they weren't Gene Genies. Their skin was nearly the same colour as the fog from which they were emerging, a toxic green that looked far more unnatural than Rogue's own blue. Their faces were bubbled and boiled away, great folds of flesh on one side and bare bone on the other.

They looked like the victims of some horrible industrial accident, but on top of their heads was the same thin strip of white hair that sat atop Rogue's own.

"They're GIs!" said Bagman, his voice thick with revulsion.

"Yeah," Rogue said softly. "Genetic rejects. I guess the Gene Genies didn't manage to make us straight off. They had to experiment first."

Bagman couldn't tear his eyes away from the freaks. The mutant GIs seemed equally fascinated with them. One of them stepped forward, head tipped to the side so that its good eye was almost level with Rogue's. "Brudder?" it said hesitantly. "Thought we only GIs. Waiting here. Waiting to be used. But now you here, you GIs too." Its voice was mushy and awkward, as if its mouth wasn't made quite right on the inside.

"Yeah," Rogue said, grabbing Bagman's arm and dragging him backwards towards the airlock door. "We're GIs too, just like you."

The mutant smiled, the expression distorting its face still further till it looked hardly human at all.

Another mutant, larger than the first, stepped up beside it. "But so different," it said. "Why you so different to we?"

Subtly, the atmosphere changed, and the creatures which had seemed so pitiable a moment ago suddenly seemed threatening, dangerous. Rogue became uncomfortably aware that the mutants were nearly twice the size of him and Bagman, and that neither of them had thought to bring their weapons, an unforgivable oversight for a GI. Rogue knew that they had to get out of there.

But it was too late. The lead mutant's face lit with sudden, angry understanding. "They normal, like creators!" it said. "They replace us, brudders!"

"No!" the other mutant shouted. "We only GIs! We still needed! You not take our place!"

An arm lashed out, faster than Rogue would have believed possible, to catch Bagman across the side of his face, and the other GI went down with nothing more than a soft grunt of pain.

Rogue saw Bagman's death, and his own, in the mutant's one good eye.

The Gene Genies would have been proud of him. Without thought or hesitation, he lashed out at his enemy, aiming instinctively for its most vulnerable area. His thumb hookied into its eye socket, reached in and gouged out.

The mutant gave a terrible, high-pitched scream of agony, and while it was still reeling from the shock, Rogue slung Bagman over his shoulder and ran.

Bagman and Rogue never spoke to each other or to anyone else about what they'd seen, but Rogue saw a change in his friend after that. Where before his humour had come from a light-hearted, uncaring place, it now seemed to come from somewhere darker. He worked harder, too, striving to excel in everything they learnt. The Gene Genies were delighted: it seemed to them that one of the weakest of the squad had suddenly found his fighting spirit. But Rogue knew why Bagman was really trying so hard, why his jokes were so barbed. Every day, he lived in fear that he'd fail, that the Gene Genies would find him as obsolete as the mutants hidden behind the airlock, and he'd be sent to live there with them, waiting forever for a call which would never come.

Bagman feared this, but Bagman didn't know what Rogue knew. When Rogue had emerged through the mutants' airlock door with Bagman slung unconscious over his shoulders, it had been to find the Gene Genies waiting for them.

They were furious – and they were scared. First, they forbade Rogue to speak of what he'd seen. Then, with Rogue watching, they jettisoned the lab holding the mutants from the station. When it was free, floating in space, they blew it up.

"We made it detachable as a contingency," one of the Gene Genies told him coldly. "Perhaps we should have done this long ago. Erased our mistakes." The Genie's icy blue eyes bored into Rogue's, making sure he understood every implication of his words.

And Rogue did. He knew then why the Genies would never use their names. They didn't want to see the GIs as people, because people weren't expendable, and the GIs were.

After that, Rogue kept as close an eye as he could on what their trainers were doing and saying, and made sure to pass every test with flying colours. He did what he could to help his friends do the same.

The training got harder each year. When they were thirteen, military prisoners, deserters scheduled for execution, were shipped over to Milli-Com from one of the many battlefields of the war. The prisoners were given knives and told that if they could kill one of the GIs, they could walk free. The GIs weren't armed.

The other GIs weren't scared. They'd been told often enough that they were the best of the best, superhuman, a match for ten ordinary men, but Rogue was wary. He knew that a knife could kill, in anyone's hand.

One of the GIs lost an ear; another had the tough tendons in his knee severed. Both injuries could have been healed, cloned flesh regrown, but the troopers were flunked out of the programme. Rogue never saw them again.

When he saw a knife plunging towards his own chest, he ducked under the swinging blade to bring himself out behind his opponent's head, a great hulking man with ebony skin and a desperate expression on his face. Then Rogue took the man's head in his hands and snapped.

It was his first kill. The Gene Genies told the GIs they were real soldiers. They said that they'd grow to love the kill, that there was no feeling like the feeling of ridding the universe of one more filthy Nort. Rogue didn't think that this was something he'd ever grow to love, but he could already tell that it was something he was good at.

When they were fifteen, they met the Dolls for the first time. The Gene Genies must have been keeping them on some other satellite base, away from the GIs and their all-too-human adolescent hormones. For some reason, they had decided that the time was right for the GIs to meet their female counterparts.

The GIs were lined up, standing at attention, then the Dolls marched in. Rogue felt something like a collective indrawn breath from his fellow troopers. They'd seen women before, of course; many of the Milli-Com personnel were female, but they'd never seen women who were like *them* before: blue skin, white hair, muscles bulging beneath their standard military-issue jerkins.

They were clones, just like the GIs. And just like the GIs, they couldn't have been more different from one another. Rogue spotted her straightaway, the Doll he'd later learn called herself Venus Bluegenes. They all had names like that, names with a sense of humour, creative names that they must have spent some time thinking up. It made Rogue slightly ashamed of the unimaginative names the GIs had all given themselves.

The Gene Genies told them that the Dolls were strictly support personnel. They were getting weapons training as a precaution, nothing more. But Rogue looked at the way the Dolls handled their guns, so competently, and the ease with which they passed every test, and he wondered. He looked at Venus in particular. The way she smiled with just half her mouth, as if smiling too much would reveal secrets she wasn't willing to share. The way her eyebrows curved over her eyes like question marks. The way she walked.

Helm caught him looking. "She's mine," he said, one hand clasped to the hilt of his belt knife in a threatening gesture that might or might not have been conscious.

Rogue laughed. "Don't think she belongs to anyone."

But Helm didn't find it funny. "I mean it," he said. "I like her, Rogue, and she likes me."

"In that case," Rogue said, "what have you got to worry about?"

After that, he stayed away from Venus. He didn't want to cause any trouble with Helm, who often seemed to be looking for a reason to pick a fight with Rogue. No one mocked Helm for his obsessions any more. All his knowledge, as he'd told them it would, had cohered over the years into a tactical mind that was second only to Rogue's. But that wasn't good enough for Helm. He wanted to be first. Rogue had no intention of ceding that position to him, though if letting him win Venus would keep Helm off his back, he was willing to do that.

Sometimes he'd catch Venus smiling at him, looking at him with considering eyes.

When they were eighteen, they graduated from "school" to full military drill. Gunnar loved it. He loved the smell of real ammunition, the mock battles they fought, the adrenaline surge. But he wasn't satisfied with war games, he wanted the real thing.

"When are we gonna see some action?" he asked. "I want to shoot something for real."

"They'll send us planetside soon enough," Rogue told him. "They didn't spend all these years training us just to let us stew in space."

But Gunnar didn't look satisfied. His white eyes were narrowed into angry slits, trying to see into a future where he'd be firing real guns into real enemies and spilling real blood.

When they were twenty, finally ready to face that future, Rogue discovered that for Gunnar it might never come.

"Computer reveals a slight instability," Rogue heard the Gene Genie say, and when he peered around the doorway he'd been leaning against, field-stripping his gun, he saw that the man was looking at Gunnar's file.

"Can't risk him in the field," said a second Gene Genie, one of the highest ranking on the station.

The first Gene Genie frowned. "Guess he'll have to stay on Milli-Com then," he said. "Talk about a waste of resources." Then they seemed to sense Rogue loitering outside and the door hissed shut on rusty hydraulics.

Rogue didn't tell Gunnar. How could he? He waited for the hammer to fall, and wondered how his friend would take it.

Weeks went by, nothing happened and it came to the day before their passing out ceremony. No official announcement had been made, though they knew through the sort of process of osmosis that seems to operate in all military establishments that they were due to ship out very soon. The blue-green planet that had hovered below them for all of Rogue's life had disappeared six weeks ago. Shortly after that, great shutters had been brought down over all the station's viewports. Milli-Com was on the move.

The satellite, stationary and hidden for so long, was finally heading for the heart of the war, taking its precious cargo with it. The GIs would soon see some real action.

Everyone tackled the routine drills, the monotonous training exercises and the endless equipment checks with renewed vigour. For years, the Gene Genies had told them not to slack off, not to grow bored, that one day their lives would depend on getting these things right. Finally, they really believed it.

There was a jittery, hopped-up atmosphere on the station. Everything, everyone, felt on the edge of violence. Gunnar's hand twitched constantly a few inches from the energy gun at his belt, itching to draw it. Bagman couldn't stop talking, as if terrified of what might come to fill any silence he left. Helm glared at Rogue whenever he was within ten feet of Venus, just waiting for an excuse.

Finally, from under their feet, subliminal but felt deeply , came the muted roar of the station's thrusters, bringing it to a halt at its final destination. The top brass arrived to witness this momentous event. An array of generals, medals they'd probably never earned glittering on their chests, paraded through the corridors that the GIs had thought of as their own. They watched the GIs train and they watched them fight and they watched them eat. Though they didn't say anything, Rogue tried as hard as he could to read their expressions and decided that they seemed pleased with the result of their long experiment.

When one of the generals walked into the room where Rogue, Gunnar and three of the others were reacquainting themselves with the digi-map of Nu Earth (though they'd memorised every hill and river long ago), Rogue thought that he didn't look so pleased. The general was a good-looking man, probably no older than forty, young to have reached his rank and with the look of smug satisfaction that went with that achievement. His eyes, a light grass green, glittered in the light of the halo-lamps overhead.

Rogue found that he didn't like him. Maybe that was because he'd guessed what the general had come to say.

The wall of the chamber was lined with canisters of gas toxins, all of which Rogue and the others had been exposed to at one time or another. A normal human would find them lethal, most within a matter of seconds. Rogue had found them no more than unpleasant. The worst they'd left him with was a tight itchy pain in the back of his throat.

"Trooper G," the general said, when they'd all snapped smartly to attention, "front and centre!"

Then, before he could say any more, the station juddered violently. The general was thrown to the floor with a loud gasp of shock and pain. The troopers tumbled to their knees, rifles leaping into their hands to face the threat.

"Asteroid storm! Asteroid storm!" the intercom blared out loudly, and the troopers relaxed, re-holstering their guns. The general began to climb back to his feet, his face sharp with annoyance to have had his dignity compromised in this way.

Then the second rock struck and the impact knocked one of the canisters of toxin from the wall.

Without conscious thought, Rogue flung himself towards it, but he was simply too far away. His fingers just brushed the edge of the metal frame as it struck the floor and the glass within it shattered.

The cloud of toxin it released was colourless. Rogue was only able to detect its presence by a faint tang of apple in the air, but the effect on the general was instant. His hands leapt to his throat, clasping it in agony as he let out a bubbling scream of pain and a pink froth erupted from his lips.

With cold, clinical detachment, Rogue thought: Agent PDP, death in three seconds. He saw Tank dive for the door and knew that he was heading for the chem masks, but no matter how quick he was, the general would never be able to mask-up in time. Rogue's mind working at speed, considering then rejecting possibilities. Blocking the general's airways, shooting a hole in the station's hull to let the gas out, breathing the clean air from his own lungs into the general's.

The general's face was already breaking out in the virulent red pustules of the toxin, the symptoms which had given it the nickname of the "polka-dot plague", when Rogue saw the answer. And the moment he saw it, he saw that it was the answer to another problem, too.

"Gunnar, shoot out the de-chem flasks!" he shouted. "All of them!"

Obeying orders was something else they'd all had drilled into them for longer than their memories went back, and while Rogue wasn't Gunnar's commanding officer, his unmatched tactical skill and combat abilities had earned him the other GI's respect. Gunnar didn't even hesitate – he just brought up his rifle and fired. The general was writhing in fear and pain, limbs flailing into the path of Gunnar's rounds, but not one of them hit him. There was no marksman among the GIs more accurate than Gunnar.

The deafening roar of rifle fire was soon joined by the sharp reports of glass vessels imploding. A second later, Rogue felt the cool rush of the antitoxin filling the room, and he saw the general's hands fall away from his face, where the vicious red welts were already fading. Strangely, the antitoxin had a far less pleasant smell than the toxin itself, something like the musty odour of a uniform that had been worn for a week, then left in a locker for a month.

Rogue saw the general's expression unclench as the man realised that he would live to preen another day. But when he looked at Gunnar, his green eyes filled with a venomous anger, as if the toxin had somehow seeped inside them.

An instant later the expression was gone, replaced by the general's usual deep self-satisfaction, and before Rogue could think about it further the doors of the room hissed open and the room became full of Gene Genies and GIs, clustering around the general with medpacs in hand and slapping Gunnar on the back. Rogue settled back onto his haunches, satisfied. Gunnar was the hero of the hour. There was no way he wouldn't be shipping out now.

Finally, the day came. The passing out parade and, more importantly, the mission briefing. The GIs stood in ranks, rigidly at attention under the glaring halo lamps high up in the vaulted ceiling of the Parade Ground, the vast central chamber of Milli-Com. The artificial gravity was weaker here, and Rogue could feel his feet trying to drift up from the floor, as if his body couldn't wait to fling itself into space and down to the planet's surface below.

"Men, this is it," General Aitchison said, his voice stuttering over the word "men" as if he wasn't quite sure it applied to the blue-skinned beings standing in front of him.

Rogue felt a collective sound, a hitching of breath, go through the men around him. He didn't shift his position, but his eyes flicked right and left, taking in the suddenly tense muscles of those around him, the fire in their eyes. He knew the same fire was burning in his own.

"You know why you were created, you know that you alone are capable of surviving on the surface of Nu Earth, the most crucial battle zone in the whole war. Now you will have the chance to prove yourselves. Are you ready for the challenge? Are you ready to show those Nort scum what real Southers are made of?"

Rogue and the GIs let out a full-throated roar, so loud the station seemed to shake with it. "Southside, South-side, Southside – yeah!"

The general took a step backwards, as if physically pushed by the wall of sound, but Rogue saw him smile. "For twenty years we've kept your existence secret for this very moment, the moment that will turn the tide of war for the South." Then, his voice dropped, as if he was confiding in each of the GIs individually, and the noise in the room dropped with it, every soldier strain-ing to hear his orders, to finally discover where and when his first taste of battle would come.

"Tomorrow night," the general said, "you will be dropped into the Quartz Zone. I'm sure I don't need to tell you the strategic importance of that area. Possess-ing that critical wedge would allow us to drive between the Nort Scum legions and the Thirteenth Army to the south. But the Norts have never defended that land. They believe that it is impenetrable, too toxic and too wild for any frontal assault."

The general studied the troopers in front of him, a fierce smile on his face. Beside him, the long thin line of high-ranking officers shifted and looked at each other, high on adrenaline. "They're wrong," he said. "You men will take the Quartz Zone. Unprepared, the Nort defences will crumble. And then you'll spearhead the drive that will finally take the whole continent."

Gunnar grinned fiercely. "Those Norts won't know what's hit them."

. . .

They hadn't got it quite right. The skin was too blue, too much like a summer sky, the eyes glowed red rather than a blank white, and no Genetic Infantryman, even in the heat of battle, had ever worn an expression quite that deranged, as if his sanity had cracked sometime in the recent past.

But Pietr didn't know that. He stared at the cut-out shape a hundred feet in front of him, his Lazooka held awkwardly in unfamiliar hands, and wondered how he could ever fight a person, a creature, like that.

The words of the training vid they'd been shown ran in his head. "Uncovered a top-secret project... The genetic infantrymen, corrupt products of degenerate Souther science... these freaks, these genetic abominations, bred for death, able to breathe the poisoned air, able to survive in the toxic hell the Southers have made of Nu Earth, are nothing more than brightly coloured targets for our snipers."

Pietr heaved the weight of the Lazooka into position and fired at the leering head of the blue target in front of him. The energy weapon sprayed a hot bolt of death five feet wide of the target, leaving nothing to show for his shot but the stench of ionised air. He looked around guiltily to see if his brother had noticed his mistake, but the others were all intent on their own target practice, reducing the blue cut-outs to smouldering wrecks. Pietr felt a trickle of sweat veer down his forehead and into his eye, and raised his arm to wipe it off before remembering – for the tenth time – that he was wearing a full-body chem suit. He'd never get used to life on the radiation – and chem-blasted surface of Nu Earth.

So much for knowing your enemy, Pietr thought bitterly. Knowing it and being able to hit it were obviously two different things. "Through strength, through will, through purity, Nordland will prevail."

How many times had he heard that over the four months' training he'd been put through before shipping out here? Maybe he didn't have the necessary purity.

Except – he looked to his left, where his brother was putting his tenth shot straight through the target – there was nothing wrong with the purity of his blood. There was just something wrong with him.

He couldn't fight. He should never have joined up. But then his brother had returned from the battles on Epsilon 7, muscles bulging out of his uniform, a man instead of a boy. Their parents had lavished all their attention on him and made jokes about how Jaze was making Nordland safe so that soft young boys like Pietr could bury their heads in books, and Pietr had known that he had no choice. He would become the man his brother was.

His parents had been so proud, then, when he'd gone to the recruitment office on the veldt and signed himself up; prouder still when the elite Kashan Legion had accepted him to serve alongside his brother. His mother had cried, but she'd told him she'd always known there was more to him than his brother or his father said. He wondered if she would still believe that, if his father would still be proud of him, if they could see him now, losing the battle against the wooden cutout of the real-life enemy he would soon be facing.

The Quartz Zone. They had their orders. They were to defend the strategic territory between the Scum Sea and the mountains to the north against the Souther assault, which Nort spies had determined was coming. The Southers, and in particular the monstrous Genetic Infantrymen, would be totally unprepared for the Kashans of which Pietr was the most junior recruit. Their commanding officers had told them it would be a massacre.

Pietr aimed and fired again, his shot going wide four feet to the left. He was sure the officers were right. He wondered which side it was that would be getting massacred.

ONE
QUARTZ ZONE MASSACRE

Rogue had never really understood the term "hive of activity" before, but, having watched Milli-Com over the last twenty-four hours, he finally got it. The whole place was like a beehive that a child had stirred up with a stick, everyone rushing everywhere and getting in everyone else's way. And here was the honeycomb itself, the drop pods stacked ten high on top of each other, ready to be deployed through the turbo-tubes that would blast them towards the planet's surface below.

Drop time T-minus seventy.

The drop pods were tight, claustrophobic little hollows encased in memo-steel to keep out the nuclear heat of re-entry and padded with transplastic to mould itself precisely to the shape of the GI within. It would cushion them from the impact on the planet's surface and make sure that the terminal velocity they reached as they fell didn't mean precisely that.

The GIs called them coffins. Rogue inspected his: fifth from the left on the second row up. He'd done it ten times already today, although the Dolls were supposed to be responsible for servicing the equipment pre-battle. But they weren't the ones whose lives depended on them, and Rogue had learnt long ago never to trust anyone's judgement but his own. So he flipped the catch on the lid, and it hissed open with a soft whoosh of hydraulics. There was no fusion cell in it, nothing that could implode or explode during the decent through Nu Earth's toxic atmosphere. The whole mechanism was the finest clockwork, a device from another time.

When the lid had flipped open, Rogue looked down to see a single red rose lying on the transplastic moulding. He lifted it up and frowned at it, trying to work out how it could have got there, which of his buddies was having a joke on him and what exactly it was supposed to mean.

"Like it, blue?" a husky voice asked from beside his elbow.

He looked round to see Venus Bluegenes half-smiling at him. She nodded at the rose. "Picked it from the hydro-plant this morning. For my favourite GI."

For a moment, Rogue didn't know what to say. He couldn't tell if the thing he could see shining out of her pale eyes was mischief or something else. Then, just as he'd opened his mouth to reply, he saw Helm approaching flanked by Bagman and Gunnar.

He hurriedly slammed shut the drop pod's lid, trapping the rose inside it. "Very funny, Venus," he said gruffly. "But you haven't got time to be wasting on jokes. There's soldiers lives depend on you doing your job now."

Her smile dropped and she sketched a hurried salute. "Sir, yes, sir!" But there was a mocking tone to her voice, and as she sauntered away, hips swinging, she paused to look back over her shoulder at him.

Helm noticed. "What's my girl talking to you about, Rogue?" His voice was full of threat, as taut as a wire about to snap. They all were now. It was as if they could already smell the blood – their enemies' and their own.

"Just telling me to take care of you," Rogue said after only a second's hesitation.

Bagman laughed and slung his arm over Helm's shoulder. "Ooh, Venus wants Rogue to look after her little baby, hold his little hand," he said. He pouted up his lips and made as if to kiss Helm.

Helm pushed him away roughly. "Scan out, Bagman!" But his eyes followed Venus as she left the launch chamber, and Rogue saw his face relax slightly.

Only Gunnar didn't seem tense. He had been filled with an almost manic joy since the mission announcement had been made. He'd barely spent a minute outside of the shooting range, honing skills which were already near perfect. Rogue had performed Gunnar's equipment checks for him, sure that his friend wouldn't remember for himself.

Suddenly, a voice began to ring out through the room, echoing back to them from the snaking metallic corridors outside. It seemed to be emerging from the whole station. "All GIs... All GIs assemble on the drop-pod deck with weapons and equipment ready. This is not a drill. Repeat, this is not a drill."

Rogue felt every single muscle in his body clench, and relaxed them all with an effort of will. His hand, as if of its own volition, drifted down to check the hilt of his knife at his knee, and the ammo-pouch hanging above it, then across to the butt of his gun before feeling behind him for the weight of his kitbag, which hadn't left his back for the last seven days.

It didn't feel quite real. They were finally going to war. They'd spent so long preparing for it, and yet now that it had come he wasn't sure he was ready. He saw Bagman swallow once, hard, before checking his own equipment.

A tech marched past. Not one of the Gene Genies, he was a newbie brought in the last few weeks when the station staff had doubled to prepare for the coming battle. The tech frowned down at his hand-screen, then up at the GIs as if they were just another piece of unreliable equipment.

"Get moving," he ordered, his voice emerging high and thin from beneath a beaked nose. "Into the drop pods. Now we find out if you freaks are as good as you're supposed to be."

The man marched off to repeat his orders to the other knots of GIs standing around the chamber. Helm reached up, adjusting the readout monitor on his helmet to bring it closer to his eyes. Rogue saw that his fingers were trembling as he did it, just a little, but with anticipation, not fear. "This is it," he said. "This is what we were created for."

Gunnar looked down at the stock of his rifle, his finger unconsciously clenching and unclenching on the trigger. "Can't wait to get down there." His voice was hoarse with excitement. "The Norts won't know what's hit 'em!"

He and Helm grinned at each other. Rogue felt the same excitement, but his own was tempered more by caution. They were as perfect a fighting force as they could be – for a fighting force that had never seen any real action. No number of battlefield exercises or sessions in the sim-suites or wargames could fully prepare them for the real thing. None of them had yet learned what it was like to see one of their comrades die. Rogue was grimly certain that they were about to find out and could only hope that it wouldn't be one of his buddies who provided the lesson.

Bagman was squatting on his haunches, obsessively checking through the contents of his kitbag as the robot arm pulled them out and packed them back in again. He echoed Rogue's own thoughts. "Just remember, guys, this isn't another training run." Then, mouth twisting in a half-smile, he repeated the mantra they'd been taught again and again in training. "Let's watch each other's backs down there."

"Always," Gunnar said as he and Helm and Bagman slapped each other on the backs. The call to enter the drop pods continued to blare in the background, filling the huge space with sound like a physical presence, and the air was choked with the peculiar smell of the GIs' sweat.

After a moment, Helm seemed to realise that Rogue wasn't joining in. He looked across at him, his forehead creased in a curious frown. "What do you say, Rogue?" The others looked too, as Rogue's words really mattered to them. Time and again, in training sessions and outside, he had pulled their bacon out of the fire, and somehow that had given him some authority in their eyes. The responsibility weighed heavily on him.

He wished he really did know what they seemed to think he knew, that he could impart some final words of wisdom that would keep them all safe. But he didn't, so he just shrugged and said, "Let's be careful down there. We were bred to survive on Nu Earth, but that doesn't make us invulnerable." He gave his equipment one last check, then straightened his back. "Good luck. I'll see you on the battlefield."

Then he turned away and slid nimbly into the drop pod beside him. The transplastic instantly moulded itself to his body, like being hugged too hard by someone you didn't know that well. "Ready," he said to Bagman, and with a quick grin and a thumbs-up Bagman slammed down the lid on the drop pod.

Rogue found himself shut in darkness, the transplastic pressed right up against his face. He could smell the rubbery scent of it where it squeezed up into his nostrils. And his own heartbeat echoed loudly in his ears, transmitted directly through the material around him.

Sealed into my coffin, he thought. He felt a slight jerk, a short acceleration, and then he was falling towards Nu Earth and the Quartz Zone.

Pietr had heard the name a month ago, the Quartz Zone, when the new recruits to the Kashan Legion had first heard what their mission would be, but he'd never really thought about what it meant until now.

The whole place was made of crystal. It glittered in the moonlight. Every few seconds his breath would huff out in a gasp of barely suppressed terror, and the field of his vision would fog out for a moment to a diffuse light, the sort of light you were supposed to see after death. But the eye guards were designed to be self-cleaning, so a fraction of a second later the mist would clear and the rainbows would be back, and beyond them the shattered landscape of giant, twenty foot tall crystals towering over the pools of stagnant chem.

This was it. It was really happening. Until now, he realised, he'd been able to kid himself that it wouldn't. It had been ridiculous, he knew, but some small part of him had always assumed that he'd be sent home before any real fighting began. He just wasn't cut out to be a soldier. He'd realised that within a week of joining up, and surely his commanding officers would realise that too and send him back out of harm's way.

Except that they hadn't. And the one time he'd tried to bring it up, subtly, with his brother, Jaze had looked at him with such contempt that Pietr had never mentioned it again. It was only the thought that he might yet win his brother's respect that kept him from running away into the chem-blasted wilderness and taking his chances.

His brother, their squad leader, was to his left, binoculars pointed up at the sky, rock steady, as they had been for the last two hours. Around him the rest of the squad were standing, weapons slung for instant combat readiness, scarlet chem suits bleeding into the darkness. They were laughing and joking and talking about how many of the blue freaks they were going to kill, and whether blue ears counted for more than pink ones when you took them as trophies.

Into the distance, the thousand men of the Kashan Legion, the best legion in the whole damn Nort army, were all saying exactly the same thing.

Pietr had tried to join in, but they'd just looked at him in disbelief, as if they knew he didn't mean it, and turned away.

He wanted to kill Southers, of course he did, they were scum and they deserved to die. He just wasn't sure that they wouldn't kill him first. And if they did, what good would that do for Nordland? His gaze swept over the glittering moonlit landscape, as jagged as a serrated blade. It wouldn't be a good place to die.

"Visual contact!" his brother suddenly shouted. "We have visual contact!"

Pietr jumped so hard that his Lazooka fell out of his hands to land with a musical ringing sound against the crystal ground. He fumbled it back as quickly as he could, but his hands were shaking so hard that it took him three tries. By the time he'd got the Lazooka up again and pointed toward the sky, his brother had noticed.

Pietr couldn't see the contemptuous sneer wrinkling his brother's handsome face beneath the insectile mask of his chem suit, but he could imagine it. "What's the matter, Private Pietr? Scared?" he asked.

"Don't be stupid," Pietr said, but his voice was shaking even harder than his hands and his helm mic broadcast it round to echo brightly from the crystal rocks.

Jaze, scenting weakness, moved in for the kill – as he had done since he was seven and Pietr was three. He walked up to his brother and thrust his face as close to his as his chem suit would allow. "Pull yourself together, private!" he shouted. "You're a disgrace to your family and a disgrace to your uniform!"

Around him, Pietr could hear the other Kashans snickering. He felt himself flushing. As if embarrassment mattered at a time like this. If his brother still despised him, after he'd given up everything to fight for his country, when he was probably about to die for his country, then what had been the point of it all?

Jaze grabbed Pietr's Lazooka, his muscular arms pulling it from Pietr's leaner frame with nonchalant ease. Then he thrust it back into Pietr's arms sighted straight up at the sky. "The enemy's coming from the sky, not the ground," he said. "Just point it and pull, and if you feel like soiling your suit, try to do it quietly."

Pietr gripped the weapon as hard as he could and walked back to his own position, trying to straighten his spine and not slink away as the mocking laughter of the other men followed him.

He did as his brother said, pointed the Lazooka up and rested his finger against the trigger. He had to resist the urge just to pull it down, to let go with a wild stream of fire. He couldn't see anything, though. The sky was pitch black, the moon shining only thinly through the roiling mass of yellow and green chem that was the planet's atmosphere, colours he'd learnt to loath with a passion since coming to Nu Earth.

"I see 'em," a voice suddenly shouted from his left. Then another from his right. A third said, "Sweet... There are thousands of them!" And at first Pietr couldn't work out what they meant. There was nothing in the sky, just some high black dots and a flock of birds making their way across the blasted landscape. He remembered that no birds ever flew over this land, and he knew that the dots were all men. Every one of them was an enemy who wanted him dead and every second they were getting bigger.

In the seconds he watched, frozen, they started being the recognisable silver rockets of drop tubes heading for the ground.

Before he'd even realised what was happening, Pietr's finger tightened on the trigger. With a roar, the Lazooka spat out a shrieking trail of fire towards the sky. By dumb luck, the fire lashed against one of the descending pods.

The drop pod beside Rogue's burst into a bloom of flame too bright for even his eyes to watch and he knew that another GI had died. The front screen of Rogue's drop pod had cleared for landing, giving him a perfect view of the slaughter all around. His hands strained against the enfolding transplastic, itching to do something, but he was entirely powerless. All he could do was watch as GI after GI died.

It was like target practice for the Norts below, he thought, the easiest kind of turkey shoot. He wondered bitterly why it hadn't occurred to the Souther high command that if, by any chance, there were Nort forces in the Quartz Zone, the GIs would be entirely unprotected as they came down.

Didn't quite care enough to worry, he reckoned. The risk to our lives didn't figure into the equation the same way it would have if we were real men.

To his left, another drop pod went. He wondered with a jolt of fear if it contained Gunnar, or Bagman, or Helm. How could he hope that it didn't? If it wasn't them, it was some other GI. There was no good option, nothing to hope for.

For too long all he'd been able to see were the green-yellow clouds of the sky lit by an occasional brilliant flash as another drop pod went. His own drop pod tilted and he felt a sharp jerk even through the protective transplastic moulding as its grav-chute deployed. Finally, he could see the land below him, the sharp crystals stabbing upward into the sky like knives ready to cut any surviving GIs to shreds.

He was only thirty metres above it now. Twenty metres, and there didn't seem to be any Lazooka fire heading his way, all of it concentrated upward at the GIs still deploying from the tubes. I'm going to make it, he thought, feeling the intense selfish joy of survival.

Then he didn't have time for thought at all as the drop tube hit the ground with a force that would have pulverised the bones of any normal man. It was rolling so fast that even Rogue felt his head spin and his teeth clatter together, then there was a smaller impact and he felt it come to a stop at the bottom of the gully where he'd landed.

Rogue's training took over, aided by the self-preservation instinct carried by every life form, even one bred in a tube. He punched the door release button but it didn't shift, the mechanism jammed, so he kicked it open then leapt and rolled, trying to get himself clear of the drop pod in case any enemies had seen it land.

It was a good thing he did because he was only ten metres clear when a rifle beam shot into the heart of the pod. He saw the outer metal of the pod glow from dull red to white. Rogue only had time to roll himself into a shallow hollow in the quartz before he heard it explode with a muffled boom and a shower of molten metal sprayed out over the crystal rock, hissing and sinking into it as it landed.

A moment later the Nort marksman seemed to realise that Rogue had already left the pod. The energy beam swung round, hitting a few inches from his head. Rogue had already realised that his targeting computer was fried, both the heads-up display in his helmet and the auto-lock-on in his gun. Probably frizzed by the Nort bombardment as they descended, he thought, maybe by something designed specifically to do so.

Rogue told himself that it didn't matter. He didn't need any computer to tell him how to find an enemy. After twenty years of training, his mind was its own targeting reticule. He continued his roll to take him out of that hollow and into the next and in the same movement he brought his gun round and let off one round. Even over the din of battle he heard the muffled cry as his shot hit home.

He didn't hang around to enjoy the kill. Even in the one brief look he'd taken to find his mark, he'd seen that they were hopelessly outnumbered. The battlefield was a seething mass of chem-suited Norts clustered around lone, desperate blue figures like white blood cells congregating to eliminate an unwelcome infection.

As soon as his drop pod had landed, he'd begun to acquire his own clot of enemies. They were closing in fast. Their rifles let off such a continuous stream of fire that even through Rogue was managing to dodge the individual beams, the air was heating so fast around him that he could feel it scorching his lungs and singing the thin brush of hair on his head.

But the advantage wasn't always with the numbers. Rogue had been told that often enough and now he could see why. The Norts were too close together. They were encircling him completely and soon they'd be unable to fire at him without firing at each other. As he dodged and weaved and let out seemingly random shots that actually had a tight pattern, he saw a few of the Norts realise this and start to back away. But the others were still advancing and all that accomplished was more confusion for the enemy. Some of them stopped firing altogether, frightened they'd be taking out their own side. Others continued and did kill their own men.

Soon it was utter chaos. Rogue continued weaving and shooting, until he'd finally achieved his aim. He'd cleared a zigzag path through the encircling force of Norts, and by the time the Norts had realised what he'd done, he'd already taken it. Some swung their rifles to follow him, but Rogue was gone before they fired and all they did was shoot their own men.

But though he was out, there was nowhere to run, nowhere to hide, and Rogue's blue skin stood out like a convenient target in the bleak crystalline landscape around him. Another mistake the Gene Genies made, he thought. They were so proud of their creations that they made us stand out rather than blend in.

He'd broken through one circle only to find himself still surrounded by enemies, the shattered quartz of the battlefield stretching as far as the eye could see and the legions of Nordlanders stretching with it.

There were fewer blue forms among the white now, and there'd been few enough to begin with. Most of the GIs had died in the air. Died without firing a shot. Their bodies would never even have a grave. They'd lie on the cold stone of this hellish battlefield until eventually even their altered flesh would rot and fall away, and all that would remain would be chem-scoured bones, finally, in death, indistinguishable from normal men.

Rogue put all that from his mind and for a while did what he'd spent his life preparing for. He fought. It became a routine, almost a mantra: aim, dodge, fire, reload. Aim, dodge, fire, reload. Sometimes it felt like there was a haze hovering over his mind, but every time it descended he fought it off. One nanosecond of distraction and they would have him and there would just be one more blue corpse without a name on the battlefield.

Then, when he really wasn't sure that he could go on any longer, he saw a blue form ahead of him. It took him a moment to recognise the face, screwed up into a grin of manic battle rage.

"Gunnar!" Rogue shouted, surprised to find his voice still strong and clear.

Gunnar's head snapped round, and in that moment of inattention a Nort machine gun locked on, but Rogue was quicker and the Nort died with a strangled gasp before he could fire.

"Rogue! Hey – over here!" Gunnar shouted. "I think I see a path through."

Rogue leapt the mound of quartz in front of him. This time it was Gunnar who saved him, taking a Nort sniper in the shoulder before he could get a clean shot. Then they were together, back to back, and though there were only two of them Rogue felt ten times better than he had before.

He scanned the horizon, but all he could see was an unchecked mass of Nort troops and a few, a very few, GIs fighting a desperate battle for survival among them.

"Don't see any way out from here," Rogue said.

Even with his back to Gunnar, Rogue knew that his mouth was stretching in the over-wide smile he always wore when he was being most dangerous, the smile that made him look a little mad. "Yeah, well, we might have to kill a few Norts first," Gunnar said. "That a problem for you?"

From the edge of the battle, the soldiers looked like toys carelessly knocked over by a bored child. Well, they are my toys in a way, thought Bland, mine and Brass's private little sandpit. And when everything's finished we'll sweep up the pieces and see what we can make of them.

"Care to take a wager, Mr Bland?" his partner asked, gently stroking his moustache through his chem suit as he surveyed the carnage beneath them.

"I'm always amenable to a little flutter, Mr Brass," Bland said. "I assume you don't intend it to concern the outcome of this particular conflict."

Brass tipped his bowler hat lower to shade his eyes from the glare of the midday sun. Beneath the hat he was wearing a customised chem suit, skin-tight and nearly invisible. They'd designed it a month after they'd first joined forces, to allow them to wear their own suits below, which were so much more elegant than the military issue suits the soldiers wore. And besides, when you were innocent merchants plying your trade in a war zone, it was extremely beneficial not to look too much like you belonged to either side. It paid to appear harmless, too, and perhaps a little absurd. One didn't want to look like a threat.

"The outcome is, of course, a foregone conclusion," Brass said. The screams of the dying only drifted thinly up here, like the distant cries of birds, but it was clear which side most of them were coming from. "I was referring to the profit we are likely to make from this little contretemps. I personally believe that we'll find richer pickings here than after the Dixie Offensive."

"Ah, happy days," Bland replied. He remembered that time very well. The Norts had been developing their new Hell Cannon. They'd cut down the Souther forces like wheat. Then an accident had happened: an overheating fusion cell had exploded in the centre of the Nort ranks, and at the end of the battle there was no one left alive but Bland and Brass themselves.

They'd pried the Hell Cannons from the clawed, scorched hand bones of the Nort soldiers and sold them to the Souther High Command for enough to let them take a five-month holiday away from Nu Earth. "I very much doubt we'll be seeing that kind of money, Mr Brass," Bland said.

"Now, now, when have my instincts ever been wrong?" Brass said. "There's a pricking in my thumbs that always means money. I shall forgive your doubts, however, as we're likely to find out for certain very soon. It seems to me the battle is reaching its conclusion."

Bland looked back down and saw that Brass was right. There were only a very few specks of blue in the sea of green and red. The intelligence which had led them here, telling them via their extensive spy networks that the Norts had a surprise in store for the Southers, had clearly been spot on. "I suppose then that it is time we showed our true colours," he said, turning reluctantly from the spectacle of the battlefield to their vehicle.

It sat five metres away, a great, squat, dark crab of a machine. It had never, Bland thought, been terribly aesthetic, but alas matters of aesthetics sometimes had to be set aside when lives were at stake, especially their own. The metal fortress, bristling with armour and guns, had kept them safe in the middle of many a firefight.

He pressed his eye against the aft door, pausing a second for the retinal scan, then stepped back to allow the door to heave open. Once inside, he slipped with comfortable ease into his co-pilot's chair and pressed the button marked "Nordland".

He could just barely hear the strains of the Nordland national anthem beginning to blare from the speakers at the four corners of the vehicle. He couldn't see the

Nordland flag run up the pole at the front, but he knew it was there.

"All set, Mr Brass," he said. "Now we must simply wait for those strange new Souther troops to hurry up and finish dying."

Rogue was beginning to believe that Gunnar really might have seen a way through. With two of them fighting together it was much easier. The years of training had fused them into a fluid fighting unit, almost like two bodies with one mind.

When Gunnar twisted to his left, Rogue knew that he should fire into the sudden gap, taking out the Nort trooper behind Gunnar, at the same time twisting to his left so that Gunnar could do the same for him. For the first time, he started to imagine fear in the faces of the Norts behind the masks of their chem suits.

When it happened, neither of them was prepared for it. The drill probe burst out of the ground right between them, a great churning lethal knife of a thing. They backed hurriedly away from its whirling, diamond-sharp blades – Rogue going in one direction and Gunnar the other.

Gunnar recovered himself quickly, turning to run round the thing and bring himself shoulder to shoulder with Rogue. He turned – and found himself face-to-face with a Nort. In the microsecond it took Gunnar to bring up and target his weapon, he saw only a shadowy impression of the man's eyes, hidden behind his insectile chem mask. They were blue, pale and cold, filled with the cruelty of someone who has never experienced weakness and can't forgive it in others. They didn't blink once.

These are the eyes of the man who's going to kill me, Gunnar thought. Because my gun isn't ready, and his is. The energy beam went clean through his head.

Rogue emerged from the behind the drill probe just in time to see Gunnar crumple to his knees. He couldn't see the face of the Nort who'd shot him, but he didn't really care. His gun was up and he took the Nort trooper straight through the heart. The man let out a choked, gasping scream.

Rogue didn't bother to watch him finish dying. He rushed to Gunnar's side, glad at least that the drill probe gave him enough time to tend to his comrade. But Gunnar was already fading. "I was slow, Rogue," he said, his once powerful voice little more than a whisper. "Too damn slow. I..." Then he was gone. The light in his white eyes faded till they were the colour of pearls, blank and lifeless.

Rogue couldn't allow himself to feel anything. "Don't worry, you'll get another chance," he said to the fallen body of his comrade. "We're Genetic Infantrymen. Even when we're dead we don't escape from war."

Rogue knew what he had to do, and that he only had seconds to do it. For the first time in the battle he felt a brief shudder of nausea, which he suppressed quickly . He rolled Gunnar's body over roughly. It flopped like a rag doll. Then he snatched his knife from his knee and applied it to the back of Gunnar's head. A fountain of blue blood shot up, some of it splashing in Rogue's face. He ignored it and dug deeper, twisting the knife around to find his target.

He felt his palms grow sweaty as the knife found nothing but Gunnar's flesh. Finally he felt it, a metallic resistance against his blade. He twisted the knife around till it was underneath the obstacle, then flicked it up. The little microchip, buried deep in Gunnar's head, shot into his hand, slick with blood and the spongy remnants of his friend's physical brain, but though Gunnar's brain was gone, his mind remained. Stored in the chip, ready to be re-genned in a force-grown clone body when they returned to Milli-Com. The Gene Genies had planned for every contingency. Not that they were concerned about GI fatalities, Rogue thought bitterly. They just didn't want to see their eighteen years of training go to waste.

"Sixty seconds, Rogue," a voice said from the tiny chip. It was tinny and mechanical, nothing like Gunnar's, but something in the inflection identified it as his. "Install me into my rifle before my biochip expires," Gunnar said urgently.

Rogue snatched the rifle from the ground, yanking it to release the straps from beneath his friend's corpse. The hole was easy to spot, just beside the clip for the magazines. He slotted the biochip into place, taking what time he could, terrified that he might damage it and deny his friend this second chance at life. Then, as soon as he felt it snap home, he flicked the clear cover over it and slung the rifle over his shoulder, flinging his own to the side after he'd liberated all the remaining ammo.

"You okay?" he asked gruffly.

There was a brief, heart-stopping pause. Then Gunnar's voice sounded out, more resonant now that it was emerging from the metal of the rifle. "Apart from being dead, you mean? C'mon, let's go find some Norts."

Rogue couldn't argue with that.

Cowering behind a rock, Pietr had watched as Jaze crumpled to the ground.

I should do something, he thought. I should…

But he didn't know what he should do. He couldn't imagine taking on the blue monster that'd killed his brother. The monster that now seemed to be talking to his gun. He just remained, crouched in his hiding hole, the back of his hand pressed against his mouth through the thick material of his chem suit.

Even though Gunnar was still with him, Rogue felt exposed again, lonely without the physical body of his friend beside him. And the Nort scum had stepped up their assault since Gunnar had died, as if the taste of blue blood had got them baying for more. Up ahead, Rogue saw a cannon emplacement that was decimating a group of GIs below.

"Gun's causing a lot of damage, Rogue," Gunnar said. "We should take it over."

Still working as a team, Rogue thought. He turned to the cannon, cleared the Norts clustered around it and used it on the rest of them. And with Gunnar in his weapon, he suddenly had a full heads-up-display, all the feedback that had been frazzled on his old gun. Once the cannon was used and discarded, he headed higher, not letting the Nort drill probe and the four Norts it discharged stop him, more determined than ever to get himself out of the battle in one piece now that Gunnar's life depended on it too, and less sure than ever that it was possible.

Then Rogue saw a cluster of blue bodies only a hundred metres ahead of him – long after he'd thought there were no more to come – and he was filled with renewed hope.

His hope burned even brighter when he saw the familiar figure of Bagman take out three Nort troopers before Rogue had crossed half the distance towards him.

Bagman was showing his crooked grin when he saw Rogue and sketched a salute. "Damn good to see you, Rogue!" he said. "What the hell's going on? How did they know we were coming? Something's wrong, very wrong."

"I know," Rogue said. Bagman's words had crystallised his own unspoken fears, that there was more than bad luck or bad timing to the Nort presence at their exact landing site.

"Any sign of the others?" Bagman suddenly asked, as if he'd read something in Rogue's expression.

"I'm right here, old buddy," Gunnar's strange new mechanical voice said.

It took Bagman only a second to work out what that meant. Rogue saw his expression twist into one of anger and grief. "Damn this war."

Another second, and Bagman was all business again. He nodded towards a Nort bunker ahead of them, the heavily fortified point where their underground network of tunnels broke through to the surface. "We've got to take that stronghold," he said to Rogue. "They'll keep on rolling reinforcements through it until we do."

Rogue looked around at Bagman and the other GIs, Fisher, Tank and Twitch, and he felt confident that it wouldn't be a problem.

It wasn't, but it wasn't easy either. There were Kashans inside the bunker, lots of them, and by the time they'd cleared it out and mined it back into the dust, Tank was down and Fisher was injured. Then the Blackmare tank came. Huge, vast and dark, it seemed to blot out half of the sky behind its bulk. A fist shot from its front cannon and shook the ground like an earthquake, but the artillery man had aimed wide, and instead of taking out the GIs, it opened an escape route for them, a bolthole in the crystal rock ahead. Without any prompting, the GIs headed straight for it, and the Norts followed them, determined not to let their prey get away.

By the time Rogue and Bagman were through the quartz tunnel and safely out the other side, there were no more GIs left with them. Neither of them said anything – they both knew what they were thinking. And looking at the field of battle below, it was clear that it was far from over.

There were bunkers everywhere, heavily fortified with gun emplacements. The individual Norts they could take out, one damn soldier at a time, but the big guns were another matter. They needed to be put out of commission.

By unspoken consent, Bagman and Rogue headed for the nearest bunker. If they could destroy this one they might just have a narrow corridor outside the firing range of the others through which they could escape.

"Wait here, Rogue," Bagman said. "I'll take this one out." Before Rogue could protest, he'd pulled a micro-mine from his kitbag and was loping across to the thick compcrete wall of the bunker. "Cover me," he snapped out to Rogue over his shoulder.

Rogue didn't need to be asked. Trusting Bagman to cover any forward fire, he concentrated on protecting the flanks and rear. The Norts must have realised what they intended because they were coming thick and fast, a great red swarm of them.

Rogue didn't care. More Norts meant easier pickings for his rifle and with Gunnar in place, the targeting system was back with a vengeance. He didn't miss a single shot, and every one was a headshot, as if Gunnar was getting a vicarious pleasure from visiting his own death on all these enemies. Rogue was so intent on the fight that for a second he didn't see it. What happened to Bagman was only a blurry event at the periphery of his vision, something that shouldn't distract him from the task at hand.

But there was something about the colour, about the blue spray spreading in every direction that told Rogue this was something he *should* pay attention to. So he spun round in time for the final act, as the drill probe's blades sliced round through Bagman's flesh one final time, leaving him nothing more than a scattered heap of flesh and bone.

Rogue snapped. Gunnar, he could take. The whole damn situation he could cope with. It was war. Drek happened. But Bagman too, the one Rogue had always somehow felt it was his duty to protect... Was he really going to end this day with all his friends dead?

Letting out a roar of rage, he leapt onto the platform of the drill probe, heedless of the blades as they spun inches from his exposed flesh. He saw the door that led in; it was sealed. There was no way it should have been possible to open it from the outside. But Rogue did it anyway. He flung the door open, kicked the Nort manning the entrance viciously in the face, then flung a grenade inside and slammed the door shut again.

"Stak!" he heard the Norts screaming as he leapt clear. "Stak! Get it out!"

They were right out of luck. The whole drill probe shook then exploded in a welt of fire.

Rogue saw it on the edge of his vision as he knelt to examine what was left of Bagman. It took him a horribly long time to find the head in the mass of gore. When he did, little of the face was left and for a horrible moment he was afraid the biochip had also been destroyed in the carnage.

But it hadn't. The head was pulped, so he used his fingers to dig it out this time. Once it was free, he hesitated a moment, then smiled and slipped it into the slot on Bagman's kitbag. Where else could it go?

"Second lease of life," Bagman said. "Lucky you were here." Even emerging tinnily from the speakers in the side of the pack, the sarcastic intonation on the word "lucky" was more than evident.

"GIs make their own luck," Rogue said. "I'll get you clear of here, Bagman, Gunnar. You're going to live through this, even if your bodies didn't."

Then, as if it had heard him, his helmet mic crackled into life. "Rogue," Helm's voice said. "I'm getting a signal from Milli-Com. They're ordering a full-scale retreat." Rogue ignored the snorts of disdain from Bagman and Gunnar. It had taken the brass an awfully long time to notice that things weren't exactly going the GI's way. "We're to rendezvous at the Orange Sea Coast for rescue craft pick-up." The mic hissed into silence.

"What did I tell you?" Rogue gritted to the others. "We're getting out."

He wished he felt half as confident as he sounded.

TWO
TWO DOWN

Pietr couldn't believe that his brother was really dead. Just couldn't believe it. Jaze had been there his whole life. His first memory was of his brother stealing his teddy bear out of his cot and his parents laughing when he told them about it. It didn't seem possible that Jaze should be dead. Pietr had been the one who was meant to die. He *deserved* to die. His brother had as good as told him so. And how was he going to earn Jaze's respect now, finally see his brother regard him through eyes glowing with pride, when his eyes were dim and dead? How come it was Jaze's body that was lying here on the ground?

After a few minutes just squatting in the hollow behind the corpse, Pietr staggered to his feet. He could barely see; the tears scalding his eyes felt as toxic as chem. But he made his way to his brother's corpse and no one stopped him. The battle had long since moved off, the ebb and flow of war which Pietr hadn't known about until today carrying the fight far out of his sight towards the coast.

Jaze still looked alive. His body was unharmed. Only the black stain on the breast of his chem suit showed what had happened, and that could just have been mud. Maybe it was mud.

Pietr took the sleeve of his chem suit and tried to rub the mark away, but nothing would shift it. So instead he tried to wake his brother up.

"Jaze," he said. "Jaze, come on, stop kidding around." He nudged his brother gently, then harder when there was no response. "Don't do this to me, Jaze. Don't do it," he said, and he was sobbing so hard that he couldn't speak any more.

But this time the tears were of anger. How dare those blue-skinned Souther freaks take his brother away from him? How dare they?

Pietr staggered to his feet, pulled his beam rifle from where it had remained slung across his shoulders for the entire battle, and clasped it in his hands. The weight felt good. Dangerous. He could make this right. He could take on the Souther scum, kill them all, kill the one who'd killed his brother, then there'd be no one to kill his brother and his brother would be alive again.

Somewhere, hazily, he thought that there might be something wrong with the logic of this. He shook his head. Didn't matter. For the first time since the battle had begun he had a clear sense of purpose. He knew what needed to be done.

The fight was on the shore, so that must be where the Southers were. If he could just find them he could put this all right.

He'd taken only five paces towards the Orange Coast when a voice rang out behind him. "Soldier, halt!"

He carried on walking.

"Halt, I say!" the voice snapped, and some vague part of Pietr recognised it as Lieutenant Kurn. As the recognition sank in, reality began to return and Pietr hesitated and turned to face his commanding officer.

Kurn took a step back when he saw him, as if something in Pietr's posture unsettled him, but he quickly steadied himself. "There are new orders, soldier," he said. "You're to follow me."

"But I want to kill those Souther scum," Pietr said. He noticed that his voice sounded weak, as if he didn't really mean it. Did he? He wasn't sure any more.

But Kurn heard only the words. He smiled, the first approving look Pietr had ever received from him. "Don't worry, Pietr," he said. "That's exactly what you're going to be doing."

Rogue couldn't believe that luck really did seem to be with them. Shortly after receiving the message from Helm, they'd found a cave system burrowing through the quartz cliffs. The Norts must have known it was there, but they had passed through and moved on. There was enough salvage in the cave, broken equipment and disabled armaments, for Rogue to provide Bagman with the raw materials to manufacture him more ammo and as many micro-mines as Rogue was likely to need. A few more med kits would come in handy too. Rogue knelt and tossed it all into the kitbag, where the nanites could get to work on it.

"Great! Food," Bagman said.

Rogue smiled. "Thought you were looking hungry."

It actually seemed like things might be looking up until they emerged from the caves. "Damn it, Rogue," Bagman said when he could see the view. "Don't we deserve one break?"

The coast was visible, toxic orange waves beating against a blackened shore. There were other GIs too, more survivors than Rogue had anticipated. Still, even from this distance, Rogue could see that many of them were wounded, keeping going only through the iron will and inhuman stamina that had been bred into them.

There were Norts too. The GIs hadn't made a clean escape. The enemy had followed and they had the upper hand here as well. For a moment the view was obscured as a gas bomb exploded a hundred yards from their position, and when the choking black smoke cleared Rogue could see that there were a few less blue forms left standing. There was another Blackmare tank, too, blasting sizzling bolts of blue death at the retreating GIs.

"Almost at the coast," Bagman said. He made it sound like a hope rather than a certainty.

"Yeah, I can already smell the pollution," Rogue replied. He didn't like the lie of the land at all. Up here they had the advantage of height, but as soon as they ventured back onto the battlefield they'd be bright blue targets for all the Nort armaments.

His helmet mic crackled into life and Helm's voice came through again. "Guys, I'm getting a lot of readings up ahead, and I don't think they're friendly."

"You don't say," Bagman said sarcastically, as Rogue eyed the massed Nort forces below.

Gunnar's rough voice, emerging from the stock of Rogue's gun, sounded entirely serious. "Norts?" he said. "Cool. A trip to the beach and Norts to kill. I love this war."

Rogue didn't say anything, but he felt a first stirring of unease. Gunnar's bloodthirstiness had always been constrained by the fierce military discipline they'd spent years learning. The GIs were designed to be killing machines, but by giving them human form the Gene Genies had ensured that they could never be only that. Now Gunnar's consciousness was embedded in something that really was nothing more than a killing machine. Could his humanity, or even his sanity, survive it?

"I believe all is clear, Mr Bland," Brass said. He looked down at his shorter partner, then they both rose carefully to their feet from behind the quartz mound where they had been hiding as the last of the fighting passed them by.

The ground in front of them was like an abattoir, except that much of the blood sprayed across it was blue. Pausing only to collect the weapons of the fallen and flip them into the hovercart, Bland towing behind him, Brass made straight for the first blue-skinned corpse.

He knelt beside it, fascinated to see how human it looked. From their vantage point above the battlefield, it had been impossible to tell the exact appearance of the new Souther troops. Up close he saw that the thing could almost have been a man. Except, of course, for the muddy blue skin, the brush of white hair on the head and, perhaps most disturbingly, the strange blank whiteness of the eyes.

"No chem suits," Bland said. His heavy lidded, deceptively tired-looking eyes turned to Brass. "It disturbs me that we knew nothing of these creatures."

Brass nodded. "They must have been bred this way, possibly from birth. For the Southers to have run such a programme without our knowledge... Well, it is clear we shall have to step up our surveillance operations on Milli-Com."

"But what are they?" Bland asked. He knelt down beside the body and prodded the cut in its side cautiously with one gloved hand. A gout of blue blood shot out towards him from the wound and he jumped hurriedly back before climbing thoughtfully to his feet.

"I think that further research is required, Mr Bland," Brass said. "Will you take the feet?" He grasped the body's head, unnaturally heavy in death, and with some effort he and Bland heaved it onto the hovercart. They could study it later, in the safety of their vehicular base. A thorough dissection was clearly called for, but there was no time. Others, inimical to their own purposes, would soon be on the battlefield.

Brass wasn't worried about the Norts' own clean-up operation. He knew from experience that they had hours before that was likely to occur – typical military inefficiency, which Brass was all too familiar with after the ten years he'd spent slaving thanklessly in Nort computer intelligence. No, it was other body looters Brass was worried about. Although, he flattered himself, his hacking skills were second-to-none, not to mention his in-depth knowledge of Nort cryptography, it was possible that others would have gathered the same intelligence he and Bland had. Not to mention that the firefight they'd just witnessed must have lit up the chem clouds for miles around. The vultures would be descending soon. And when they did, Brass intended for them to find the corpses already picked clean.

He was therefore in such a hurry that he almost missed it. At first, he took it for just another blue-skinned corpse. But then he saw the gaping wound in the back of its head that hadn't been caused by any beam rifle he'd ever seen.

"Mr Bland, would you pause a moment?" he said. Bland turned to look at him, his hand still on the hovercart's pull-chord, as Brass knelt down beside the body.

He looked at the hole in the back of the head and came to the conclusion that it had been caused by a knife. A quick peek with his nanoscope and he established from the pattern of serrations that it was a standard-issue Souther Infantry knife. Which meant that this soldier had been killed by one of his own side. Except, Brass realised quickly , the wound in the blue trooper's head hadn't been the fatal one. It would have bled far more profusely if it had been inflicted ante mortem. When Brass flipped the body over, he saw that its death had been brought about by an energy beam between the eyes.

There was only one reason that Brass could imagine for the wound. Something had been removed from it. "Curious," he said to his partner. "Mr Bland, I believe this warrants further investigation."

Before he'd got far out of the cave system, Rogue managed to hook up with Helm. He'd guessed Helm must have been looking for him. He was grinning at him, clearly pleased to have found at least one of his buddies alive, whatever rivalry he'd felt with Rogue in training put aside in the crucible of battle. Rogue wondered if he'd still be pleased when he heard the news Rogue had to tell, how badly he'd let their other buddies down, that he'd been too slow to save them.

Helm's smile was slipping as he looked around Rogue, clearly expecting to have found him with Gunnar and Bagman. "Where are the others?" he said to Rogue after a moment. "Couldda sworn I heard them talking over the radio."

"They're dead," Rogue said.

Helm's eyes widened, then narrowed as if to stop them spilling out any emotion that wasn't suitable in a GI.

"Hey, watch who you're calling dead," Bagman's voice rang out from the robot arm of Rogue's kitbag.

Helm looked shocked for a moment, and comprehension lit his eyes. "You got him out in time."

Rogue nodded. "Gunnar too. Quick enough to get them out of their bodies," he added bitterly, "not quick enough to keep 'em in them."

"Don't beat yourself up about it, Rogue," Gunnar said gruffly. "Wasn't for you, we wouldn't have made it at all. Now I get to kill another day."

Helm opened his mouth to reply, then spun round as he spotted something out of the corner of his eye. He dropped to his knees, swung his rifle up and looked down the sniper scope latched to the stock. Rogue saw him breathe in, hold the breath in his lungs, keeping his body entirely steady, and squeeze off a shot. It was too far away to see if it had reached its target, but Rogue was willing to bet money that it had. Helm was second only to Gunnar as a marksman.

"Nort Lazooka unit," Helm said shortly.

"Way to go," said Gunnar. "Do it to them before they do it to us."

Helm seemed to hesitate a moment, then he unsnapped the sight from his weapon and handed it over to Rogue. "Take this. Makes more sense for Gunnar to have it anyway." Rogue didn't like to deprive Helm of what edge he had, but he knew that he was right. With Gunnar in charge his weapon could auto-fire, making it far more useful than Helm's simple rifle. The scope just made it that much more deadly. And like they'd always told them in training, the best get the best – 'cause they'll know what to do with it.

"Thanks," he said gruffly. "You know, would make a lot of sense for you to take one of the guys. That way, if one of us gets cut down at least half of us'll make it out alive." He held Gunnar out towards Helm.

"Hey, buddy, what do you think you're doing?" Gunnar said indignantly.

"Looking out for you," Rogue said, but he drew the rifle back a little.

"I can look out for myself," Gunnar said. "And I'm not some bit of equipment you can trade around like an object. There's a mind in here, in case you'd forgotten, and it gets to decide where it goes."

Rogue felt ashamed. "Sorry, Gunnar. Guess I'll keep you then, if that's what you want."

"I'm happy where I am," Gunnar confirmed. Helm nodded that he understood and Rogue slung the weapon back over his own shoulders. He knew that Gunnar was right. Subtly, he had already begun to think of his two old buddies as less than human, without real feelings. Only their bodies were lost, not their spirits or their wills.

"Big words," Bagman muttered to Gunnar. "But you just wanted to stick with Rogue 'cause you know he's more likely to get us out alive than Helm."

Rogue hissed at Bagman to silence him and hoped that Helm hadn't heard, but he thought from the suddenly tense set of the other GI's shoulders that he probably had. Great. Their situation was bad enough as it was. The last thing they needed was to reawaken old rivalries.

Helm didn't say anything, he just continued scanning the battlefield before them like a chess grandmaster studying the board before making his move. "We've more chance of surviving if we save our ammo," he said. "Stealth's the best strategy here." Then he turned to face Rogue. "If you jump across that gap, you could sneak up on the tower lookout. I'll cover you from here."

For just a moment, looking into Helm's eyes as the crump and shrieking of heavy artillery sounded below, Rogue wondered if Helm *would* cover him. His doubts evaporated as soon as he saw the white fire in his comrade's arms. They were GIs; they could trust each other absolutely. Because they only had each other.

And Helm did cover him. With Gunnar's sniper sight in place it was almost too easy. Rogue took out the Norts before they even saw him coming, headshots every time, and behind him Helm mopped up any survivors. Even another Blackmare tank proved no obstacle – Rogue just found himself the Lazooka unit

Helm had downed earlier and used the Norts' own weapons against them.

It looked like they might make it back to the coast unhindered, until the quartz hillock in front of them suddenly erupted into molten lava and the same Hell Cannon that had nearly finished them off swung round and took out a small cluster of GIs only a few short metres from the shore and safety.

Helm fell to the ground beside Rogue, instinctively placing his back to him, ensuring a three hundred and sixty degree range of fire. The air around them was thick with the smell of the nearby sea, a hint of brine masked behind the stink of lethal chem. Even GIs might not survive the waters of that ocean very long.

"Rogue, another message coming in from Milli-Com," Bagman said. "The rescue craft can't come in until that Hell Cannon is taken out."

"And that bunker," Gunnar said. "The machine gun emplacements there will make mincemeat of our guys trying to get down to the shore." He couldn't point, of course, but Rogue knew just where he meant. It lay right between their hideout in the rocks and the shore. Other groups of GIs had spotted it too. Rogue could see them holed up around the rocky escarpment, calculating the odds that they'd make it down to the shore alive. The odds weren't good. And if Rogue could see them, then so could the Norts. They'd be sending in forces to wipe out those last, pinned-down pockets of resistance before long.

Rogue calculated that the bunker was doable. The cannon was the problem. The Norts knew that it was their prize possession, and they'd defended it accordingly. "You take out the bunker," he said to Helm. "I'll take care of the cannon."

But Helm had clearly performed the same calculation as Rogue. "No way," he said. "It's a suicide mission, Rogue. Let me do it."

Rogue looked at him, at the steely look on his blue face, and knew that he wasn't going to back down. "Fine," he said. "We'll draw for it. Give me your tag."

Helm didn't like this either, but it was too fair for him to argue with. He pulled out the dog tag from his belt pouch and handed it over to Rogue. Rogue slipped out his own and dropped them both into the helmet of a nearby Nort casualty. "Pick," he said to Helm.

Helm dipped his hand in – and when he pulled it out it was holding Rogue's tag. Reluctantly, he handed it back to Rogue. "Fine, take the cannon. But if you die trying I ain't putting you in my equipment. You can rot in the ground."

"Got that," Rogue said as Helm marched off without a backward glance. He tossed the Nort helmet back on the ground.

"Hey," Bagman said. "What about Helm's tag?"

Rogue unclasped his fist to show the tag still held within it.

"You cheated!" Bagman said indignantly.

Rogue shrugged. "It was for his own good. Now boys, you ready for that suicide mission?"

By the time Pietr had rejoined his unit, he'd recovered his mind enough to know that he was lucky that Lieutenant Kurn had stopped him before he had a chance to embark on his suicide mission against the Southers. The rage had gone, but it left in its place a terrible shame. His brother had died a hero while he'd been cowering behind a rock.

His fellow Kashans were in high spirits, almost dancing around the huge shards of crystal that filled the ground around them. He could hear snatches of the Nort national anthem being shouted out, and the men nearby were slurping surreptitiously from a flask of synth-brandy. He could smell the slightly chemical tang of it on the breeze.

"We showed 'em," Private Schulz said. "We showed those blue freaks what a real man is!" His chem suit was splattered with blood, blue and red, but he was too filled with the manic joy of battle to care.

"Hey," Sergeant Wilnerz called out when he spotted Pietr. "How many Southers did you bag?"

"I, err..." Pietr stumbled, and the others all laughed.

"I took seven," Schulz said. "Better than any man here, I'll wager – except maybe Jaze."

"Where is Jaze?" somebody else asked, and every eye turned on Pietr, the weight of their gaze like a physical burden.

Pietr almost couldn't get the words out. His tongue felt too big for his mouth. "He's dead," he managed to stumble out eventually. "One of the Southers killed him."

"Stak," Wilnerz said, but the others greeted Pietr's words with a cold, accusing silence.

"And what happened to the Souther who killed him?" Schulz asked eventually. "You must have seen him, if you know how Jaze died."

"Nothing, I don't know," Pietr said, unconsciously backing away from him and half lifting his hands in a warding-off gesture.

"So you let him walk away from your brother's corpse alive?" Wilnerz's voice was as cold as Jaze.

Pietr didn't reply, just continued backing away straight into Lieutenant Kurn. Kurn grunted in annoyance and pushed him away. Pietr stumbled back, and when he'd regained his footing he saw that Kurn had deposited a pile of chem suits on the ground. There was something wrong about them and it took him a moment to realise why. They were Souther. The Souther insignia, a white arrow on red, stood out on their breasts.

"Put them on," Kurn said. "Don't ask why. It's classified. Just do it."

Schulz pushed past Pietr, digging his elbow into his ribs as he passed. "Why are you waiting, Pietr?" he said, loudly enough for the others to hear. "Seems to me this is the uniform you ought to be wearing."

Brass paused with his vibro-scalpel inserted into the skull of the blue corpse laid out on the metal slab in front of him. He'd already dissected the muscles, seen how thick they were, the strengthened tendons and ligaments joining them to the super-dense bone. He'd removed and cut open the organs and estimated that they must work at five to ten times the efficiency of a normal human's. The heart which pumped the strange blue blood had two extra chambers, though he couldn't quite work out why. They should know more when Bland had finished his chemical analysis of the blood itself. And the liver – in there, somewhere, lay the secret of these creatures' ability to live unprotected on the toxic surface of Nu Earth.

But here, in the skull, he was quite sure lay the real prize. After a moment his blade encountered some resistance and he carefully pried it out using his finest forceps. A chip – biomechanical by the look of it.

Bland drifted over from the chromatoscope to peer over Brass's shoulder. After a moment, he frowned. "It appears to be non-functioning, Mr Brass," he said.

Bland was no doubt right. There was a blackened edge to the chip which hadn't been caused by any injury the blue trooper had sustained. "Programmed to self-destruct, I'll warrant." Absent-mindedly, the tapped the forceps against his mouth, hardly noticing the stain of blue blood they left on his lips. "But what is it intended to do, eh? And how much might the Norts be willing to pay for it?"

"Far more if we had a working one," Bland said. "Any thoughts on how we might acquire one?"

"As a matter of fact," said Brass, "I have. Someone had very carefully removed the chip from that other body we found. If we find him, we'll have found our prize."

It nearly was a suicide mission. Rogue felt like he might have every single gun in the Nort army pointed at him. A little while ago a few of them had been pointed at Helm, but he'd succeeded in taking out the machine-gun emplacements and was herding the GI survivors together, ready to make a run for the shore as soon as the Hell Cannon was taken out. This would leave the Norts free to focus everything they had on Rogue.

He definitely wouldn't have made it if it hadn't been for Gunnar and Bagman. Bagman had eyes in the back of his head – literally – sensors that detected enemy lock-ons before Rogue even had the Norts in visual range, and when he needed breathing space to plant some micromines he just set Gunnar loose on his tripod to cover his back.

But Rogue still didn't see any way that he was going to be able to take out the troopers round the Cannon itself. They were clustered too tight, and whatever armour they had seemed to be impervious to both bullets and micro mines.

He stumbled over an inlet of the sea, ignoring the froth of chem that rose up round his knees, and took out one of the Norts, a lucky shot as the man stuck his head out from behind the defences. One down, who knew how many more to go? Rogue fell to his knees in the water, using the shallow bank as cover. The stream itself ran up within a few feet of the Hell Cannon, but there was no way he could use it for cover. Any closer and the Norts would have a clear line of sight over the bank.

The water felt hot against his legs, as if it was so used to burning its way through flesh and bone that it hadn't quite accepted that this was a body it couldn't touch.

Rogue thought about the bodies it could touch. Crouching in what they thought was safety only a few feet from the stream.

Before he could consider whether it was a good idea, he ran down the stream straight towards the Cannon. "Cover me, Gunnar!" he shouted.

"What–" Gunnar began, but then he was too busy to talk, firing every round he had to keep Rogue safe. The only thing that saved Rogue was the Norts' surprise. It hadn't occurred to them that he'd make such a point-less, sure-to-fail move.

"Tent, Bagman," he shouted.

"Rogue, are you feeling okay?" Bagman asked, his voice echoing over the deafening roar of machine-gun fire.

"Now!" Rogue bellowed, and Bagman didn't argue any more. His robot arm dipped into the kitbag and pulled out the ultra-dense material of the one-sheet tent, the only protection a GI was supposed to need in the wild.

It was resistant to everything. Waterproof. Wind-proof. Chemproof. As Rogue approached the Cannon, feeling the burn of ion fire as the big gun itself swung round to annihilate him, striking mere inches from his furiously pumping legs, he dipped the sheet into the water, scooping up as much of the toxic stuff as he could. He snapped it up and out – flinging the chem straight over the heads of the Nort gunners.

They screamed in pain, and he saw them fall and flail, tearing into each other in their haste to get away from the burning, acidic stuff. It was enough. In the few seconds it bought him, he vaulted up to the Hell

Cannon, took every last micro-mine Bagman had left and flung them inside. The explosion was strong enough to blast Rogue off his feet and ten feet through the air, but it was enough to kill every single Nort defender and to put the cannon permanently out of commission.

"Way's clear," Rogue shouted into his helm mic, too loud probably – he was still deafened from the explosion. "Get our guys down to the shore. I'll meet you there."

But first he was going to have to wait until the world stopped spinning around at quite such a crazy rate.

As soon as Helm got Rogue's signal he was up and running, the other GIs at his shoulder. He might think Rogue was a tight-ass who had far too high an opinion of himself, but when it came to battle Helm trusted him completely. If Rogue said the way was clear, then it was. They'd already covered half the distance to the frothing orange shoreline and Helm could see the sleek shape of the Hoverfoils arrowing over the water towards him.

He picked up his pace, pausing only to pick off the occasional Nort trooper who'd escaped the explosion of the Hell Cannon, and soon he was wading out into the water. He was pleased to see that every GI who'd come with him was still with him. The foils were almost there, which was just as well, because the close up the stench of the roiling toxic waters was almost overpowering.

"Here they come," he said into his mic. "Hurry up, Rogue. Our ride home's here."

"Almost there," Rogue's voice crackled through to him, and he could see his comrade pick himself up from beside the wreckage of the Hell Cannon and half walk, half stagger towards the shore.

The Hoverfoils were almost on them before Helm realised something was wrong. And by then it was far too late.

The deck cannons opened fire, the Nort flags were suddenly unfurled above the ships – as if mocking the GIs for trusting them – and the men in Souther uniform who were no Southers at all began to scream and laugh as their guns mowed through the last GIs left on Nu Earth.

"They're Norts!" Helm screamed to the GIs behind him. "It's another trap! Get out of the water!"

On board the foil, Pietr clasped the deck cannon and found that his hands were frozen solid. If he hadn't been able to see the Souther troops, if they hadn't come so close that he could see their faces as their expressions turned from hope to confusion, anger and despair, he might have been able to do it. But the targets were too easy. It just didn't feel right to kill them.

The blue-skinned freaks seemed so human when you saw them close up.

None of the other Norts seemed to have the same qualms. He saw fountains of blue blood as the guns mowed through the ranks, cutting the bodies of the soldiers to shreds of flesh, flaying them almost like knives.

There was one GI he noticed in particular, taller than the others, who seemed to be miraculously avoiding the carnage. He'd gathered a knot of men around him and against all the odds was leading them back to the shore. One blue-skinned trooper fell, then another, but still the leader kept on walking. Pietr found that he'd clenched his hands around into fists, willing the Souther on, willing him to make it. Then the controls of the cannon were wrenched out of his hands and the voice of Private Schulz said,

"You useless Souther-loving scum coward," before the cannon was swung round and a blast of fire sent off straight towards that one remaining group of blue-skinned troops.

Helm floated in the water. For a while he'd thought the floating was death, that he was floating away to the spirit realm that he'd heard the Gene Genies talking about, although it wasn't a place that they'd said GIs would ever go.

The pain began, the terrible pain of multiple shrapnel wounds, and he thought that he couldn't possibly be dead, and that the reason his vision was so blurred was probably because it had been damaged in that last, all-encompassing explosion.

After a while, he tried to move. It was useless. The feeble twitching of his limbs just served to upset him in the water and he ended up swallowing a burning mouthful of chem before he stopped.

He felt the water move as a Hoverfoil eased towards him, and he saw the face of a Nort trooper peering down at him through his Souther chem mask. He started struggling again, hopelessly, trying to force himself to turn around and get away.

"Stop!" the Nort said. "Bring this one aboard. Surgeon-Kapten Natashov wants one of these genetic freaks alive."

Rogue saw it all from the shore. For a moment he moved forward, his legs striding towards his fallen comrade without conscious thought, as if GI loyalty was so deeply bred into him that even his muscles felt it. He soon stopped. He was too far away. There was nothing he could do but die or be captured too.

"They're all dead," Bagman said. His new synthetic voice wasn't built to convey much emotion, but Rogue knew his friend well enough to detect the despair in his tone. "It was another trap."

Gunnar just sounded angry. "The Norts have been second-guessing us since before this op began."

"But how?" Bagman asked.

Rogue thought that was a very good question, but not one they had time for now. "Worry about that later," he said. "First of all we need to get our comrade out of there." He didn't finish the sentence because he didn't need to. Then, he thought, we'll get revenge for all the comrades who didn't make it.

THREE
SURGEON-KAPTEN NATASHOV

Helm was in a world of pain. His eyes kept fuzzing in and out of focus. Not good. A GI was supposed to be damn near indestructible. For that kind of thing to be happening he must have suffered some serious damage. Terminal damage.

Then he felt a wet slapping against his chest and a sudden easing of the pain, as disconcerting as the silence after a scream. His vision cleared, and he saw that a Nort with a red cross emblazoned on his chem suit was leaning over him. A medic. They wanted him to live, then. That couldn't be good news.

Once the pain had passed, he became aware that his hands and feet were shackled, spread-eagled against the deck of the Hoverfoil. His back was pressed to the damp metal surface of the thing, damp where the foul-smelling chem had washed over the shallow sides of the vessel. He could feel it eating away at the material of his fatigues. If he'd been an ordinary man, it would have eaten away at his flesh too.

Gently, keeping his face carefully neutral, he pulled against the restraints. No go. They were rock solid, far stronger than they needed to be. It looked like they'd been expecting to pick up a GI survivor and had forward planned. That wasn't good news either.

Helm tried to reassure himself that Rogue would be looking for him. If Rogue didn't die on the beach, too, he thought. If he can find a way to track the Hoverfoil to wherever the hell it's going.

His thoughts were interrupted by a shadow that suddenly loomed over him, blocking out the sun. It was wearing a cumbersome Souther chem suit, but Helm was damn sure it was a Nort. Helm squinted up at him, but he couldn't make out the face in the shadowed hood. Then the figure stepped to one side and a beam of sickly early morning sunlight glanced in through the side of his visor, illuminating a face that was almost comically young. Round cheeks, lips just a little too full for a man, startled-looking blue eyes, studying Helm with an expression of fear, as if he was the one who was lying on the deck in chains.

"Trying to see what a real soldier looks like, Nort?" Helm sneered.

The Nort soldier jumped back, his hands half lifting as if to push Helm away. Helm heard a wave of laughter from the troops around him. So, this one was the butt of the outfit. There was always one. Bagman had been theirs, except he was also a damn fine soldier. The Nort looked barely strong enough to lift a gun, and without the killing instinct to fire it. Helm filed all this away, human recon, useful if he should ever be in a position to plan an escape.

The Nort's expression tightened as the mocking laughter continued and Helm heard one voice say, "Look at Pietr, chatting with the Souther like they're best friends." "Maybe they are," another one said, to renewed laughter.

"You aren't a real soldier. You're a… a freak!" the Nort called Pietr said. His foot lashed out towards Helm's exposed stomach.

Chained down as he was, Helm couldn't evade the blow. It caught him against an open knife wound. He let out a grunt as the air whooshed out of him, but carefully kept all other expressions of discomfort suppressed. When he could be sure his voice would emerge sounding sufficiently nonchalant, he said, "Yeah, striking an injured prisoner, that's about the level of you scum."

He saw Pietr flush under his visor, a red stain on his pale cheeks. But the mocking laughter had stopped and at the periphery of his vision Helm could sense the other Norts watching the little scene unfolding before them with interest.

"You filthy pigs killed my brother," Pietr said. He sounded a little more convinced of his own words this time.

"Yeah, well, sorry to hear that," Helm said. As he saw the startled expression settle on Pietr's face, added, "If we'd been doing our job right we would have killed you too."

That got him another kick in the guts, harder this time. Then Pietr dropped to his knees beside him and thrust something towards his face. It took Helm a moment to realise it was a little holo-cube, projecting the wavy image of some square-jawed Nort creep into the air above it.

"That's him," Pietr said. "Recognise him? I want you to tell me who killed him. Was it you?"

Helm thought about pointing out that there had been several thousand men on the battlefield and the chances of him recognising one of them were slim, even if they hadn't all been wearing chem suits. Besides which, whoever had killed this boy's brutish-looking brother was probably floating face up somewhere in the scum sea himself. But the boy was beyond that sort of rational argument. His pale eyes looked wild, and Helm guessed that he wasn't really in control of what was coming out of his mouth.

So he just said, "Couldn't tell you. You Norts all look the same to me. But I killed a good hundred of you scum, so I guess your brother might have been one of them."

Pietr lifted a fist, preparing to smash it down into Helm's face. Helm looked up at him impassively. "What you waiting for, Nort?" he said. "Not like I can fight back."

Pietr lowered his hand, looking at it as if puzzled to find it acting in that way. He stood up and stumbled away from Helm, pursued by more mocking laughter from the other Norts.

Helm carefully breathed out. He could only hope the Norts where he was heading were as easy to control.

Surgeon-Kapten Natashov surveyed the table in front of her with pleasure. She'd had to modify it in a hurry – they'd only given her a few hours notice that they were bringing the GI prisoner to her – but she thought she'd done a good job of it.

Everything was gleaming, surgical. The surfaces, the knives, the other instruments. She didn't want to risk any infections, anything that might give her prisoner a premature release from her ministrations.

When she was satisfied that all the instruments were ready, ranked in neat rows, gleaming wickedly up at the high metal ceiling of the base, she turned her attention to the toxins. She prided herself on her collection. For a fan of poisons, and Natashov considered herself a fan, there was no better place to be than Nu Earth. Two thousand seven hundred man-made toxins had been released into the atmosphere in the last year alone. And once there they'd bred, mutated, transformed. Poisons were a form of life, Natashov thought, always multiplying, always changing.

Only the fittest survived. She smiled at the array of tubes in front of her, then turned to the Nort commander beside her. "The GI prisoner, he is ready for me?"

The foil commander nodded, then grimaced. "You'll be lucky to get anything out of him," he said. "The Souther scientists created their Genetic Infantrymen to endure anything."

Natashov smiled. "Excellent. I enjoy a challenge." Her eyes returned to her poisons as she continued, "Grand Admiral Hoffa ordered the complete destruction of all the GIs, but that doesn't mean I can't do a little experimentation first."

A body was wheeled into position on a heavy steel trolley scored with grooves to carry the blood away. Natashov looked down into the taut face of her prisoner, blue skin shining dully in the bright lights. "Shall we begin, GI?"

Rogue only had to take one look at the base to realise that a frontal assault was out of the question. The base itself was large enough, hugging the shore like a steel limpet. And after that he still had to get to the heart of the huge Nort ship docked there, as big as an island.

They'd had stealth and infiltration training, but that had relied on them getting into places where everyone was suited up. Here they were all walking bare-faced, the scum sea the one place on Nu Earth where the poisonous atmosphere was burned clean away by the chem of the water itself.

The first area proved easy, just a matter of avoiding the Norts, navy men in blue mask-less chem suits, who were clustered in small groups shifting cargo around the enormous docks at the heart of the base, loading and unloading the small patrol boats which lived in there.

Then, there was a problem. There was a gate he needed to pass to get through to the section of the base that led to the ship, and the gate was up, leaving a precipitous drop to the water below. He could see the controls – on the other side, completely inaccessible even if he did come out of hiding. He had to find a way to get the Norts to lower that gate themselves.

"Bagman," Rogue said. "Get me some micro-mines ready."

"You can't blow the place up, Rogue!" Bagman said worriedly. "If it goes, Helm might go with it."

"Don't worry," Rogue hissed, "I'm not looking for anything major, just a little distraction."

After a second's hesitation, Bagman's robo-arm popped out and deposited one of the tiny grey micro-mines into Rogue's palm. Rogue put it in his mouth to keep his hands free, carefully guarding his teeth with his lips. The Gene Genies had assured them that the devices were safe until primed, but then the Gene Genies had told them the Quartz Zone offensive would be a walk-through, so what did they know?

There was only one soldier defending the nearest patrol boat below him in the water, a bored-looking Nort leaning against his rifle rather than holding it to attention. They'd obviously gotten cocky since taking out the GIs.

Rogue ghosted towards him, sticking to the shadows, letting his blue skin work for him. Gunnar was strapped to his back, too noisy for a stealth mission.

He was only a foot away when the Nort saw him and by then there was nothing he could do about it. He opened his mouth to shout an alarm, but before any sound came out Rogue's hands were around his neck and with a sharp jerk he snapped it. The only sound the man managed to let out was a choked gurgle, too quiet for anyone to hear.

Rogue took the micro mine out of his mouth, spitting out the metallic taste along with it, and dropped it into the belly of the patrol boat. Then he ran like hell.

For a second he might have been conspicuous. Then the boat exploded: a vast gout of fire belched up into the night sky, and suddenly everyone was running. Men sprinted from the other side to see what had caused the explosion – and they were lowering the bridge across the water to do it.

"Good one, Rogue," Bagman said.

As he'd hoped, they seemed to be treating it as an accident. Too sure of themselves, unable to contemplate that the Southers might have struck back so soon. Stupid. And stupid got you dead.

Rogue wasn't in the killing business at that moment. He planned to remain undetected at least until he located Helm. An officer he passed in the shadows shouted out to him to turn around and help with the patrol boat, but Rogue ignored him and that seemed to be okay. When there was an emergency, a lot of soldiers disobeyed a lot of orders.

"You really think we're going to get away with his?" Bagman whispered.

"Nope," Rogue said.

"Don't see why we just couldn't go in shooting," Gunnar grumbled quietly, but not quietly enough.

The Nort squadron who'd been marching past turned to stare at Rogue. Then the leader stepped closer and stared even more carefully.

"Soldier," he said suspiciously, "just what happened to your skin?"

It seemed like a genuine question. These must be base personnel, Rogue realised, not veterans from the Quartz Zone fight. He guessed that the GIs had been kept secret from them too. Armies generally liked their left arms not to know what their right arms were doing.

Making his voice into a desperate rasp, Rogue said, "Got splashed with chem from the explosion before I could suit up. I need... I think I need to go to detox, sir."

The sergeant frowned and for a moment Rogue thought he wasn't buying it. But then he pushed Rogue gently in the back and said, "Hurry along then, soldier," and Rogue realised that the expression was because the sergeant thought Rogue was a goner and didn't know how to tell him.

Rogue sketched a Nort salute and trotted off. So far, so good.

Elsewhere on the base, two visitors were annoyed to find their attempt to get an audience with Surgeon-Kapten Natashov delayed by this unexpected calamity.

"This is most inconvenient, Mr Brass," Bland said.

"Indeed." Brass surveyed the room, considering trying to chivvy things along, but he could tell he would meet with short shrift. He sighed. "Well, I suppose our information will keep for a few hours."

Bland, his face squashed slightly under the transparent gel of his chem suit, didn't look happy. "But this is Natashov we're talking about. If reputations are to be believed, the soldier in her... care, may not *have* a few hours. And as you know, it is imperative that the chip be removed from him while he is still alive."

Natashov was enjoying herself. She'd heard the alarm going off, but had ignored it, secure in the knowledge that her operating room was safely hidden in the heart of the huge ship. Nothing would be allowed to interrupt her fun.

She looked down at the face of the Souther experiment, the so-called Genetic Infantryman. It already looked ten years older than when she'd begun work on him a few hours ago. There were deep lines of pain scored into his cheeks and beside his eyes, though he had yet to utter anything above a muffled gasp. She could see what his silence was costing him in the tight white squeeze of his fists as she brought the scalpel down again and carefully severed the middle finger on his left hand. There were only three left now. Soon she'd have to move on to something else.

He didn't make any sound of protest, just glared fiercely at her out of his blank white eyes. "You'll never get me to tell you anything," he snarled.

The foil captain had been right – these GIs were tough. That was fine with her: breaking the strong was always more satisfying than breaking the weak. But maybe it was time to move on to her favourite toys.

She pulled the rack of toxins nearer and selected a tube of thick red gel. On a normal human, it caused an agonising and drawn-out death as all the blood leeched from the body through the pores. It would be interesting to see what effect it had on a GI.

Pietr knew he should be back with his platoon. The all-clear had sounded a few minutes ago. It seemed there'd just been an accident with one of the patrol boats. Everyone else would be drifting back to the Kashan quarters on the vast troop carrier. They'd be wondering where Pietr had got to.

Pietr didn't know what was the matter with him, and he needed some time alone to figure it out. He'd failed on the battlefield, on the Hoverfoil. He knew that. He hadn't been the man his brother would have wanted him to be.

But that could change, he told himself. That had to change. He could become a better soldier, the soldier his brother would have wanted him to be. The soldier who could avenge his brother's death.

Pietr lifted his chin, trying to put pride and determination into his step. He hefted his beam rifle in his arms, testing the weight of it, convincing himself that he could grow used to it, that it would become his friend. Head high, gun at the ready, he marched down the corridor to rejoin his squad.

Pietr saw him.

His blue skin was quite visible, even in the dim corridor lighting. Pietr was amazed that no one else had spotted him, but then he guessed that everyone had been busy dealing with the alarm, an alarm which suddenly made a lot more sense. Pietr swallowed past a lump of fear in his throat and pressed himself against the wall as hard as he could, as if he could actually melt away into it and out of danger.

But the Souther's attention wasn't on him. He was peering round a corner, no doubt scanning the way ahead. Pietr had a very clear view of his profile, and he was suddenly absolutely sure that this was the man who had killed Jaze. He didn't know how he was so certain — they were clones, they all looked alike – but there was something, some subtle cast to the creature's face, that put it beyond doubt.

Pietr couldn't believe it, couldn't credit that his chance for revenge had come so easily. His hands tensed, ready to lift and target his gun. But then he started looking at the Souther, really looking at him. The thing's whole body was nothing but wiry muscle. The training video had said the GIs were ten, twenty times as strong as an ordinary man, and looking at this one Pietr could believe it. And their reflexes were super-fast, too, their senses hyper-fine.

What if I move and he senses me before I can target him? Pietr thought. What if I'm too slow and he kills me before I can kill him? He could hear my breathing now. He might have some sixth sense that can detect my presence when I don't even make a noise. So in the end Pietr just turned and ran, and only when he was well away, a hundred feet from the blue soldier, did he sound the alarm.

When the alarm changed in tone, Natashov lifted her head from her work. She knew that sound. It was an intruder alert. As if on cue, her radio crackled. "Surgeon-Kapten, there's an intruder on the ship," the foil commander said. Then, flatly, as if this shouldn't matter, "It's another GI." He ended the message just after she heard him barking orders to bring the blue-skinned scum down.

She looked down at her own personal GI. He had proved disappointingly resistant to her poisons. And she could tell that her time with him was drawing to a close. "One of your comrades coming to rescue you?" she said to him. She looked back at her poisons, at the one vial she had yet to use, and smiled. "A pity you won't be alive when he gets here."

She removed the vial from its case and carefully slotted it into the back of her strongest hypodermic; the first two she'd used had snapped off without penetrating the GI's skin. The vial had a small symbol on its side: a skull icon, rather like the one the GI wore on his equipment. Appropriate, really.

"You Genetic Infantrymen are supposed to be immune to every kind of poison." She squeezed out a little liquid from the end of her syringe, being very careful to keep it away from her own skin. "Let us see how true that is."

She plunged the vial straight into the trooper's neck.

She had one second to enjoy the expression of agony on the man's face and the helpless scream that was wrenched from his throat as the skin around the point of contact bubbled and burst.

Then blue hell burst into the room and all she could concentrate on was keeping herself alive.

Helm was in agony, the deepest pain he'd ever felt. The wounds he'd received after the Quartz Zone were nothing compared to this. He could feel himself burning up from the inside. It shouldn't be possible, but the Nort torturer's toxin was killing him.

Damn it! He didn't want to be just another piece of Rogue's equipment. He tried to make the most of the last feel of his body, agonising as it was. He pressed his arms back against their restraints, thinking: This is what a limb feels like, this is what cold feels like, don't forget it. He knew it might be a while before he experienced those feelings again.

Then he caught sight of Rogue's battle with Natashov and realised that he might not ever feel them again. The Surgeon-Kapten was clearly skilled at more than torture. She seemed to anticipate and dodge every shot Rogue sent off. And she had weapons of her own: knives, whirring blades, spiked balls. Helm had felt them all in his own flesh and now he saw them being used on Rogue.

As he watched, Rogue dodged just a fraction too late, and one of Natashov's knives caught him under the ribs, leaving a thin trail of blue blood. Rogue dodged round and away, but a second slower and the knife would have bitten lethally deep.

"What the hell are you doing, Rogue?" he heard Gunnar shout. "Finish the bitch off!" Helm remembered that it wasn't just his own life that depended on Rogue's survival.

He realised that there was something he could do to help them all. Natashov had left one of her vials of poison next to the tips of Helm's manacled right hand. There was barely anything left in the tube, but that didn't matter. All he wanted was a distraction.

He clawed his fingers desperately towards it, and was terrified for a moment when they didn't move at all, as if the scorching toxin in his system had already severed all the nerve connections there. After a second, his hand seemed to wake up. It was still horribly weak, but he gritted his teeth – feeling them crunch and crumble in his mouth – closed his fingers around the syringe, and flung it towards Natashov.

She was about to plunge her knife into Rogue's exposed thigh, but at the sound of the syringe clattering to the floor her head snapped round. In the second it allowed him, Rogue emptied Gunnar into her with everything he had.

He paused only to check that she was dead, then strode straight towards Helm. Helm didn't know how bad his appearence was, but from Rogue's expression he could tell it wasn't good.

"Hurry up, Rogue," Gunnar said. "He's dying."

Helm knew that Gunnar was right. His vision was already starting to go, showing him the world only in shades of grey. Rogue moved towards his head, ready to remove the biochip. Then he saw the empty vial of toxin with the skull icon on it.

"Some kind of toxin," Bagman told them, as if that wasn't obvious. "One even we're not immune to." His voice sounded suddenly worried. "Where'd the Norts get it from?"

"Good question," Rogue said. His face and voice were grim. Even in the half-light of his fading life, Helm could tell that Rogue was having the same thoughts he was. But there was something else he wanted Rogue to know, while he was still a man.

"Rogue... I didn't give her anything," he gasped. His voice was just a thin thread, but he could tell that

Rogue had heard him. He nodded. "Just like we were trained," Helm whispered.

Rogue bent towards him, knife in hand. "Take it easy. We'll take care of it." The grey faded to black and Helm was gone...

He returned, seconds later, seeing the world in a completely different way. He knew, instantly, that Rogue had used the slot in his helmet to house him, and he would have smiled if he'd been able to.

He'd been right to try to remember what pain and cold and touch felt like. They were all gone now. He'd lost all ability to move, and for a moment he couldn't escape the thought that he'd been paralysed and he had to fight the urge to scream. He could still see, areas of the spectrum that had been invisible even to his GI eyes, and he had a whole new set of senses, too. His hearing could pick up vibrations as well, and his sense of smell was tied in to a chemical monitoring system, a spectroscope that told him the exact composition of the air around him.

Best of all was the computer. Inside the helmet he was plugged into resided the limited AI that kept all Rogue's equipment running and fed into his HUD. He felt like he was swimming in a pool of information. He knew that if Rogue connected him to any information system, any computer on the planet, he'd be able to swim in a whole sea of it. The primitive hacking he'd carried out as a human paled in comparison.

"There," Rogue said. "Now we're a team again."

"What now, Rogue?" Bagman asked.

"Now we find out who was responsible for the massacre at the Quartz Zone."

"Rogue," Helm said urgently. "That Nort, before she started torturing me, she mentioned a name."

Listening as Helm relayed the words Natashov had

spoken to him, Rogue carried him out of the room where he'd died.

A few seconds after they'd gone, two figures stepped out of the shadows. They looked rather foolish, with their bowler hats and waxed moustaches, but that was all on the outside. On the inside, they were every bit as ruthless as the surgeon-kapten who lay dead on the floor.

"Well, Mr Bland," said one. "It seems we know where to find a living biochip."

FOUR
DESERTER

Steel watched the film through narrow, slitted eyes. It showed a Souther flag fluttering in the breeze. The sky behind it was blue, dotted with white clouds. It was nowhere on Nu Earth, that was for sure. Then the picture faded and was replaced with one of a soldier, a strange blue-skinned creature wearing Souther insignia. Steel knew that this was a Genetic Infantryman, though he'd never seen one himself, and the information about them had only been released to the rest of the Souther army after the genetic freaks had botched the Quartz Zone offensive so spectacularly.

Bred for war, the other Southers had been told. Bred to be failures, Steel reckoned. Bred to be less than real men. The viewscreen was showing pictures of the infantryman in action, clearly shot during his long training at Milli-Com. Above the pictures, the caption "HAVE YOU SEEN THIS DESERTER?" appeared.

Then a voice, the sort of voice Steel was used to hearing in this sort of film, spoke. "Be alert, Souther!" it said, as if Steel wasn't alert twenty-four hours a day, never letting his guard down for a moment. "One of the Genetic Infantrymen, the last reported survivor of the Quartz Zone Massacre, has gone renegade, refusing to obey orders to return to Milli-Com. This cannot stand. He's a deserter, and must be treated as such."

The screen faded to a still shot of the deserter as the voice continued, "Learn this face well. If you encounter him, approach him with extreme caution."

Steel almost laughed out loud at that. Caution wasn't a word in his vocabulary.

"Alert the military authorities, and let military justice deal with this dangerous renegade."

The shot changed to one that Steel recognised. Nu Atlanta. He'd fought a battle there during his first year of service, had nearly lost an eye and taken the eyes out of seven Norts in revenge.

"In other news," the voice continued, "Nu Atlanta has finally been declared pacified and safe from Nort attack. To celebrate, Milli-Com Command has ordered R and R facilities to be set up for our victorious boys."

A ragged cheer went up from the hundreds of troops from the East Continent command post who'd been gathered to watch the film, but Steel wasn't really paying attention. He couldn't get the picture of that deserter, that filthy traitor, out of his mind.

Traitors made him almost as sick as Norts did. He touched the necklace around his neck, made from twenty-three trigger fingers of the Nort snipers he'd taken out, and resolved to add a blue finger to his collection.

Further towards the back of the room, another figure was watching the film with interest. Colonel Kovert looked round at the faces of the other Southers, flushed with anger at this desertion by one of their own, and knew that some of them would not be satisfied to leave the matter to the military authorities, whatever the film had instructed.

He turned to the operative behind him, still lurking in the shadows. "The Rogue Trooper," he said. "I want him found."

Rogue had been crouching in the shadows, staring at the small base for so long that Bagman was beginning to wonder if he'd fallen asleep. The chem clouds were low, blocking out the sun almost entirely and turning day into night, as if the black hole that filled one quarter of the sky was slowly eating away at the rest of it. Helm, Bagman had discovered, could see even in the dark now that he'd lost his physical body.

Bagman couldn't. He guessed the extra senses they got came from the piece of equipment they were plugged into. It made sense. Bagman's vision was no better than before but unlike Helm he almost felt like he had a body of his own: arms, legs, head, fingers, toes. Only trouble was, they were Rogue's arms and legs and head. The kitbag he controlled was the source of everything Rogue needed, so the intelligence implanted in it had been granted detailed information about its carrier. Bagman would have bet good money that he now knew Rogue's body better than Rogue knew it himself.

He knew when Rogue was hungry and gave him food. He sensed the slight tear in the ligament of his shoulder, the place where the muscle was lifting away from the bone, and he fed him the nano-tube which would target and cure that precise injury. He looked after Rogue better than his mother would have, if Rogue ever had oner.

On the whole, he thought Helm and Gunnar had got the better deal. Being a nursemaid just wasn't that much fun.

"You sure you can do this, Helm?" Rogue said, snapping Bagman out of his reverie.

"No problem," Helm replied. "You get me in there, hack me into their communications net, and I'll pull everything I can on Grand Admiral Hoffa."

"You ready for this, boys?" Rogue said.

Bagman and Gunnar said they were, though Bagman didn't get the point of Rogue asking. They'd be going in whether Bagman and Gunnar were ready or not. Rogue had the body, so Rogue called the shots.

The stronghold had a small crew, some machine-gun units, a few NCOs running them, one sniper, and a whole load of fly-by Hoppas ready to drop more Norts and the odd decapitator along with them, but none of them knew what had hit them. Rogue went in strong and hard, taking out a sniper first with a bullet through the head, before turning to the Hoppa landing pad. He didn't want them bringing in more reinforcements before Helm had done his job.

For the brief but intense minutes of battle, Rogue was in another world, a world of reflex where thought wasn't needed or welcome. In the days since he'd marched away from the Quartz Zone in search of Admiral Hoffa, he'd found himself thanking the Gene Genies for the brutal training back on Milli-Com. There was no room for fear in battle, they'd told the GIs. Rogue hadn't realised how true that was until he'd started putting his life on the line down here on Nu Earth. Fear slowed you down, it made you cautious, and caution got you killed.

Rogue wasn't cautious at all. He went straight in, Gunnar blazing, dodging and weaving but never wavering. A moving target was harder to hit, and he knew his body could take some punishment before it caved. He was shooting all the time, not a constant stream, stopping to target, wasting no shots. By the time he was halfway into the control centre, thirty Norts were dead.

When he'd reached the corpse of the radio operator, they all were dead. Afterwards he allowed the fear to take him, the knowledge that any second out of the last thousand might have been his last. He noticed a burn on his arm and realised how close a beam had come to getting him, but he'd felt nothing at the time.

"Medpac, Bagman," he ordered, and slapped the nano-infused pad onto the scorched flesh. Then, before it had even sealed to his skin, he put Helm down next to the radio terminal and jacked him into the nearest port. He took a few seconds to secure all the doors, then went to crouch in the one that he knew wouldn't remain sealed for long, the one that led deeper into the base and towards the rest of the Norts.

In the seconds while he waited for the Norts trapped inside to bypass the door-control he'd blasted shut, he took a look around the place. It was a dump. The equipment all looked second-hand and third-rate. There was no strategic importance to this little scrubby section of Nu Earth, Rogue knew, so the Norts hadn't committed any decent resources here. This was exactly why he'd picked it. It might be a backwater place manned by troops the Norts couldn't be bothered to equip properly, but it still needed to keep in touch with Nort Central Command. That's the beauty of networks. Point A is connected to points B through Z.

Or at least Rogue hoped so. Helm was still working away, and so far he hadn't shown any sign of making progress. Maybe the Nort network had security protocols even Helm couldn't crack, in which case they were back to square one as far as tracking down General Hoffa was concerned.

Rogue stopped worrying about it when the small chamber was suddenly filled with the acrid smell of metal melting, and a second later the first Norts became visible through the glowing hole they'd bored into the thick steel of the doors.

He took three of them down with Gunnar before they'd even realised that they'd made it through the door. After that they took up defensive positions and started firing back. Rogue was sheltered behind a good strong steel partition, but he knew it couldn't last through a concerted barrage, and there was always the chance that a stray shot would take out Helm.

"How you doing, Helm?" Rogue asked him.

"Almost there, Rogue."

It was funny, the voice sounded like Helm's now, with all his inflections and personality in it. Rogue wasn't sure if that was because in the days since he'd possessed it, Helm had been altering the helmet's speaker to reflect his speech patterns, or if it was just that Rogue was getting more used to the strange mechanical grate of his friend's new voice.

He picked off another Nort trooper who'd been foolish enough to poke his head round the upended bench they were using for cover. His head exploded in a bloom of blood, and Gunnar let out a whoop of satisfaction – until he saw the horde of reinforcements pouring in behind the fallen man, clutching Lazookas and other artillery heavier than Rogue was equipped to deal with.

"Take your time, why don't you?" Gunnar shouted back at Helm. "It ain't like we got anything else going on here!"

Helm ignored him and just shouted out, "Got him! Let's get out of here, Rogue."

Using Gunnar to lay down a steady stream of suppressing fire, Rogue dived out of the back entrance, the one he'd carefully tunnelled down to give himself a clear escape route.

When the Nort troops made their way cautiously into the central chamber he'd vacated, they had one second to enjoy the regained territory. Then they had another second to notice the micro-mines scattered across the surface of the floor.

A second later the micro-mines went off and they weren't noticing much of anything.

• • •

"Where to, Helm?" Rogue asked as soon as they were clear of the explosion. The land surrounding the base was featureless scrub, all life wiped from it by the pervasive chem, save for the hardiest plants and ugliest insects.

"Nu Paree," Helm replied. "According to what I picked up, he's scheduled to have a meeting there in three days' time."

"Nice job," Rogue said, and instantly regretted it. If Helm had still had a face, he knew from the second of lethal silence that followed that it would have been twisted into a furious scowl. As it was, the anger was confined to the voice.

"Don't patronise me, Rogue," Helm said. "Just cause I haven't got a body doesn't mean I haven't got a mind. I'm a GI same as you."

"I know," Rogue said as calmly as possible. "It was a good job. I couldn't have hacked into those systems with a body or without one."

"Too right," Helm said, but he sounded mollified.

They both stopped speaking when they saw what was in front of them: an entire Souther squadron. Every one of them pointing their weapons at Rogue.

Rogue had his gun at the ready too, he always did, but they were Southers, damn it! Even if he could take them all out, he wouldn't want to.

"Drop your gun, deserter!" the lead Souther said.

"Forget it, soldier!" Gunnar said, but Rogue ignored him and threw the weapon to the ground. Gunnar let out an indignant squawk.

Rogue held his hands carefully away from his sides. "What is it you boys want?" he asked the Souther soldiers.

Their leader smiled nastily and took a step nearer. As soon as Rogue could see his face through the distorting lens of the chem suit, he knew that he'd made a mistake. It was the smile of a man who could only find pleasure when someone else was experiencing pain. His eyes were a blank green, devoid of feeling. And around his neck Rogue could see a necklace of human finger bones –some with the flesh still clinging to them.

Helm saw them too. "Good move, Rogue," he said. But by then there was nothing Rogue could do about it. The other soldiers in the troop had moved round behind him and secured his arms to his sides with razor wire. Helm was taken from his head and tossed casually into a corner.

They couldn't know about the biochips, he realised, which gave Rogue some sort of advantage, but he couldn't begin to see how to use it.

"I'm Sergeant Steel and I've got orders to take you in," the leader said. Then his smile widened, looking even crueller and a little crazy. "Hope you don't mind if I bring you back in pieces."

Pietr couldn't figure out why the others were treating him like a piece of dirt. A small squad of Southers had been spotted approaching from the chem-river valley on the other side of the mountains, and the Kashan Legion – fresh from their victory at the Quartz Zone – had been sent to intercept it.

Easy in, easy out, their commander had told them, though Pietr still found himself shaking with fear. It didn't help that he was alone, the other Kashans leaving a space around him as if he had some kind of infectious disease. He could see them talking to each other, laughing, and he was sure it was about him. Maybe he was just being paranoid, but then why did they keep looking over at him?

He told himself not to worry about it. Battle was coming, and he needed to concentrate on that. Concentrate on not getting killed.

A good start would be to stop his hands shaking. He could see his beam rifle, wavering as he held it, the muzzle pointing at the ground one minute and then weaving towards the lowering green-yellow clouds the next. He tightened his fist until his knuckles whitened and the gun steadied.

It was just in time, as the first wave of Southers broke over the brow of the hill. These were nothing like the blue-skinned devils they'd fought in the Quartz Zone. They were just ordinary men, in chem suits like Pietr, but they still terrified him. He tightened his grip on the rifle still further and fired. Ahead of him, one of the Southers stumbled backwards, a blackened hole in his chest. Pietr didn't know if it was his shot which had taken him out, but he told himself that it was and it gave him the confidence to go on.

For a while, he didn't think, just fought, and he found that when his own life was on the line he didn't have any hesitation about killing. For a while, he even found himself smiling, or at least his mouth was set in a rigid grin, as he ducked and weaved and somehow miraculously came through the hell of machine-gun fire and micro-mines unscathed.

Then he saw a cluster of five Southers heading straight towards him and he knew he couldn't take them on alone. He looked around, expecting backup and found that there was no one there.

For a second, he thought that all his comrades must somehow have been killed. Then he flicked a desperate glance to his right and spotted them, standing aside, watching. Watching and deliberately leaving him to face these Southers alone. He opened his mouth to shout for help, then shut it again. Even at this distance, he could see in the other soldiers' stances that they had absolutely no intention of helping him.

He looked back at the Southers, terrified. They all had their weapons trained on him. He could see the leader grinning, a white slash in the brown oval of his face.

Suddenly a stray burst of ion fire caught them from another corner of the battlefield. For a moment, they were just black silhouettes, shadow puppets on a stage of blinding white. Then there was nothing but a smear of soot on the red rock of the hillside.

After that the battle was over fairly quickly. Pietr didn't fight, just stood shivering on the sidelines. He knew that he should be dead. Worse, he knew that his comrades *wanted* him dead.

As soon as the all-clear was sounded, he strode up to Schulz, one of the figures he'd recognised watching him as he faced a squadron of Southers alone. So angry he forgot that Schulz outranked him, Pietr grabbed the other man by the shoulders and spun him round to face him.

"What the hell were you doing out there?" Pietr shouted.

Schulz shook Pietr's arm off contemptuously. "Doing out where?" he said nonchalantly. Around him, the other members of the squadron all gathered, facing Pietr. It wasn't difficult to guess which side they were on.

"You left me to die!" Pietr shouted.

Schulz laughed, amused by Pietr's anger. "Sorry, but we thought you'd just walk away." There was a slight pause, then he added, "You know, the way you did when you saw that Souther freak who killed Surgeon-Kapten Natashov."

Pietr felt his blood freeze in his veins. He took an unconscious step back from Schulz. They'd seen it. How had they seen it? But of course there had been sur-veillance all over the station. No doubt someone had been reviewing the tapes to see how the Souther had breached their security and had ended up witnessing Pietr's humiliating inability to face the man who'd killed his brother.

"I raised the alarm," he said, trying to cover the catch in his voice.

"Yeah – to call other men to do your fighting for you," Schulz said contemptuously. Then he just walked away, as if Pietr wasn't worth talking to.

Pietr remained frozen to the spot. They'd seen it. They knew what a coward he was. And if he'd thought his life in the legion was unpleasant before, he was sure it would seem like nothing to what came now. For as long as his life actually lasted.

Rogue could feel the razor wire digging into his skin, breaking through the flesh so that he felt a tickle of his blue blood oozing over the top of it. They'd tied it much tighter than they needed to, tight enough to wound. There was absolutely no way he was getting out of it.

He looked around, but even his sensitive eyesight couldn't spot anything helpful in the night-darkened landscape of low hillocks and scrubby bushes.

"What are we gonna do, Rogue?" Bagman whispered in his ear. "Just tell me the plan."

Rogue almost laughed. "Hey, buddy, your idea is as good as mine," he whispered, though he didn't really need to. Steel and his men were standing a good ten feet away, laughing and drinking and having a heated debate about the best way to kill Rogue and how they were going to torture him first. The discussion was the only reason Rogue wasn't dead already. He'd even hoped for a while that it might escalate into the kind of argument where shots got fired and Rogue could slip away in the confusion, but the other men seemed too scared of Steel for that.

"Oh," Bagman said. After a while, he added, "But you have got a plan, right?" There was a slight edge of panic in his voice.

"Yeah," Rogue said wearily. "I've got a plan."

"Well, maybe you'd like to listen to my plan first," a voice said behind Rogue.

Rogue instantly tensed and tried to turn, jack-knifing himself against the hard ground, but he was tied too tightly.

"Relax Rogue, she's one of ours," Bagman whispered.

"She?" Rogue felt the figure behind him begin to press something against his bound wrists. He really didn't like the feeling of helplessness; it was one thing the Gene Genies had never trained him for. Almost snapping his back with the effort, Rogue managed to twist his head round on his shoulders and get a look at the newcomer.

It *was* a she. A chem nurse, to be precise. He could see the white of her uniform glowing palely in the light of Nu Earth's fractured moon. If Steel and his men had been watching more and drinking less, she would have been very easy to spot. She still might be. All it would take would be one person looking at the wrong moment.

As soon as his arms were free, Rogue rolled to cover and pulled the chem nurse down with him. "Thanks, sister," he said. "Now get away as fast as you can."

"Only if you come with me," she said. "They still outnumber you, and I didn't free you for you to fight Southers."

Rogue *had* been considering taking out Steel and his men. He reckoned the Southside would be better off without them, but he saw the pleading look in the nurse's big dark eyes and decided that revenge could wait. Besides, the Southside needed all the men it had after what had gone down at the Quartz Zone.

"Sure, sister," he said. "But I gotta get my equipment back first."

She frowned, a neat row of wrinkles on the forehead of her smooth white face. "You can get new kit as soon as you're out of here," she said.

Rogue shook his head. "Not like this. This kit's got my buddies in it."

"Too right!" Bagman said.

He saw her jump, a brief startled expression on her face, before she schooled it back to calm. "Biochips, got it. Okay then, trooper, I'll meet you over on that far ridge." And as quick as that she was gone. Rogue liked that. No messing with unnecessary talk, just going straight for the mission objective. The girl would have made a good soldier if she hadn't been a nurse.

He didn't waste any time himself, just began crawling over the ground on his belly. He knew where Helm was, a few feet from where Rogue had been lying, tossed away when they'd first captured him. Gunnar was more of a problem. They hadn't wanted to leave a weapon by their prisoner, no matter how securely tied he appeared, so Gunnar had been taken by their mess fire. Fortunately they'd moved a few feet away from that as their discussion about Rogue's death had begun, but that was still a few feet too close.

For a moment, Rogue went through the cold calculation: should he risk himself, Helm and Bagman to rescue Gunnar? Was that the best use of his resources? But he found that he couldn't carry on thinking that way, not even after twenty years of training from the Gene Genies. Gunnar wasn't an asset, he was a friend and there was no way in hell Rogue was leaving his friend to Steel's ministrations.

As it turned out, getting Gunnar was a breeze. The fire they'd lit in a pile of the scrubby, dried-out bushes had robbed the men of their night vision. Rogue, who'd been designed to adjust to changing light levels faster than thought, didn't have any such problem. He crawled to within feet of the men who were plotting to kill him, as silent as a snake, and not one of them even glanced round.

Gunnar had the sense to stay silent, unless he'd been damaged in the fall, so Rogue was in and away within seconds. He heard the words, "burn off his feet, make him walk on the stumps", and then he was out of earshot.

But when he snagged Helm off the ground, it all hit the fan. Steel must have finally decided on a plan – maybe the whole walking-on-his-stumps thing had taken his fancy – because suddenly the Southers were all looking over to where Rogue's body ought to be and wasn't any more.

Rogue used their second of shouting confusion to hightail it out of there. He could have used Gunnar to take them on, and in fact Gunnar was quietly urging him to do just that. But he'd told the chem nurse he wouldn t, and he'd rather make a clean break and not give his situation away.

So he just ran, silent, weaving through the dry, tangled vegetation on the ground. To his eyes, the landscape before him was as clear as daylight, but bathed in a blue light that made it look slightly unreal, as if it was all part of a dream from which he might soon wake up. Behind him he heard Steel and his men blundering and shouting. Their vision was nowhere near as good as his, but they'd managed to follow, and they were heading towards him. Good. He'd kept his promise to the chem nurse. He hadn't attacked them. But if they were going to attack him… Time to clean some scum out of the Souther forces.

The first soldiers didn't know what hit them. They'd expected Rogue to be on the run, not waiting to ambush them as they blundered about looking for him. They didn't know he could see in the dark. Ironic, really, that the Norts had turned out to know more about GIs than their own side.

The Southers' blood was black in the moonlight as it sprayed out of their bodies, but they died all the same. Steel wasn't so easy, though. He saw Rogue instantly, picking him out in the darkness with an old soldier's instincts and heading straight for him. Even when Rogue had riddled his torso with bullets, he kept on coming. At first Rogue thought he might be wearing some kind of new body armour, something the Southers had developed to be proof against their own weapons. But then he realised that Steel *was* getting hit. His body was juddering with the impact of the bullets.

He just kept on coming. His mouth was set in a stiff grin of agony but his eyes burned with hate. It was hatred stronger than any Rogue had seen in the eyes of the Norts he'd battled. This was personal. This man thought Rogue was a traitor. Fair enough. Rogue thought Steel was a traitor – to everything the South stood for, everything that made it worth fighting for against the Norts.

He put a bullet straight through Steel's mask and into his hate-filled eyes. The big man collapsed at his feet, still reaching out for Rogue. His hand touched Rogue's foot, grasped hold of it convulsively, and then relaxed.

After that it was a mopping-up exercise.

A few minutes later, Rogue was sitting in the lee of the hill, his wounds being tended to by the chem nurse, who'd given her name as Sister Sledge. For her sake, they'd lit a small night-globe. In its reddish-pink light he studied the shape of her face. Her lips were full and curved, and there was a downward tilt to them that spoke of a concealed amusement. Her eyes were huge and very dark, the same polished brown colour as her hair. She was pretty, he guessed – he hadn't had much experience of normal women. He found himself suddenly thinking of Venus, very glad she'd been spared the massacre in the Quartz Zone.

"You haven't asked who I am. You haven't asked why Steel and his men were holding me prisoner," he said after a few minutes of silence. "Don't you think there might have been a reason they had me trussed up like a pig?"

She shook her head, her smile emerging fully onto her face. "I know who you are," she said. "You're the Rogue Trooper. And I know about Steel, too. Every chem nurse does, we've all had to deal with the messes he's left behind, and I'm not talking about on the Nort side. The guy's warped."

"Get no argument from me," Gunnar said. "Should have just taken him down straight off."

Sister Sledge didn't seem phased by the biochips now that she knew what they were. "He was still on our side," she shot back at Gunnar. "And my job's about saving lives, not taking them."

"Yeah, well, mine ain't," Gunnar grumbled, but he subsided into silence.

"The orders were to bring you in, not kill you," Sister Sledge said to Rogue. Her expression grew self-mocking. "I'd try to bring you in myself but I don't rate my chances."

"So Milli-Com's after us too," Helm said. "Figures."

"But we're only doing our job," Bagman protested. "They ought to be cheering us on, not sending psychos like Steel out after us. We're heading after the Nort who ran the Quartz Zone campaign," Bagman said to Sledge. "Make him pay for what he did to our buddies."

"She doesn't want to know that," Rogue growled at Bagman.

"Doesn't need to know that, you mean," Sledge said, but she was laughing. "It's okay, I'll just patch you up and send you on your way. Where you go is your business." She slapped a final medpack onto the raw, oozing wire cuts on his arm. "Well, that's you done. I'm sorry I can't do more for your friends, but I don't carry that kind of equipment around with me."

"It's okay," Helm said. "We didn't expect you to be carrying re-gening gear into the field."

Sister Sledge frowned. Rogue felt a sudden stab of unease at the expression. "I wasn't talking about re-gening," she said. "I was talking about the, well, the degeneration."

"What degeneration?" the three biochips said, pretty much simultaneously.

Sledge suddenly looked very uncomfortable. "I'm sorry, I thought you knew. Of course you must have left before they found out."

"Found out what?" Helm snapped impatiently.

She seemed to wonder whether she should go on, then realised there was no way they were going to let her stop. "It's the chips," they said eventually. "There's a fault in them. A… an electrical seepage, I think, it's not really my field. Anyway, if you get yourselves re-gened within a fortnight or so it shouldn't be a problem, the degeneration won't have taken away any crucial memory functions."

"And if we wait longer than a fortnight?" Bagman asked, his mechanical voice tense.

Sledge looked even more unhappy.

"Just tell us, sister," Rogue said. "We're soldiers, we can take it."

"Speak for yourself, Rogue," Bagman said. "You're not the one who's falling apart."

"Shut up, Bagman!" Helm snapped. "Just spit it out, lady!"

"There'll be permanent deterioration in your personality. They'll still be able to re-gene you, probably, but what gets put back into those bodies might not be the real you."

A cold, dead silence followed her words. Rogue was sorry when a few minutes later she slipped off into the chem mist, her white-clad form soon lost, a ghostly after-image in the pale light of a new dawn.

"Hell, Rogue," Bagman said as soon as she was gone. "What are we gonna do?"

"We're gonna get ourselves straight back to the nearest Souther station and turn ourselves in, that's what!" Gunnar said.

"You only died three days ago," Rogue said. "There's plenty of time to hunt down Hoffa before anything happens. And if we leave it now the trail will go cold. Not to mention that as soon as we go back to Souther High Command they're gonna throw me in the brig, and you too probably as soon as they've put you back in bodies they can lock up."

"You're not the one risking your life here, Rogue!" Gunnar snapped. "We might not have two weeks like she said. They might've got that wrong."

"I am risking my life, every second," Rogue snapped back. "And unlike you, if I fall there'll be no one to put me in a biochip and give me at least a second chance."

"Well..." Gunnar growled, but Rogue knew he'd got to him. "What do you say, Helm?"

There was a long silence. Rogue wished he could see his friends' faces. He'd never realised how much he'd relied on them, how adept he'd grown at reading their emotions from the slightest flick of an eyebrow. Without those cues, he had no idea what they were thinking. He didn't like that feeling at all, as if his friends were drifting further away from him, lost in the mist like Sister Sledge.

"Rogue's right," Helm said eventually. "We have to keep on. We owe it to Ape and Killer and Sandman and all the rest. They'd do it for us, if the situation were reversed."

"Fine," Gunnar said reluctantly. "We'll keep on. For now."

"Hey, doesn't anyone wanna know what I think?" Bagman protested.

"You're outnumbered, buddy," Gunnar said. "And we stick together, don't we?"

"Yeah, yeah, course we do," Bagman said, but there was a hint of uncertainty in his voice.

Rogue knew that he had them with him. But he also knew that it might not be for long.

FIVE
GAY PAREE

Nu Paree was just the sort of city that Nu Earth was full of. Half-wrecked, riddled with bullet holes and missile craters and still lousy with corpses and the things that fed on corpses. But underneath it you could see what the place had once been, the hope with which it had been built. People had come here to make something, Rogue thought, and it was only after a while that they decided to tear it all down again.

Subliminally, he heard a low roaring sound growing in his ears, and before he'd even registered it as a fleet of Nort hoppas he'd ducked under cover, sheltering in the derelict remains of an old café. There were still half-eaten meals on one of the few tables that had remained standing after the roof collapsed. Judging by their state of decay, they were a good few years old.

The Hoppas took their time, travelling so low that the roar of their engines shook some china off a tilted shelf to smash on the tiled floor. They were searching, Rogue knew. For him? Probably not, but he had to plan the operation as if they knew he was coming. That way he'd be about as careful as he needed to be.

"Monsieur," a voice said from beneath a fallen beam, "I really must ask you to 'urry up with your order. We 'ave others waiting for the tables."

Rogue ignored it. It was just a service robot, still carrying out its programming long after there were any customers left to insult. He waited until the noise of the Hoppas had faded completely, and gave it another ten minutes before poking his head out of the shattered doorway.

In the distance, he saw the dark shapes of the Hoppas floating in to land by the largest building in the city, the giant, dark hulk of the cathedral. They seemed to have come from somewhere in the direction of the Mitterand tower. He'd passed the impossibly tall spike of it as he came into the place, close enough to see that its struts had been hung with the decaying bodies of Souther troops. Bagman had wanted to wait and pull them down, give them a decent burial or at least some dignity in death, but Gunnar had reminded him that they didn't have the time.

"Lots of Norts," Gunnar said.

"Yeah," Helm agreed, "looks like our Grand Admiral doesn't want his meeting to be disturbed."

Rogue thought Helm was probably right. It was hard to think of another reason why the area would be so infested with Norts. It wasn't like Nu Paree held any strategic importance. He shot another look round at the shattered remains of the once elegant town. The kind of real estate only chem rats valued.

"Wonder who he's expecting?" Bagman said.

"Not us, that's for sure," Rogue told him, hoping it was true. Then, before he could start worrying about that, he added, "C'mon, guys, let's go pay our respects."

Grand Admiral Hoffa was trying to study his face, peering at him curiously from beneath heavy brows, but he preferred to lurk in the shadows. It wasn't that he was ashamed – why should he be ashamed? He'd done what he did for the good of the Southers, for the good of the whole damn human race. But he'd always preferred the shadows, like the puppeteer he was, trusting to the darkness to keep the strings he pulled hidden. And he'd pulled Hoffa's strings most successfully. The Nort general had done exactly as he'd wanted.

"Congratulations, my friend," Hoffa said. The man certainly liked the sound of his own voice. He didn't think Hoffa had risen to his rank from the field. Born to it probably – that was the Nort way. "Thanks to the information you provided," he continued now, "the massacre of the GIs in the Quartz Zone has been almost a hundred per cent success."

He knew he was expected to respond. The admiral thought he had done this for the money, as if he would be motivated by so low a thing, but he was prepared to keep up the pretence. He liked to be underestimated. "Your praise is appreciated, Grand Admiral Hoffa," he said. "As is your fine Nordland brandy." Actually the stuff was vile, no match for the clarets his home planet's vineyard produced, but he wasn't going to tell this cretin that. "But what I really want from you is the payment I was promised."

Hoffa smiled, seemingly pleased that he was playing the part expected. No one wanted their tools to have minds of their own. "Full payment will be received once we can confirm that all the GIs have been eliminated."

He frowned at that. As far as he knew there was no question that all of the blue-skinned freaks were gone. And when he went back to Milli-Com to resume his day job he intended to make sure that no more would ever be created. He figured it shouldn't be too hard to persuade his fellow generals of that, not after their dismal performance at the Quartz Zone, and once they were gone, the Southside would be pure again, human. That was one thing the Norts got right: the importance of purity.

"According to some reports, it's possible that at least one of them may have survived," Hoffa said, almost smiling at the disquiet he knew must be showing on his face. Before he could say anything else, a huge explosion shook the foundations of the building. A screen fell from the wall to shatter against the floor, sending shards of glass shooting lethally through the air.

Hoffa staggered, struggling to keep his feet. "What's happened?" he shouted into his head mic, his voice shrill with fear.

A voice crackled through on the radio. "Admiral, we're under attack from a Souther Genetic Infantryman!"

Now Hoffa wasn't the only one who was panicking. He hadn't counted on this, hadn't imagined that any of the inhuman monsters could have escaped the trap he set for them.

"Seal the building!" Hoffa screamed.

He only hoped it wasn't already too late.

The battle was fiercer than any that Rogue had yet fought. The shattered landscape of Nu Paree was a nightmare to traverse, offering concealment for Nort snipers, or targets for Hoppa missiles that threatened to bring the shattered masonry down on top of him. There were decapitators everywhere, the whirring blades of the little flying robots buzzing like insects as they swarmed towards him, hungry for his flesh. He took out a cluster now, aiming for the leader, knowing that once it was gone – seared into a ball of fire – the rest, mindless without it, would soon follow. He didn't wait to watch it happen. He just kept on moving forwards, fighting, racing along the dry riverbed that ran like an artery right into the heart of the city.

He knew that the important thing was to keep going. If he ever lost his momentum, the Norts would work out that he was only one man and that there was no way he should be able to be taking out so many of them unopposed. They were firing wildly, and not well. They'd even managed some friendly fire incidents, and he'd seen a stray round from a Nort hell cannon barrel into the wall of the cathedral itself.

Ahead of him, he saw a pile of ammo crates and he was about to drop a micro-mine or two into them, leaving a surprise for the Norts behind him and maybe taking out a couple more of the Hoppas that were closing in fast when Helm said, "I'm picking up a strange signal from those crates. It's some kind of weapon."

Rogue almost didn't bother to check, but the Hoppas were nearly on him now and any weapon he could find had to be good news.

Especially when it turned out to be a Sammie launcher. Grinning in triumph, Rogue strapped it the bottom of Gunnar's barrel and took down the nearest Nort with just two shots.

"Woo-hoo!" Gunnar shouted. "Now we're cooking!"

Rogue felt good about it too, but he knew they shouldn't get cocky. At the moment they had the advantage of surprise. The Norts thought they'd kept the area clear with their Hoppa air surveillance and the constant ground patrols, but it had made them careless. Even better, it meant that the bulk of their forces were stationed on the perimeter they thought they'd established.

Rogue had a few clear minutes until they all came piling back in, and he intended to make full use of them.

He threw himself to the side and rolled forward, and then ran on, not stopping to look at the deep crater the missile meant for his head had made in the compcrete

of the fallen wall. Gunnar was constantly moving in his
hands, spraying fire left, right, behind him. Gunnar
could aim for him even when he couldn't see.

The dying screams of the Norts were muffled behind
their chem suits, but Helm helpfully amplified them for
him, just so he'd know he was doing his job well. It
gave him no pleasure, just a grim sort of satisfaction.

A whole company of Norts rose ahead of him suddenly. They'd been hiding in a crater in the street he
hadn't even seen and now they were almost close
enough to touch. Before he even had time to ask for it,
Bagman's robot arm had pulled a micro-mine from his
pack and flung it towards the Norts.

"Jump, Rogue!" he shouted.

Rogue didn't need to be asked. Using the superhuman strength of his specially bred muscles, he vaulted
over the heads of the startled Norts, clearing them by
a good three metres. Still, when the mine went off
beneath them, the force waves from it pushed him
unstoppably through the air, throwing him into the
wrecked remnants of what must once have been a rich
man's playcruiser. He rolled with the fall and kept on
running, ignoring the searing pain from where the
blast had scorched the skin of his back.

The cathedral was in sight now, looming darkly over
the streets like a curse. But always there were more
Norts. One emerged from a side street, and as Rogue
ran, he took him out with a casual machine-gun round,
having only a second to see the startled look on his
round, babyish face as the bullets tore the chem mask
right off him.

"Should'a got us re-gened before this," Helm said.
"That way, if you don't make it through, we'd still have
a chance."

Rogue didn't say anything. He needed to conserve
his breath for the frantic run. There was no way the

people in the cathedral hadn't heard the firefight. Hoffa was probably already making plans to escape. Rogue had to expend all his energy, use every breath in his body to get there before Hoffa did.

Besides, Helm was right. Rogue was risking all of their lives and he hadn't really given them much choice, which meant he owed it to them not to die. He flicked out a shot that took one Nort through the heart, then another that blasted the one behind him through the head. And he kept on running.

In a scrubby landscape that wasn't quite desert nor grassland, a figure bent over a Souther corpse. After a moment, it reached out and flipped it over, wincing at the blood that oozed out of the many wounds. It pulled open the chem suit – this soldier didn't need to worry about toxins now – then drew out the dog tag from beneath his fatigues and read the name.

Sergeant Steel.

So, it looked like Rogue really had gone rogue, finally living up to the name which had never quite suited him back on Milli-Com. Back when he'd been just another GI, a good one, maybe the best. One who'd obeyed orders, smartly, not dumbly, just the way he'd been trained. Now he was killing his own side, killing the men sent to bring him back in. That had never been in his training.

What would Colonel Kovert make of that?

Pietr had to spend three hours psyching himself up for it, and then another two preparing the speech he was going to make in his head. It wasn't like he didn't have the time. Now that the action was over, he found himself with a permanent halo of space around him, no matter where he went. If he walked into a tight group of soldiers, all laughing over some joke with post-battle relief, they'd mysteriously part around him, as if he was surrounded by some sort of personal force field.

Or, more likely, as if he was suffering from some affliction that none of them wanted to catch. He knew what the affliction was. Cowardice. Well, he would show them. He would prove that he was no coward, and no traitor either. He would prove it to them, and more importantly he would prove it to himself – and to Jaze.

When he strode towards the group eating their rations round the burning remains of a Souther tank, he saw them look up, and then look down again, pretending he wasn't there. That he wasn't even worth noticing.

He almost gave up at that point. But then he remembered what Jaze always used to say about him, that he was a quitter, that he didn't have the guts or the balls to see anything difficult through to the end, and he cleared his throat. "Listen," he said.

There was absolutely no reaction from the men in front of him. He could see the bald patch on the top of Schulz's head as he bent to his plate of grey slop, and the clicking of their jaws seemed unnaturally loud in the silence they'd left around his word.

"Listen," he said again. "I know what you all think. About me. I know you think I'm a coward. But it's... it's not true. It's not fair."

Schulz did look up at that. "Go away, Pietr. There's nothing you can say to us that will make up for what we saw you do."

"I'm going to hunt him down," Pietr said.

That did get a reaction. Some of the other soldiers looked up. Schulz frowned. "Hunt who down?"

"Him, the Genetic Infantryman. The one who killed Natashov. Who killed my brother."

"Yeah? How'd you know he killed Jaze?" Schulz asked. "They all look the same."

"There are some faces you don't forget," Pietr said, and for once his words were treated with respect. "I know I should have got him before, but I wasn't ready. I am now. I don't care how long it takes, or how hard it is. I'm going to hunt him down and get my revenge for what he's done." He felt his confidence growing as he spoke the words. He knew it was the right thing to do. It was what Jaze would have wanted him to do.

Schulz laughed at him. He turned away from Pietr to face the other men. "I get it. He's planning to desert and he's making up his excuse ahead of time." Then he lowered his head and carried on eating, as if Pietr had disappeared again.

Furious, Pietr lashed out, striking the mess plate from Schulz's hands. The grey gruel splashed onto the soldier next to him who leapt up with a cry of annoyance. Pietr ignored him. "Think what you like," he shouted, to all of them. "But you'll think different when I come back with the Rogue Souther's head in a bag."

Then he strode out of the camp and he didn't look back. All he had to do was prove that he really was right.

Far away from the battle, in a little cafe that was still miraculously standing, Bland and Brass sat sipping coffees.

They'd brought the usual portable field generators with them, so they'd been able to slip out of their chem suits. A robot walked over to the table, servers chugging as legs that hadn't moved for decades were pressed into reluctant service. Bland had mended it as soon as they'd found the restaurant. No point eating out if the service wasn't up to scratch.

He regretted it now, of course. It was the rudest thing he'd ever come across. He really should have remembered what he'd learnt about Nu Paree back when he was in intelligence.

"Will messieurs be vacating the table soon?" the machine asked, its voice scratchy from long misuse. "Only as you can see we are very busy." The place was, of course, entirely deserted.

Bland ignored the machine and turned to Brass. "So, what odds will you give me on the Rogue Trooper surviving this conflict?"

Brass frowned at him as he sipped his mint tea. "Don't be vulgar, Mr Bland. One should never bet on a man's life. Particularly when our entire plan depends on him surviving. To make a bet would be tempting fate."

Bland decided that Brass was probably right, and returned to eating his croissant in silence. It would all be over soon enough anyway.

Hoffa couldn't believe it had all gone so wrong so quickly. His men had assured him that the whole place was secure, the whole town, damn it! And yet he could hear the sound of gunfire somewhere in the outer corridors of the cathedral base. The enemy hadn't just breached the perimeter – he'd annihilated it!

And all this in front of the Souther traitor, a man who was supposed to be impressed with Nort might, not seeing Nort forces routed by one single man. Still, he reminded himself, it was the traitor's fault that the man was free at all. There was no way he'd be getting the remainder of his fee after this. There was another round of machine-gun fire outside – this one sounding like it was only feet from the door.

"What's happening?" Hoffa shouted into his radio. There was no reply. "Answer me!" he screamed. He got back nothing but static, and behind that the sound of gunfire and screams. Hoffa was coldly certain that they were the screams of dying Norts. For his entire military career he'd managed to stay well back from any battles, directing from the rear. And of all places, at the absolute centre of his power, the battle was coming to him!

The static continued for a moment as Hoffa screamed into the radio. Then, ominously, it all went completely silent.

"Your men are dead, admiral," the traitor's voice said from behind him. "And I'm afraid our arrangement has changed."

Hoffa spun round to face him. His heart was racing so hard he really feared it might burst. Too many years of good living on the kind of rations you only got when in high command. "What... what are you talking about?" He felt a sudden cold fear when he looked at the Souther's face. He'd never noticed how cruel it was before, how utterly lacking in any human warmth.

Then he looked down and saw the pistol the traitor general held in his hand. Before Hoffa could really register the reality of that, or the fact that it was pointed directly at his chest, the traitor reached up a hand and pulled down the visor of his chem suit to cover his face. Behind the plasglass mask, his face suddenly looked like a reflection, just an echo of a real person.

"I can't allow any chance that my identity could be discovered," the traitor said calmly. Then he moved his gun away from Hoffa's chest and towards the wall and fired.

For a second, Hoffa thought he'd been spared. Then he realised that the round the traitor had fired was a seal-burster. It had punched a hole clean through the wall of his base. Through it, the toxic atmosphere of Nu Earth rushed in with an audible whoosh, a yellow and green cloud that meant only one thing to anyone not already masked.

"No!" Hoffa screamed. He tried to say more, but he could feel his throat closing up, swelling as the toxins hit it. He fell to his knees, choking. Through eyes that were already boiling in his head, he saw the traitor turn calmly and walk away.

If Rogue hadn't paused to collect enough salvage for Bagman to make him a couple of Sammies, he might have been finished. As it was, he didn't rate his chances.

The inner door to the cathedral was guarded. He'd expected that, but he hadn't expected the two huge mechanical suits the guards were wearing, doubling the size of the Norts within them, casing them in almost impenetrable steel armour.

The first one fired off a round towards him and when he dodged to the side, there was a hail of bullets from the other one waiting for him, two of them searing agonisingly through the soft flesh of his forearm.

"Sammies, now!" he screamed at Bagman, but even the seconds it took to fit them to Gunnar might be too much. Another spray of bullets splashed towards him. They missed, but the shattered compcrete they blasted from the walls and floor flung shrapnel into his unprotected shoulders.

"Done!" Bagman shouted.

Rogue's hands were numb; he almost couldn't feel the missile Bagman thrust at him, and for a terrible second he fumbled it and almost dropped it to the ground. Then it was on, slotted into Gunnar, and he got one quick look at the mechanical arms of the Nort's war suit reaching towards him before it blew up in a gout of red-hot molten metal. Then he spun and took the second one and he didn't even care that shards of the explosion blasted into his flesh, flaying it from his bones, because he'd cleared the way and now there was nothing to stop him from getting into the cathedral and to Hoffa.

Except something, some twinge in his gut, told him he was too late.

Inside the chamber was the man that Rogue recognised from the hacked Nort transmissions as Grand Admiral Hoffa. He didn't look capable of engineering the death of every friend Rogue had ever had. In fact, he didn't look capable of engineering anything. He was obviously dying. As Rogue ran up to Hoffa, Gunnar trained on his desperate, gasping form, he saw that the skin on his face had boiled and split, ravaged by the chem which was leaking in through a large hole in the pressure dome.

When Rogue got close enough, he saw that the admiral's lips were working, but the sound that emerged was little more than a harsh whisper. He had to bend his head down to hear it. "Help... help me," the admiral pleaded. For a moment, the remnant of one of his eyes caught Rogue's.

"Help you?" Gunnar grated. "The scum who murdered our buddies!"

Hoffa's ruined eyes flicked round the chamber, as if trying to find the source of the voice. After a moment, they settled back on Rogue. He heaved in a breath, and Rogue could hear the toxins bubbling in his lungs as he did it. "I... I gave the orders, but the information came from one of your own."

Rogue felt the words like a shard of ice stabbing into his heart. "A traitor? Who?"

Hoffa shook his head, though Rogue wasn't sure if he meant that he wouldn't or couldn't say.

Rogue took hold of the admiral's shoulder in a grip that would have been agonising if the man hadn't already been overwhelmed by the pain of the toxins. "Tell me," Rogue said to him, loud enough to be sure that he heard, "and I won't kill you."

Another coughing fit took hold of Hoffa, leaving a red froth of blood around his lips. For a moment Rogue thought that he was already gone, but then he lifted his arm and pointed towards the airlock door on the other side of the chamber. A moment later his hand reached up to clasp his neck, desperately clawing at it as if he could force a way through for the air which could no longer make it past the swollen constriction of his throat. "Please," he said.

Rogue released him and stood up. "I said I wouldn't kill you. I didn't say anything about helping you live."

He paused a moment longer, to make sure that Hoffa really was finished, then raced towards the airlock door. Outside it, he ran straight onto a Hoppa landing pad. One of the Hoppas, a great brute of a flying machine, was already lifting off from the pad. The air beneath it was churning, blowing up a miniature whirlwind of chem that choked even Rogue.

"The traitor," Gunnar shouted. "He's escaping!"

The Hoppa was already fifty feet into the air by the time he'd finished speaking, and receding fast. It left behind the ravaged ruins of Nu Paree – and another empty Hoppa.

"He's trying to escape," Rogue said. "Let's make sure he doesn't succeed."

SIX
CRASH COURSE

There was a moment of discomfort that Helm might have experienced as pain, had he still had a body, and then he was in. The Hoppa system wasn't like anything he'd yet hacked. They'd had some training in Nort technology back on Milli-Com, but studying the schematics of the big machines was very different from being inside the wires and circuits, his consciousness floating through a landscape that was nothing like the human mind.

"How you doing?" Rogue's voice asked. It was like a faint echo of a sound, intruding into a world where it didn't belong, then out again, threatening to take Helm's mind back out with it. With an effort that was like clenching a muscle in his head, Helm held himself inside the virtual world of the Hoppa's onboard computer. With an even greater effort, he sent his own voice out of that world and into the real one which at the moment seemed little more than the memory of a dream to him. "I'm working on it as fast as I can, Rogue." I'd like to see you do it faster, he thought but didn't say. The man who'd taken his body away from him was within their sights; it was no time for the team to be squabbling, however much Rogue's take-charge tone might piss him off.

He let that thought go, let all external feelings float away, and concentrated on the present situation. He needed to break the security protocols on the Hoppa to enable him to fly the thing.

At first, he couldn't make sense of anything. He just experienced a blaze of light and snatches of sound whizzing past in either direction, too quickly for him to understand them. It was almost too much, and he had to fight the urge to retreat from it, to close off his mind from this alien mechanical one and reassert his sense of self.

He fought it with every soldier's instinct that had been bred into him for an entirely different sort of battle. Then he used the thing which hadn't been bred into him, the thing which set him apart from the other GIs: an ability to impose order on chaos, and to make sense of things that human minds weren't designed to grasp.

Even before he'd been able to insert his mind into the machines he was studying, he'd learnt to solve this sort of problem by visualising it as something concrete, something his mind would find easier to manipulate.

Now that he was nothing but mind, he found that visualisation still worked, but he ended up participating in his own imaginings. He'd quickly learned to stop seeing the insides of computers as battlefields – there was enough fighting on the outside.

He thought strongly of a city – one laid out on a grid, a very logical city where the pattern of lights in the huge towers and the height of the skyscrapers themselves all possessed meaning.

After a few moments, he was in the city. He took a moment to marvel at it – something from his mind that was out in the world. There were no people in it, just the buildings, straight and tall, reflecting the light backwards and forwards between them. Perfect. But he wasn't here to look, didn't have time for it. He was looking for – that. The vast opaque wall dividing the heart of the city from the rest. That was what he needed to take down. In the real world outside the machine, the wall was the security protocols, the black ice preventing unauthorised access to the Hoppa's controls. That didn't matter. He'd seen it as a wall, so it was as a wall that he'd have to deal with it.

Sounded like a job for some high explosives. Just as well he'd imagined himself into this world too, in his old, true form. He pulled a batch of mico-mines out of his kitbag and headed towards the cliff-face of darkness.

In the cockpit of the Hoppa, it felt like only a second had passed before Helm said, "It's done, Rogue. Access all areas."

Rogue nodded and squinted down at the Hoppa's control console. The one to gun the engine was pretty obvious, and he flipped that first, but after that it was hard to tell which of the serried ranks of dials and levers actually made the damn thing take off. He shrugged and twisted a purple knob. There was an enormous growl, the machine heaved, jerked and the engine cut out. Well, obviously not that one.

"Err, Rogue," Bagman's voice said. "Do you actually know how to fly one of these things?"

"Nope," Rogue said. "Guess I'm about to get a crash course."

"Literally," Gunnar muttered.

"I'll fly, you fire," Helm said, as some outside force seemed to take over the controls and they assumed a healthier-sounding hum. "We got two Hoppas on our tail already and we aren't off the ground yet."

It was only now that Pietr was away from the camp, far enough away to be sure no one was pursuing him, that he realised he had no idea where he was going.

Under the sickly yellow stars of the Nu Earth night, he sat down on the ground and put his head in his hands. He'd taken supplies and he'd taken his weapons, but he hadn't really thought beyond that.

He found himself fighting the urge to cry, something he hadn't done since he was eleven years old and Jaze had broken the model Hoppa that he'd spent weeks assembling and painting. Jaze had laughed at him, calling him a baby, and Pietr had sworn never to cry again. He wouldn't cry now. He swallowed back the lump in his throat and swiped an arm angrily across his eyes – before realising that he couldn't touch them because the visor of his chem suit was in the way. That was something else he hadn't thought to bring. Without a field atmos-tent, he'd be stuck in the chem suit twenty-four-seven. It was designed to recycle everything his body produced, but that would still only see him through a few more days.

He stood up again, gazing out over the silent, humped landscape. Okay. This wasn't a problem. He just needed to find another camp, a small one somewhere back behind the battle lines where security should be lax. And how was he going to find that? For a moment he despaired. He wanted to just sink down onto the ground and stay there, sitting, until he died of hunger, or chem-poisoning, or – if he was lucky – a Souther patrol took him out. But that would just be proving everyone right about him. It would prove Jaze right about him. He just needed to think. He might never have been much of a soldier, but he'd always been a good thinker – if he hadn't signed up for the infantry to follow Jaze he could easily have found himself a job in intelligence. It was time he started using some of it.

He realised that there was a sound on the periphery of his attention: a rushing, trickling sound, somewhere to his left. It must be the river he'd passed after he'd first left the camp. Vague memories from basic training came back to him, lectures about the importance of securing all supply routes, aerial, land and aquatic. Where there was a river, somewhere along its length there would be a base. He smiled for the first time since Jaze had died. Jaze had always said that thinking got a man dead, but maybe Jaze hadn't known everything.

Two hours later, he was trotting away from Base Camp Delta Xeta with a new atmos-tent and a crypt-enabled radio unit.

He flipped open the radio as he walked and tuned it to the general news channel. Almost immediately, he found a report about a lone Souther's brutal murder of Grand Admiral Hoffa. The monster had somehow broken through the defences of Nu Paree and killed the admiral in his own command centre, cruelly letting him choke to death on the chem-tainted air outside.

Pietr felt his heart contract with a feeling that he told himself was excitement. It could only be the Rogue Trooper.

Helm pushed the left wing so far down the Hoppa was almost flipped onto its back, and by about a centimetre the machine managed to avoid crashing straight into the tall spike of the Miterrand Tower.

"Jeez, Helm, watch where you're going!" Bagman shouted.

"Scan out, Bagman," Helm said tightly. "I'm concentrating."

"Could've fooled me," Bagman countered, but he shut up after that.

Rogue could tell Helm wasn't finding the Hoppa easy to steer. The machine moved like it had been designed to do something else entirely and some halfwit had reconfigured it to fly at the last moment.

There was another building approaching, what might once have been a look-out tower but was now just a decaying concrete odalisque. Helm steered away from it early this time, and the building whooshed by his left flank, clearing it by a good three metres.

Then the traitor's Hoppa was in Rogue's sights and he didn't have any more time to worry about Helm's driving. He laid down a tracery of fire, saw some of it catch the wing of the traitor's Hoppa, and prepared for another strafing run. Then the two Hoppas that Helm had been trying to shake closed in and by the time Rogue had disposed of them, the traitor's Hoppa had pulled away once again and their own was signalling damage to its aft engine.

Helm ignored the damage and gunned the engines to full power, surging after the traitor's craft.

"Err, Rogue, there's–" Bagman said.

The blast hit the Hoppa from underneath. The cockpit was filled with the acrid smell of burning plastics and the machine bucked and swayed like a wild animal with a mind of its own. Its left wing brushed against the high side of an old public building, dislodging bricks and mortar with a horrible grating noise, then the right sheered clean through the ion-power lines, loosing a shower of sparks that erupted over the wings and in the cockpit itself. Rogue smelt the crest of hair on his head singe and he risked lifting a hand from the gun controls to put out the small fire that was burning there. The automated defences in the cockpit took care of the rest, spraying a clinging foam over the area and into Rogue's eyes, nearly blinding him.

"A-A fire from the ground," Bagman said sheepishly.

"Yeah, thanks for the heads up, Bagman," Rogue said sourly, turning his guns downwards, trying to pick out the tiny targets of the anti-aircraft guns below and hoping that Helm would be able to evade their fire until he did.

The fire from below came thick and fast, flashes surrounded by clouds of black smoke that blinded him. And up ahead the sun was rising, sending fierce rays towards him through the sullen yellow atmosphere.

"Rogue–" Helm said.

"Later," Rogue snapped back, cutting him off.

"Rogue," Helm said. "There's pursuit, ten Nort Hoppas coming up fast behind."

Rogue swore. They'd made up some distance on the traitor's Hoppa ahead, but now it looked like the problem would be finishing the pursuit in one piece. "Can you get me a visual on that, Helm?"

"Comin' up," Helm shot back.

A second later, Rogue's forward viewscreen had a second image superimposed over it. He had a moment of disorientation, then his mind, as it had been trained to do, separated out the two images and he studied the second, a view of the looming dark shapes of the enemy craft closing in on him from behind. He swore again and sent out a stream of white-hot plasma, taking two of the Nort craft down in one searing blast.

"Nice shot," Bagman said.

"Yeah, but I ain't gonna be able to stop 'em all," Rogue said. "Two of 'em are trying to flank us."

He saw them curving out from one of the two images superimposed in front of him. He didn't wait till they were square in his sights, just calculated where they were heading – trying to force him downwards into the A-A fire, he calculated – and shot there. His guess was right. The fist exploded in a ball of ionised metal, droplets splashing onto the viewscreen of Rogue's own Hoppa. He saw the red cloud of the Nort pilot's vaporised blood puff out from the wreckage. The second Nort Hoppa swerved at the last minute, but not far enough. The ion fire caught against its left wing, and it limped out of the battle towards the ground.

Helm used the time it bought him to gun the craft forward, redlining the thrusters until they were back on the traitor's tail. They were almost close enough for Rogue to see the face of the traitor, his dark form visible in the clear plastic dome of the Hoppa's cockpit.

Rogue suddenly realised that he was dreading seeing the traitor's face. Dreading finding out that it was someone he knew, someone he had trusted. Dreading most of all that it would be his own face staring at him, the face of another GI who had led all his brothers to their deaths.

The Hoppa in front swerved left where Rogue had expected it to go right, straight into one of the wrecked buildings, and before Rogue could protest Helm had taken them in after it. It twisted straight towards the ground, and Rogue had a moment of panic before he saw the wide dark mouth of an underground chamber yawning to swallow them. Then they were in, flying through what must once have been Nu Paree's sewer system, and the chase took on a whole new complexion.

It was like flying through a vast, three-dimensional maze. The traitor was a good pilot, Rogue gave him that, but Helm was better now that he had mastered the controls. In the central chamber of the sewers – a huge room, dominated by waterfalls of rank green water – the traitor had to turn and fight.

Rogue lashed stream after stream of fire after him, but nothing seemed to quite find its mark, and the traitor was firing back, forcing Helm to dodge and weave in turn. Finally, Rogue had a clean shot lined up, and the traitor's Hoppa shot straight up, out of range, out of an exit that Rogue hadn't even noticed.

"Damn him!" Helm swore, and took them up after him, but Rogue had lost his shot.

The exit took him out over a vast dam, and there was more A-A fire here, and Lazooka units too, but Rogue took them out easily because this time there was no way the traitor was getting away from him. At last, there was nothing between him and the traitor but clean air.

"We've got him now," Rogue said. While he was speaking, he brought his forward gun round to bear on the craft in front of him. It took one second to line up the shot: the left wing, underneath the engine mounting, disabling but non-lethal. He wanted to take this bastard alive.

The shot sped off on a trail of ionised air. Just before it hit, the shock wave from the last Lazooka round he'd taken out hit the traitor's vessel. The explosion bounced the Hoppa up and left, putting the cockpit itself straight in the path of the oncoming missile.

The traitor's craft screamed towards the ground, the figure within engulfed in fire.

"You got him, Rogue!" Helm said.

The traitor's Hoppa continued its precipitous descent, greying out into a vague silhouette as it fell into the chem that hugged the ground. "He's disappearing into the mist," Rogue said to the others. "Track him down, Helm. We'll land and check the wreckage."

There was nothing living in the wreck. If Bagman had still had eyes he might have been tempted to search anyway, pawing through the molten metallic ruin for any trace of the man who'd betrayed them all. But his new internal sensors which were intended to monitor Rogue's health status, told him that there were no life signs aboard.

Fine. They'd been revenged. Why didn't it feel better? Shouldn't he feel like it was over, like he'd done his duty as a GI and could feel proud? But of course nothing had really changed. Their friends were all still dead. And so was he. Then he saw Rogue reach into the wreckage and pull something out: a blackened strip of cloth. No, not just cloth, uniform.

"Souther insignia," Bagman said, using his sensors to peer through the burnt surface to the cloth beneath.

"And those are general's stars on it," Gunnar added. His voice, even mechanical and filtered, was thick with disgust. "It really was one of our own commanders who sold us out."

"Picking up signals from a Nort base nearby. Could be where he went," Helm said.

"Went?" Bagman said. "There's no way he survived that. He didn't go anywhere, apart from being smeared over the surface of Nu Earth."

"No, Helm's right," Rogue said. "If he'd died in the crash there'd be something left, some organic trace. And you're not picking anything up, are you?"

Bagman realised that he wasn't. It wasn't just that there were no life signs, there weren't the right sort of molecules around to account for the remains of a man. "No," he said reluctantly. "I guess not."

"C'mon, guys," Rogue said. "Let's go bag ourselves a traitor general."

He strode off through the still smouldering vegetation around the wreckage.

"Now hang on, Rogue," Helm said. "I thought this mission was going to end when we killed Hoffa. Now we're tracking off to who knows where to find a man who might not even have survived."

Rogue stopped walking. Bagman could tell from his elevated heart rate that he was either surprised or angry, or maybe both. "What, you're saying we should let the guy who betrayed us just walk away free?"

"No," Helm said. Bagman knew that if he'd had teeth he would have been gritting them. "I'm saying we should go back to base, get re-gened, then go after him."

"But by then it might be too late," Rogue said. "You've still got a clear week before any trouble starts in your chips. And you know we've got to follow while the trail's hot."

"Rogue's right," Gunnar said. "We're GIs. The last GIs. It's up to us to get this traitor general, no one else."

After a pause, Bagman added, "Yeah. We go after him. It's what Sandman and the others would want us to do."

"Fine," Helm said. "I guess I'm outvoted."

Rogue just nodded and began to march again, blue legs swinging through the yellow chem mist and the white smoke of the crash.

A second later, Helm's voice spoke again, but this time Bagman knew it wasn't vocal: he was saying words that only Bagman and Gunnar could hear. "You know he's never going to stop, right? He'll keep on going till we're all dead, him included. We'd be doing him a favour by bringing us all in."

"Scan out, Helm," Gunnar said uncomfortably, "Rogue's made the decision. And since he's the only one here with a body, I reckon we're stuck with it."

"He's got a body," Helm agreed. "But he still needs his equipment. He still needs us. And what if there was to be an... unexpected failure, something crucial he'd have to go back to headquarters to fix."

"No way!" Bagman said, shocked. "And you say he's the one who's gonna get us killed!"

"Oh, I'm not talking about during battle," Helm said. "I'm just saying, somewhere where we're safe, if Gunnar was to jam, or your micro-mines suddenly fused–"

"Forget it!" Gunnar roared, a painful electronic spike through their circuits. "I ain't doing it, Helm, and that's final."

"Me neither," Bagman said, and Helm shut up. Bagman clamped down tight on his transmissions, making sure nothing leaked through on the comms band they all shared. The last thing he wanted Helm to know was how very close he'd come to convincing him.

Out in no-man's-land, the pursuing figure had no idea of the argument that had silently raged between the gun, the kitbag and the helmet he could see on the blue figure caught in the sites of its sniper rifle.

All it saw was the figure itself, trudging doggedly on to who knew where. Rogue Trooper clearly had no idea he was being watched. The figure looked back through the rifle's viewfinder and readjusted the barrel the slightest bit till the crosshairs centred on Rogue's head once again. All it would take would be one tiny squeeze of the trigger, and Rogue would fall, unheeded on the blackened earth, never to kill another Souther again.

SEVEN
VENUS IN FIRE

A finger tightened on a trigger, and a bullet too fast and hard for even Rogue's skin to deflect was moments away from ploughing through his skull.

But then the finger relaxed. Better to know exactly what was going on before making any rash and irreversible moves. The figure straightened up and trotted towards the site of the crash that had so intrigued the Rogue Trooper earlier. A few seconds later, and it had found the scrap of material which had told Rogue everything he needed to know.

It told the figure everything it needed to know, too.

He'd thought the actual crash itself, the moment when the flames consumed him, would be the worst. But he'd been wrong.

This endless gnawing pain, eating away at his ability to resist it, eating away at his sanity until he thought the only way to deal with it would be by going quite mad, this was worse. Worst of all, he knew that people with the power to make the pain go away were a mere foot away from him.

The first hour after the crash was a blur. He must have crawled out of the wreckage, crawled away over the horrible grating ground, but he didn't remember doing it. His eyesight wasn't so good now, anyway. He thought one of his eyes might have started to boil before he'd managed to crawl away from the fire. He'd recognised the soldiers who'd found him by their voices. Norts.

They'd recognised him, too. That's why they'd refused him medical treatment when he'd begged for it in the dry rasp that was all that was left of his voice. One of them had even kicked him as he lay in the centre of their camp and the other had laughed. He hadn't really minded, because the pain of the kick had just registered as a pin-prick against the maelstrom of shrieking sensation that was his skin.

He knew that if he wasn't treated soon he'd die. Well, it didn't matter. He'd done what he intended. He'd elim-inated the genetic freaks, kept the Southside pure. Perhaps no one would ever recognise it, but he was a hero. So this, this agonising finale to his life, was a hero's death.

He breathed out, coughing and then screaming hoarsely at the pain of the cough, and waited for death to come. No, he wasn't ready. Damn it, he was only forty-three years old. He was far too young to die, far too important to die. He didn't deserve it. The world would be a better place with him still in it. "Listen to me," he choked out, as loudly as his ruined voice could manage.

"Shut up, Souther," the Nort said – a sergeant, he thought – and kicked him in the ribs again.

"I've got information," he said. "Classified. I was a… a general. I can tell you… I can tell you everything. Just… please… make sure I don't die."

For a while he thought they hadn't believed him. He wanted to say more but he just didn't have the energy. He could barely breathe, let alone speak. But then he felt something, a pressure against his arm, and then, amaz-ingly, a surge of well-being pulsing through his bloodstream.

They'd given him painkillers. They'd believed him.

"There's one other thing," he said.

• • •

Base Commander Tellar couldn't believe his luck. To have found such a high-level prisoner – and one willing to trade information for his life – this was the kind of opportunity that could propel you right up the ranks.

"A Souther general?" General Vard said. "You're certain?"

Tellar studied his broad face with disdain. Vard was exactly the sort of man who'd prevented Tellar's promotion all these years, an old-school snob who thought anyone who couldn't trace their family tree right back to the homeworld wasn't worth talking to.

"One of my patrols brought him in a few hours ago," Tellar told him firmly. "He's badly burned, but he's offering to trade information in return for his safety."

Vard seemed to consider this for a moment, then he nodded, as if he'd made up his mind. "Send him to me. Any information he has could be vital for our plans to assault the Souther positions in Nu Atlanta."

Tellar would have liked to complain, but he knew that there was no way he'd have been able to keep charge of the prisoner himself. The most he could hope for would be to be given at least some fraction of the credit. That was why he had chosen General Vard to inform of his find. The man was a snob, but an honest one. "There's one more thing," he told him now. "He claims the enemy soldier known as the Rogue Trooper is pursuing him."

Vard frowned. "The reports say it was this Rogue Trooper who killed Grand Admiral Hoffa."

Tellar remembered suddenly that Hoffa had been a personal friend of Vard's. He had to fight to suppress a smile. It looked like he'd done even better than he realised by bringing the Souther turncoat in. He could already feel those kapten's pips glowing on the sleeve of his chem suit.

"Prepare a suitable welcome for the genetic freak," Vard said icily. "Hoffa's death must be avenged."

The base was one of the strangest Gunnar had ever seen. It took him a moment to figure out what it was: a satellite, huge, hundreds of metres high, crashed over on its side. It was almost beautiful, glittering dully in the sun, but it was a hell of a long way to climb. Knowing their luck, he was sure the traitor would have been taken all the way to the top.

"Hold up, there's some salvage here," Helm said, and Rogue obligingly attached him to the escape pod that lay in front of the vast satellite base, hooking him up to it to hack his way in.

A moment later, there was a sharp pop and the escape pod, with Helm still firmly attached to it, blasted off the ground and straight into the lowest levels of the satellite.

Rogue swore, but Bagman laughed. "Guess he really liked flying that Hoppa," Then he sensed Rogue's annoyance and added, "We'd better get in and get him back."

There was a Hoppa to take care of before they could do that. Fortunately, they'd already found enough salvage to put together a few Sammies. Gunnar had always loved firing them, back when he was just carrying the weapon they strapped onto. Now that he actually *was* the weapon – it was a hell of a buzz, firing off something that big and powerful.

He was almost disappointed when they were past the Hoppa and into the lowest reaches of the base. It was corridor to corridor action, even if the corridors were all inverted at ninety degrees to true, so that they were walking on the steel mesh walls with the floor to their left and the ceiling – spitting sparks from shattered lights – to their right. There weren't too many Norts left, but enough to keep Gunnar on his toes, and the way up seemed like an endless spiral through corridors that never changed. A third of the way up they picked up Helm again and that was about as exciting as it got.

Until they reached the top. In the upper reaches of the fallen satellite – exactly where Gunnar had guessed it would be – was the base proper. The rusted, ruined walls of the satellite gave way to gleaming new steel and plascrete, and suddenly there were lots of Norts around and none of them were feeling very friendly. Gunnar let out a whoop of joy, loving the feeling of his barrel heating up as he fired, a sensation that was like nothing he'd ever felt when he was in a human body.

Helm said something about taking out some computers to open some doors, but Gunnar wasn't really listening. Half his attention was on the battle.

Sometimes he felt like he was born to be this weapon, like the rest of his life had just been preparation for the moment when his biochip was slotted into the mechanism and he finally discovered the clean, brutal simplicity of the killing machine from the inside. When he thought this way, he saw his body as a chrysalis, something that he had to discard before he could become what he was really meant to be.

But that was wrong. His body was *him*, and he wanted it back, and that was taking up the second half of his attention. No matter how hard he tried, he couldn't stop thinking about what Helm had said to him. About how they could force Rogue to take them back to base, turn them back into men again.

As the battle raged, he thought through what he'd do. Rogue was barrelling through the stark corridors of the base, homing in on his prey with that unerring instinct he had. Gunnar chambered some shotgun rounds for Rogue to take out a cluster of Norts disappearing through the door. Never gave up, Rogue. Never stopped. Never surrendered. Implacable, that was the word for it.

But if, say, the weapon he relied on suddenly jammed, no amount of implacability would get him to carry on then. He wouldn't put himself, or his friends, into danger by heading into battle without some decent hardware. Gunnar felt a momentary stab of guilt that he was thinking of using Rogue's loyalty against him, but he squashed it. Like Helm said, it was for the good of them all.

As he helped Rogue shoot an advancing Nort in the face and another in the gut, he considered how he'd do it. With that strange inner consciousness he'd never had as a man, he probed the workings of his own circuitry. Yes, there it was. If he made *that* connection, and disabled *this* transceiver, the loading mechanism would lock and it would look like a mechanical failure. Then he'd only have to–

His train of thought broke off as he realised that they'd broken through into the base's command centre. Except for one figure, the room was deserted. But that one figure was all Gunnar needed to see.

The traitor.

He looked at Rogue with a half smile. Gunnar wanted to wipe the smile right off that handsome face. He wanted to take the face and grind it into the plascrete floor of the room until it was nothing but raw flesh and bones. They were all dead. All dead because of this one man.

"That's him, Rogue. The traitor that sold us out," Bagman said.

Gunnar could hear all his own hatred in the other man's distorted, mechanical voice.

He saw the smooth, well-fed look of the man's face. He'd be willing to bet the traitor had never seen real action himself, just sat behind a desk and sent others to their deaths. Killing the GIs had been all in a day's work for him. "Milli-Com scum," he said. "This is for all our buddies that died in the Quartz Zone."

He felt Rogue's finger tighten on the trigger and let loose the round that was already in the chamber.

But the bullet passed straight through. The traitor remained standing, still smiling, as if nothing at all had happened.

Helm understood first. "It's a hologram!"

By the time Rogue had spun round, the Nort troops were all over the room, weapons ready. Gunnar wasn't going to let that stop him. If he was going down, he was going to take as many Nort scum as he could with him.

He felt Rogue's finger on the trigger and prepared to drop a new round into the chamber.

Nothing happened.

The mechanism had jammed. Frantically, he tried to work round it, to find the circuit that was malfunctioning and bypass it. It didn't work.

"Gunnar, I need ammo!" Rogue said. The Norts were closing in on him, and they were smiling.

"I'm trying!" Gunnar said back.

"You idiot," Bagman said, inside his mind where Rogue couldn't hear. "You weren't supposed to jam up during a battle!"

With a sudden cold certainty, Gunnar realised that Bagman was right. His earlier thoughts about jamming were exactly what had caused the problem now. He still wasn't used to having his mind inside a machine, not used to the fact that in the circuitry that held his consciousness now, a thought was no different from an action.

"I didn't mean…" Gunnar said out loud, then trailed off. He couldn't let Rogue know what they'd been talking about. What he'd been thinking about. And it was

already too late. The Norts were too close. Rogue hesitated a moment, then let the gun drop to his side. His
eyes circled the room, assessing exit routes, weak-
nesses, but as far as Gunnar could see there weren't
any.

When Rogue was facing the hologram again, the damn
thing smiled. "You want to see the face of the man who
betrayed you, GI?" it said.

There was a shuffling sound in the ring of Norts, and
two of them moved aside. In the gap they left was a Nort
officer, the base commander most likely, and beside him
a face that no one would ever forget. The scarring was
lurid and fresh, flayed skin stretched too tightly over
warped bones. The smile it wore was horrible, but still
recognisably the same as the one on the hologram. Gloating and vicious.

"Here it is," the traitor said. His voice rasped harshly,
as if it took a great effort to force it out through his
scarred throat. "Do you like the new face you have given
me?"

Gunnar wanted to say yes – to tell the bastard that even
if he was still alive, thanks to them he'd never forget
what he'd done, or stop paying for it, but he was already
being taken out of Rogue's hands by one of the Nort soldiers, handled as carelessly as if he was just an ordinary
gun, and it occurred to him that he'd be far better off if
that's all the Norts thought he was. He stayed silent.

The base commander studied him closely. Gunnar
wanted to put a round straight through his smug face.
Thanks to his own stupidity, he couldn't. "Excellent," the
commander said. "His GI weapon will make a fine battle
trophy." He turned to the soldiers flanking him and gestured at Rogue. "Take him away."

As he was dragged from the room, Rogue turned to
glare at the man who'd betrayed them twice. "This isn't
over, traitor."

The traitor's smile widened. "I'm sorry I can't stay to witness your execution, but the information I have for my new allies is eagerly expected elsewhere." Almost as an afterthought, he added, "I really ought to thank you for attacking this base. Without you, I might never have been believed, but now my friends know that they can trust me."

Then the traitor turned away dismissively, and Gunnar could only watch helplessly as the friend he'd inadvertently betrayed was led from the room.

Pietr drifted through the outskirts of Nu Paree, thinking that he had never seen anywhere so dismal, not even on Nu Earth. The city was a ruin. Deep gullies ran between the shattered masonry of the buildings, and the shattered carcasses of service robots were everywhere, some still speaking in slurry, barely comprehensible voices, twisted joints sparking and hissing. There were bodies everywhere. Nort bodies. There was no doubt that the Rogue Trooper had been here.

Pietr bent to examine one of the corpses. The Souther came at him from the doorway of the nearest building. He must have lost his gun some time in the battle, because all he was carrying was a knife. The blade of it made straight for Pietr's stomach.

Pietr didn't even think. His pistol leapt into his hands with a speed and efficiency he'd never managed previously. Before he'd even registered the attack, he'd chambered and fired two explosive rounds and the Souther was lying on the ground two feet from him, blank eyes reflecting the yellow sky but no longer seeing it.

Suddenly shaking uncontrollably, Pietr knelt down beside the body. Check he's dead, he thought. Never leave a living enemy behind you.

But there was no doubt he was dead. The explosive round had left a two-foot cavity in his chest. He could see the compcrete slabs of the pavement beneath it. There wasn't any blood. The edges of the hole were blackened, seared shut with the intense heat of the fire. The man's face was completely untouched. No, the *boy's* face. He couldn't be any older than Pietr himself. His hair was sandy and mussed, and there was a smear of soot on his right cheek.

Pietr remembered how Jaze had told him about his first kill, how his brother had said that it made him feel like a real man. Pietr looked down at the boy's body and wondered what he felt. Did he feel more like a man now? Did he feel more like his brother now? The boy's unblinking gaze remained fixed on the sky. No answers there.

It was all right, he told himself. Maybe it wasn't the first one that did it. Maybe if he killed enough he'd start feeling like his brother, start being the sort of man his brother had been. Maybe.

"Do you know what's going to happen to you, freak?" one of Rogue's guards asked.

Rogue didn't reply, just kept looking, left and right, looking for the thing that would get him out of here.

The Nort paused a moment, as if hoping that Rogue would ask. When he didn't, he said with relish, "We're going to take you out of here, and we're going to tie your arms and your legs to stammels, four of them, and then we're going to send those stammels galloping away and your limbs are going to go galloping away with them. That's what your traitor general told us to do to you. How'd you like that, you Souther scumsucker?"

Rogue turned cold eyes on him. The man flinched away from his gaze, but Rogue looked away again without saying anything and after a moment the Nort recovered himself and sniggered.

"Reckon the freak's scared now," he said to the companion who was holding Rogue's other arm. Both hands were bound tight behind his back in three sets of military issue cuffs. They weren't taking any chances. The other Nort laughed, but Rogue noticed that neither of them would look him in the eye. Even bound, unarmed and helpless, they were still scared of him. Good, he could use that. He'd have to use that, because he was damned if he was going to let himself get pulled apart by stammels. That just wasn't how he saw himself dying.

"Well, you've really done it now, Rogue," Helm's voice muttered in his ear, too soft for the Norts to catch. "Now you're gonna get killed and we'll end up on some junk heap and we'll never know what it's like to actually feel anything again."

"Scan out, Helm!" Bagman whispered. "You know damn well this is your fault. If you hadn't told me and Gunnar to…" His voice drifted into silence, as if he'd suddenly realised that he didn't want to say whatever he'd been about to say. Rogue would have loved to ask him what the hell he was talking about, but if the Norts heard him doing it, they might just clue up to the fact that his equipment was a cut above the average.

"Listen, Rogue, I'm sorry," Helm said after a moment. "You were only trying to–"

After that Rogue stopped paying attention because suddenly the two hands holding him were going slack. He tensed to move, prepared to take advantage of the Norts' moment of inattention, to kill them with his bare hands before they could secure him again, but the Norts' bodies weren't where he expected them to be, they were already falling towards the ground. A micro-second after they'd done their work he heard the muffled shots ring out.

As soon as he realised what was happening, Rogue flattened himself against the wall of the corridor, cursing the cuffs that still held his hands secure. He couldn't assume that whoever had killed the guards had done it because they wanted to help him. For all he knew the shots could have been meant for him.

A figure began to resolve itself in the shadows of the corridor ahead of him. He could see the glint of its sniper rifle. It was pointed at him.

Rogue knew he had seconds at best. One of the Nort guards had fallen beside him. He dropped quickly to his knees, fumbling awkwardly with his bound hands to grab the cuff key from the Nort's belt, then fumbling some more to get it into the release mechanism of the cuffs.

"Hurry it up, Rogue!" Bagman said.

The key jammed in the third cuff. Rogue gave up, dropped the key, and wrenched the cuffs apart with brute strength. He was just up, fists clenched in a fighting stance, when the figure finally stepped forward out of the shadows and into a pool of light. His hands unclenched themselves.

"It's a female GI!" Bagman said.

She smiled at Rogue. "The name's Venus," she said, as if he might have forgotten. "I was sent here by Colonel Kovert as your back-up."

Rogue couldn't quite take in the fact that it was her. He heard Helm muttering in his ear, and knew the other GI was having the same problem. Ever since the Quartz Zone, he'd thought of himself as all alone, the last of his kind. The existence of the GI Dolls hadn't really registered. Anyway, they'd always been told the Dolls were a non-combat unit. Judging by the professional way she was handling her sniper rifle, that had been a bunch of bull. Then what she'd said registered. "Back-up?"

Venus smiled, the heart-stopping smile that had had Helm eating out of her hand from day one. "You're not the only one who wants to nail the traitor." She stooped to pick up one of the dead Nort's guns and tossed it casually to Rogue, then turned to stalk off down the corridor without even waiting to see if he was following. She had an easy arrogance that was both infuriating and provocative. "Come on," she said back over her shoulder. "You want to debate the chain of command, or do you want to kill that traitor and get your friend back?"

"That's Venus?" Bagman said. "Now I see why you were so crazy for her, Helm. She's got the kind of body that kills – and I'm not talking about with a gun."

"Yeah, well I'm still crazy for her," Helm said. "So keep your observations and your eyes to yourself. That goes for you too, Rogue."

"Hey, the only thing I'm interested in is another soldier to help get Gunnar back and nail that traitor," Rogue said.

"It had better stay that way," Helm said gruffly. Then his voice softened. "I can't believe she came back for me. Guess she must really love me, right?"

Rogue didn't think there was any safe reply to that. He quickened his pace to follow Venus and pretty soon there was nothing to concentrate on but fighting. He guessed some kind of security camera must have picked up Venus's little rescue, because the Norts were coming thick and fast. There was no time for subtlety. It was just shoot, kill, move on.

Except this battle was different from all the others he'd been fighting over the last days. He had another GI by his side – even if she was a Doll – and suddenly fighting was a pleasure again. He saw a Nort trooper training a Lazooka on Venus and took him out with an armour-piercing round before she even knew he was in danger, then spun and let off another round straight into the faces of the reinforcements coming at him from the narrow side corridor.

He didn't even see the Nort who was creeping up the corridor behind him, belt knife raised for a killing blow. The first he knew of it was when Venus fired a shot that looked like it was coming straight for him but cleared his shoulder by no more than an inch to streak through his would-be assailant's throat.

Venus grinned, the feral grin of battle that he knew he was wearing too. "No need to thank me, Rogue," she said.

Helm sighed in his ear, "What a woman!" – as he was updating Rogue's heads-up display, pinpointing every Nort biosign on the base.

The fight out to the docks was brutal and bloody, but the blood wasn't theirs. There was no way raw Nort troopers were going stand up against two GIs fighting back to back. Rogue, high on the crazy euphoria of battle, didn't think there was any force in the universe that could, not in a fair fight.

He was almost sorry when it was over. It took him a moment to register that every Nort around him was a corpse. The only one left standing was the base commander, Gunnar clutched tightly in his hands. He could see that the commander's finger was squeezed on the trigger, so hard his knuckles were a leprous white, but Gunnar's muzzle remained stubbornly inert.

"Do you want to, or shall I?" Venus asked.

Rogue grinned at her. "Be my guest."

The Nort commander had realised by now that his gun was useless. He drew the belt knife that hung at his waist and charged towards them with a hoarse cry of mingled rage and fear. Venus's shot dropped him like a sack of potatoes while he was still ten feet away.

They heard the thud of booted feet on metal behind them and by unspoken consent Venus went back to cover the doorway while Rogue strode forward to pry Gunnar free from the base commander's already cooling hands.

"Good to be back in friendly hands again," Gunnar shouted over the roar of machine-gun-fire as Venus fought back the last of the Nort troopers. Rogue wasn't sure, but he thought he detected a note of guilt in his friend's voice.

He didn't have time to worry about it. "The traitor general, where is he?" he demanded.

"Took a Hoppa out of here as soon as the shooting started," Gunnar said in disgust. "I heard him talking about Nu Atlanta."

"That must be the Norts' next target," Venus shouted back from the door. Her eyes remained fixed outside as she picked off the Norts with clinical precision. "With what the traitor knows about our defences there, the attack on Nu Atlanta could make the Quartz Zone look like a field trip."

Rogue knew that she was right. He realised that his mission had taken on a whole new complexion. Now his hunt for the traitor was about stopping a new massacre, not just revenging an old one. The patrol boat he found docked at the exit to the base couldn't get them out of there fast enough.

Bland stepped delicately over a corpse, careful to keep his shoes away from the pool of blood spreading out through a crack in the chem mask from the hole in its forehead.

Beside him, Brass let out a small yelp of surprise as the body below him let out a sudden twitch and a shuddering moan, dying but not yet quite dead.

Bland paused beside the still warm corpse of the base commander to smile at Brass. "Well, it seems that once again our friend has made his escape."

"Just as well," Brass agreed. "Can't have that Souther technology falling into Nort hands without certain people who shall remain nameless acting as the middlemen. Where would be the fun – and more importantly the profit – in that?"

Bland nodded as he pulled out his radio, already tuned to the appropriate frequency. "There would be no fun, or more importantly profit, at all." He switched the unit on, and after a moment the signal was picked up at the other end. He listened for a while, saying nothing, because signals could be traced no matter how careful one's encryption. Then he slipped the unit back into the breast pocked of his suit.

"Well?" Brass asked, raising an eyebrow.

"Our operative has acquired the target," Bland informed him. "We must simply wait for events to run their course."

EIGHT
NO CHIP IN TEAM

Rogue almost found the boat journey restful. The Orange Sea was probably the quietest theatre of the war, real estate that no one could possibly want to fight over. The waters were a virulent green-blue, brighter than any natural waters had ever been but not in a pretty way. The sky was a yellow shade of the same toxic pigment, so that where it touched the water it looked like a stained cloth, which had been folded upwards, enclosing the world in filth.

Venus was lying in the bow of the boat, gazing out over the water as if she was hypnotised. Rogue shifted to the other side of the boat, as far away from her as possible, then took a moment to brace himself. He knew what he was about to say was an accusation, and he didn't like accusing his buddies. But at the same time he knew that there was something important he had to accuse them of.

"So, wanna tell me what happened back there?" he said.

There was a pause, a tiny one, just long enough to tell him that whatever was said next wouldn't be the entire truth.

"You were there too, Rogue," Helm said after the pause. "You saw what happened."

"Yeah, I saw my gun jam up during a firefight right when I most needed it. So I guess what I should have asked was why it happened."

There was another pause, a longer one this time. "I'm sorry," Gunnar said eventually. "I let you down, Rogue. I don't know what happened."

"Scan out, Gunnar. You did let me down, no doubt about that," Rogue said harshly. "But I think you do know what happened."

"That's out of order," Bagman said, trying to sound angry but coming out defensive instead.

"It's okay, guys," Helm said. "It was my idea, I'll tell him. And it was an accident, Rogue, whatever you think. I'd suggested to Gunnar that he might want to think about, you know, jammin' up at some non-crucial moment."

"Yeah?" Rogue said. "And why was that?"

Helm started to speak but Gunnar interrupted. "I was only thinking about it, Rogue, honest! Just considering the possibility, I wasn't ever gonna do it, and then I don't know, I musta accidentally triggered some mechanism inside and it happened for real. But I'd never have left you high and dry in a fight on purpose, never. You gotta believe me!"

"Well, maybe I do," Rogue admitted grudgingly. "But that still doesn't tell me why you were even thinking about it."

"'Cause you're never going back to base!" Bagman blurted. "You're just going to keep on and on, and you'll never catch that traitor and by the time you've finished all three of us are going to be dead, only this time there'll be no coming back from it."

"I promised you I'd bring you back before that happened," Rogue said, but he could feel his anger diminishing. At the other end of the boat he could see Venus watching them under half-closed eyelids, but she didn't join in. She knew this was a discussion where she had no place.

"I know," Bagman said. From the tone of his voice, Rogue knew he'd have been hanging his head if he was able. "I know you'd never let us die on purpose, Rogue. It was just – getting bodies again was a higher priority for us than getting the traitor. You don't know what it's like, to lose all that and think that you might not get it back again."

"It's true, Rogue," Gunnar said, his tone unusually contemplative. "It's not just about not being able to eat, or breathe, or feel the earth beneath our feet. It's about losing ourselves, who we are. Too much longer in here and I'll stop being Gunnar. All I'll be is the gun, and there'll be nothing of the man left to put back in a body."

Rogue didn't like hearing his own fears for his friend echoed back at him. Maybe they were right. Maybe he had been so focussed on avenging his dead friends that he'd lost sight of the ones who were still living.

"Okay," he said. "I get where you're coming from. But now we're talking about an attack on living Souther forces, we're talking about another massacre unless we can stop it."

"Agreed," Helm said. "And after that…"

"After that," Rogue said firmly, "I'm still going after the traitor, because while he's still alive he's still a threat to the South. But I give you my word: I'll get you back to base before anything bad happens to any of you."

"Your word's good enough for me," Bagman said. He sounded like he meant it.

"You ain't never let us down before." Gunnar sounded about as apologetic as he ever got. "All I ask is that you remember we're still GIs, we're still a team

– you've not suddenly got promoted general. If there's a decision to be made, we make it together."

"Just like old times," Rogue agreed. "What do you say, Helm?"

"What the others say," Helm said. But of all of them, Rogue thought he was the only one who didn't entirely sound as if he meant it.

He didn't have a chance to press him further because Venus suddenly stood up from the bow, making the little boat sway in the rising swell. Her expression had lost the dreamy cast she had worn as she watched the water. It was now combat-sharp, like it had come into better focus.

"Potential hostile twelve degrees starboard," she said. "I'm getting it in my sights." As she was speaking she unsnapped the sniper rifle from her waist. It fitted into her shoulder like that was where it belonged, but when she'd got it there, her finger hesitated on the trigger. She squinted through the eyepiece. "Amend that," she said after a moment. "Looks like one of ours."

Treading carefully so as not to unbalance her, Rogue joined her in the bow and raised Gunnar himself. The distant black dot on the horizon suddenly expanded, filling the whole field of his vision. Venus was right. The ship – wreckage, really – carried Souther insignia. But more than that, he recognised the figure standing up in it, frantically waving a white flag.

"Sister Sledge," he said.

"You know her?" Venus sounded astonished, and maybe, he thought, just a little jealous. He didn't know what to make of the latter, except hope that Helm hadn't noticed it.

"Saved our bacon back on the mainland," Rogue said. "Guess we'd better go and pick her up."

Venus dropped her weapon and turned to stare at him incredulously. "You're kidding, right? Rogue, we're not messing around here."

"I know," he said, leaning over the control panel and laying in a new course when it became clear that she wasn't going to do it. "But I owe her. And there's no way she could last much longer out here. Her boat's half eaten-away already." When Venus continued to stare accusingly at her, he added, "I'm not leaving her there to die."

Venus shrugged and flopped back down into the bow. "Have it your way. But remember there's a legion of Southers over at Nu Atlanta who are gonna die too unless we get there in time."

Rogue did remember, so he made the trip over to the wrecked boat as quickly as he could. His eyesight was keener than any ordinary man's, so for several minutes he was able to watch the chem nurse peering anxiously towards him, wondering if the ship heading towards her was friend or foe. When he got nearer still, her expression darkened as she saw the Nort insignia on the front and back. The white flag dropped from her fingers and he thought he saw her tremble. But then she must have spotted the tall blue figurehead at the front of the approaching boat and her expression lightened again. She was grinning when he drew up alongside her.

"What's a nice boy like you doing in a place like this?" she asked.

Venus raised an eyebrow at Rogue, but ignored the other woman.

"Coming to rescue you," Rogue said. "You'd better hop on board. We're heading into battle, but we can drop you shore-side before the action starts."

Sledge did as he asked, moving far less lithely than Venus, almost tipping the boat over in her scramble to get onboard.

"I came onboard a troop carrier to treat some wounded," she explained as Rogue tried to get the vessel back on an even keel. "A second later a Nort torpedo hit. I was the only survivor and by the time I'd regained consciousness we were drifting out of sight of land."

"Yeah?" Venus said. Her gaze took in the other woman with one glance and dismissed her at the same time. "What unit?"

"Sixty-second seaborn," Sledge said without missing a beat. "They've been brought up to bolster Nu Atlanta's defences. Nort subs are crawling all over the seas around here." She didn't seem offended at the questioning, though her mouth had a slight upward twitch as she spoke to Venus, as if she found the Doll's hostility amusing.

Venus noticed it and the lines of her face tightened. She didn't say anything more to Sister Sledge, just turned to face Rogue. "Still think it would have made more sense to leave her floating," she said.

"Ah come off it, Venus," Bagman said. "You're just jealous 'cause she's hotter than you."

This comment was, of course, just calculated to promote harmony between the two women. If Bagman had still had a body Rogue reckoned it would have been laid out on the deck just about then.

Sledge clearly decided it was time to make peace. "Sorry, didn't realise you were on a priority mission. If you can just leave me a transmitter I'll go back on the boat and wait for a Milli-Com rescue craft."

"Sounds like a plan to me," Venus said. She moved subtly closer to Rogue.

"Forget it," Helm said. Rogue realised with a sinking feeling that he'd picked up on Venus's jealousy and was fuming about it. "We don't abandon someone in the Orange Sea. Let Rogue look after her, Venus, and you and me can catch up."

But as they closed in the final distance to shore, Venus went back to lying in the bow, ignoring them all, and Helm was forced to talk to the chem nurse along with the rest of them. Rogue reckoned the best thing he could do was make Helm think he was interested in making whoopee with the newcomer. It wouldn't take too much of an act: she was pretty, her high cheekbones catching the light and her hair picking up golden highlights when the late evening sun briefly burned through the toxic clouds.

Not as pretty as Venus, though, a treacherous part of him said, his eyes unconsciously flicking to the lean blue form at the other end of the boat. He ignored that internal voice. It was only going get him into trouble.

"How long you been on Nu Earth?" he said to Sledge instead.

She sighed. "Too long."

"Hey," Bagman quipped. "When you're tired of Nu Earth, you're tired of life."

"What I'm tired of is death," Sledge said. There was no hint of a smile on her face now. "I came here to help, to make a difference, but there's only so much you can do. Most of the time I'm just making the pain less."

"If you want to help, how about helping us?" Gunnar said. "I know biochips aren't your field, but do you reckon you can tell if we've started degrading already?"

The chem nurse frowned uncertainly. "Well... I can take a look at you, but I don't know... I'm no engineer." She looked at Rogue, as if asking for his permission.

He shook his head. "It's up to the guys if they want you to poke around in their heads."

"You can poke around in mine any time," Bagman told her, a leer in his voice.

Sister Sledge hesitated a moment longer, then shrugged and reached for the gun. "Okay. Give me a second. Err…"

Rogue realised that she didn't know where the biochips were. He reached in and flipped out Gunnar's for her, careful to keep a hold of it as the ship began to dip and yaw in the rough coastal waters.

"Just don't drop me," Gunnar's voice said from the chip, higher and more mechanical sounding now that it wasn't vibrating through the metal of the gun.

Sister Sledge didn't reply, already absorbed in examining him through the eyepiece of her medi-scope. She was wearing a puzzled frown, but after a while Rogue began to think that the frown meant something else. After more than ten minutes, she leant back and handed the chip back to Rogue.

Rogue slotted it back into its housing on the gun, watching her worriedly as she still didn't say anything.

"Come on lady, open up!" Gunnar said eventually.

"Well, I'm not sure," she said.

"Just tell us!" Helm shouted. "We're soldiers. We can take it."

"It looks like there is some deterioration in the bio-circuitry to me," she told them, her voice assuming a comforting tone she'd probably practised on hundreds of dying men. "It shouldn't look that bad that soon. I think maybe the degradation happens faster than Milli-Com predicted."

There was a silence after her words.

"How long?" Gunnar said.

Sister Sledge's hand was in front of her mouth, as if she could shield them from her words that way. "I think only days before it's irreversible."

"Then I'll get you back to Milli-Com in two days," Rogue said. "That's a promise."

"Here," Sister Sledge said, holding out a docu-chip towards him. "I've entered the call-out code for a mobile field hospital unit that's based in the mountains above here. If you call them when you're ready they should be able to come and pick you up."

"Though I can't figure out why you're so keen to get back inside your bodies," Venus said. "Trained to kill and then to die, to be reborn to kill and die again. At least ordinary soldiers get to end it. For us there's no escape. Maybe you should just let those chips degrade, drift away and get some peace. Bodies aren't going to bring you anything but more war, more grief."

"Yeah, but without a body how are you and me ever going to be together again?" Helm asked, sounding hurt that Venus could talk about his death so casually.

Before Venus could respond, they finally drew near the shore and they were too busy finding a safe landing spot for more talking. As soon as Rogue had pulled the nose of the ship onto dry land, Sister Sledge hopped out.

"You gonna be okay?" Rogue asked her.

"I can look after myself," she told him, smiling. "Hope you can say the same. Take care of yourself, Rogue."

"Always do," Rogue said. He watched her until she clambered over the nearest stack of boulders. She turned round at the last minute to give him a final wave, and then her suited figure disappeared from sight.

"Well, good riddance," Venus said. "Last thing we need is a civilian slowing us down." After he'd secured the boat, Rogue offered her a hand to help her ashore, but she ignored him and leapt ten feet clear onto the dry sand above the breakers with cat-like grace. The sky lowered orange above her, and the land was broken up by great granite limbs of rock arching overhead. In the distance was the sound of artillery fire, echoing strangely round the deformed landscape.

"Incoming Souther transmission, Rogue," Helm said.

There was the squawk of a distant signal being patched in, then a slightly nasal voice said, "Rogue, this is Colonel Kovert. The Norts have already started their preliminary assault on Nu Atlanta. You're the only thing I've got to stop them."

Kovert sounded supremely confident that Rogue would do exactly as he wanted. "Kovert?" he said suspiciously. "I've heard of you. You're Military Intelligence."

Gunnar seemed to be on the same wavelength as Rogue. "Yeah, more Milli-Com top brass. Why should we trust you?"

Kovert didn't seem phased by their hostility. The only emotion Rogue could detect in his voice was a veiled amusement. "Because I'm the only ally you've got."

Suddenly, Venus's voice intruded on the transmission, sounding just about as pissed-off as Rogue had ever heard her. "Not the only ally, sir. And the situation isn't exactly what you think–"

Kovert's voice cut across hers. "I know. I've always suspected there was a traitor in Souther High Command. Thanks to you, now I know I was right."

"You *knew*?" Now Venus sounded incandescently furious. "And you didn't tell us?"

"Are you saying you could have stopped the Quartz Zone massacre?" Rogue asked, his voice lower than Venus's but even more deadly.

"I didn't find out what he was planning until it was too late," Kovert said. "And even if I had, I doubt that anyone else at Milli-Com would have believed me. It's a serious accusation to make without evidence to back it up. Even now my hands are tied. It's up to you to track down the traitor general and bring him in." His voice became smoother, almost wheedling. "If you do that, I'll do everything I can to help you and your comrades."

"Typical Milli-Com brass," Bagman grouched. "He pulls the strings and we take all the heat."

"Synth out, Bagman," Rogue said firmly. No point antagonising Kovert till he'd got what he wanted out of him. "One thing, colonel. My buddies here need regening I want your guarantee that'll happen as soon as I've completed the mission in Nu Atlanta."

"You have my assurance," Kovert said. "Now go and defend that Hovertrain – if the Norts take it out, the Southers will have no escape route out of Nu Atlanta. There's thousands of our men in there who need you, Rogue." Rogue decided that he trusted him just about as far as he could spit him, but there wasn't much he could do about it right now. Even if Kovert hadn't asked him, there was no way he could have left the unprepared Souther forces to die at Nu Atlanta, yet more victims of the traitor.

"Okay, colonel," Rogue said. "You've got a deal... for now."

Even over the radio, Rogue could hear the self-satisfied smile in Kovert's voice. "Good. Now, Venus, it's time for you to return to base. I can't have an agent of mine being seen to give aid to the Rogue Trooper. That wouldn't look good at all."

"Funnily enough, Kovert, I don't give a flying decapitator how it looks. Rogue needs my help and he's getting it."

"Venus–" Kovert began warningly.

"See you when the action's over, sir," Venus said, and broke the communication.

Back on Milli-Com, Kovert looked at his radio, hissing with static now, and smiled. Everything was going exactly as he intended.

Rogue was close to the base that guarded the hovertrain station when the saw the dogfight in the sky above him, one Souther Hoppa engaged by a pair of Norts, and clearly getting the worst of it. A streak of machine-gun fire shot from the Nort to the Souther, and a moment later the Souther vessel was falling towards the horizon and the ground, belching fire from its back end as it went. Helm projected the screaming voices of the Souther crew into his ears, sending out a mayday signal they probably thought no one would attend to. Rogue could hear the flat hopelessness in their voices.

"I've got the crash sight, can get you there in less than five," Helm said.

"Someone might have survived," Bagman added, though he sounded like he doubted it. Rogue doubted it to, but while there was a chance he had to take it

Ready to rescue some Southers?" he asked Venus.

She smiled, the white slashing grin of battle. "Always ready."

There were plenty of Norts who were ready too, crawling out of their boltholes in the ground and dropping onto the Hoppa landing pad as persistent as the stinging scum-bugs who flickered around them. Rogue wasn't sure he would have made it without Venus. But whenever his back needed covering, she was there, taking out the marines who were creeping up behind him with a couple of shotgun blasts. He didn't know how he'd have done it without Helm or Bagman either, laying out the field of conflict for him, telling him where his friends and ene-mies were.

Suddenly he had to cope without them. A Nort trooper popped his weapon round an elbow of rock and loosed off a strange, lightning-looking round, and a moment later all Rogue's instrumentation went dead.

"What the hell," he growled, tapping his helmet in a vain attempt to bring it back on line.

"EMP round," Venus told him. "New Nort technology. Don't worry, it'll wear off after a few seconds."

It did, but not before a brace of Norts had nearly got the drop on him as he ran through the blackened gouge the falling Souther Hoppa had made in the granite. After that he was very careful to keep an eye out for those troops, which was hard to do when they stayed hidden and only showed their faces for the millisecond they needed to fire. They managed to get him twice more before he finally cleared the area enough to reach the Hoppa's escape pod.

"You okay, guys?" he asked the biochips as he picked his way through the still-scorching wreckage.

"Right as rain," Bagman said, but Rogue thought he detected a light glitch in the electronic modulation of his voice. He frowned but kept his thoughts to himself. If the chips were degrading, the EMP blast couldn't be helping, but worrying about it wouldn't help either.

He was startled out of his reverie by a sudden shifting in the debris around him. A moment later, a door had been kicked open from the inside and a group of five Southers spilled out onto the ground, quickly rising to their feet. When their leader saw the red Souther insignia on Rogue's belt, he smiled. When he saw the blue colour of the skin above it, the smile slipped.

"Yeah, I'm the Rogue Trooper," Rogue told him. "Want to make something of it, or do you wanna get out there and stop the Norts shooting down any more of our men?"

The Souther sergeant, his face shiny with sweat under his chem mask, hesitated a second, but no longer. "We've got to reactivate that defensive gun. A stray shot took it offline, and now there's nothing to stop those damn Norts shelling our boys to hell as they try to get on the hovertrain."

"I'm on it," Rogue said. "Where can I find the gun?"

"I'll need to get you inside the airlock. Then I'll open up the service tunnels for you. A frontal attack would be suicide. But…" His eyes swept over the rusted domes of the base ahead of them. They were crawling with Norts, more coming in all the time, heavy shotgun units and more EMPs too.

"We'll take care of it," Gunnar said. "Just lead the way."

The Souther started when he heard the voice emanating from Rogue's weapon, then again when Venus joined them, blood dripping off her bayonet from a Nort who had come too close, but he collected himself soon enough when the Norts closed in.

Only now that he was fighting side by side with normal Souther troops for the first time could Rogue appreciate his own advantages. They were so bulky, so clumsy in their chem suits – bigger and more unwieldy than the insectile, blank-faced Nort suits – and they were so damn slow. Rogue felt like having them tag along was making his job harder, not easier. Still, there was no way he was leaving them behind.

Getting through the outer airlock and into the dome which held the entrance to the power dome was a long hard slog, but Rogue was pleased that he lost only one of the Southers on the journey. He caught a brief glimpse of the boy's face, waxy-white behind his chem mask and terribly young, then vaulted over it to let off a shotgun round at a troop of Norts who'd made the mistake of clustering too close. Then he was there.

"I've sealed the main route through. You'll have to take the service tunnel," the Souther sergeant said as

Rogue and Venus paused in the doorway. He hesitated, then added, "Good luck, trooper."

"You too, soldier," Rogue said. "Get your men onto the hovertrain. I'll join you as soon as the gun's back online."

The sergeant saluted him, then trotted off without a backward glance, his men at his heels.

"Come on, Rogue, what are you waiting for?" Venus called from inside. He ran after her, through winding intestinal lengths of tunnel, until he came out into a space so large it was hard to believe it was indoors, harder still when he saw the blots of lighting shooting up and down the vast coil in its centre. Right at the very top, dwarfed by the distance but still obviously huge, sat the anti-sub cannon.

"So, we gotta go all the way up there?" Bagman said.

Rogue pulled his straps tighter on his shoulders. "Yep."

"Well, I'm glad its your legs doing it, not mine."

The climb was long, and it wasn't peaceful. There were Nort troops coming up close behind, more of them no matter how many he and Venus picked off. He was gasping for breath by the time he reached the top, his heart thundering so hard he could feel its beats like blows against his chest. Beside him, Venus had barely raised a sweat.

"I'll cover you, Rogue," she said. "Do what you need to do."

Rogue took a look at the control panel. It seemed simple enough; just some power needed rerouting to get the gun back online. He initiated the diagnostics, then patched Helm into the control mechanism.

"Looking good," Helm said. "All systems online. What do you want me to do?"

A burst of machine-gun fire ricocheted from the piping beside him, spraying rust into Rogue's eye. "Can't stay up here. You'd better set it on automatic and we'll head out and try to get our troops onboard the hover-train."

"Got you," Helm said. "I'm gonna set it to hit anything that's Nort and moving."

A second later, the protective screen in front of the gun slid open and they were given a high, dizzying view of the battle below. Suddenly, the view was blotted out by the squat shape of a Nort Hoppa squeezing through the narrow gap.

"Great," Gunnar said, sounding like he meant it. "More target practice. Get that Sammie attachment on me, Rogue."

"Can't do it," he replied. "Didn't have any time to make more Sammie rounds."

The Hoppa was so near, Rogue could smell the acrid clouds of its exhaust. Only the complex maze of the pipes around them saved them from the hail of bullets it was spraying towards them.

Venus was grinning. "See, this is why you need a girl in the outfit. Us girls plan ahead."

A Sammie missile streaked out from the end of her gun and took the Hoppa out with a fireball that lit up the whole inside of the dome, so that for an instant the lightning arcing up the coil itself was overwhelmed, flicking negative from white to black against the red.

Rogue didn't hang around to admire the display. He flung himself over the edge of the platform, vaulting two levels to land on a walkway thirty feet below, and proceeded to get the hell out of there, Venus hot on his heels. Echoing deafeningly through the chamber, the missile fire of the cannon sounded out, doing its job as well as it knew how, just like him.

As soon as Venus and Rogue made their way out of the airlock they could see that the fight inside had just been a warm-up. There were more Norts there than he knew were living, and every one of them was determined to stop a single Souther from making it to the safety of the hovertrain he could see hulking at the far end of the base.

"Subfire's the main danger," Helm told him. "You'll need some heavy artillery to take it on."

Rogue was already on it. There was a Hell Cannon to the left of him, a few Norts manning it, but that didn't matter. A shotgun round and some micro-mines from Bagman and the cannon was his. After that it was easy. The horizon was filled with the humped silhouettes of Nort subs, but the cannon was more than a match for them. Rogue concentrated on taking them out one by one, waiting out the recharge time between rounds impatiently, while Venus covered his back, putting a hole through any Norts stupid enough to think it might be a good idea to take back the cannon.

When the last Nort sub disappeared from sight, sunk by his fire or submerged prudently beneath the waves, the Souther landing craft made it in. The troops it disgorged looked weary, their faces glazed with tiredness and prematurely lined with cramping fear and the bitterness of defeat. Rogue saw one of them look up, realise the distance still to go to the safety of the hovertrain, and sit back down again on the shelf of the craft, as if he just couldn't face fighting on for that little bit longer.

The first Nort Hoppas hove into view and the man joined his comrades as they pelted through the chaos of battle away from the shore, survival instincts kicking in whether he wanted them to or not.

Rogue lost sight of him. He dropped the Hell Cannon – it was powerful but too slow – and found himself an AA-gun instead. The Hoppas were harder targets, buzzing to and fro like hyperactive wasps. Even when he took one down, chances were it managed to disgorge a pack of Norts onto the ground before it fell. Those Norts in turn fell on the Southers, cutting down the battle-weary men as they fled.

Rogue couldn't worry about the dead, only the living. He set his mouth in a hard line and carried on firing, killing, finally fighting beside other Southers where he belonged. Thanks to the traitor, Nu Atlanta might be lost, but thanks to Rogue there were going to be plenty of Souther survivors making it out of there.

"Rogue," Bagman said, after a time period that felt like hours, but could have been minutes or days. "Rogue, we're getting flanked at the back."

"Most of our men are on," Helm spoke into his ear. "Time for us to join them."

"Hey, but I haven't had a chance to kill any Norts yet," Gunnar said. "Gotta bag me a couple at least."

"You can clear a path back for us," Rogue said, reluctantly abandoning the AA-gun and taking Gunnar back into his arms. "Should be enough Norts to keep you happy."

He wasn't kidding. He and Venus had to fight their way through a horde of the troopers, a mixture of the blue-clad marines and shotgun and EMP units. Bagman used up pretty much his entire supply of micro-mines salting the ground behind them to stop the Norts taking them from behind. In front, Rogue stopped seeing individual men. He just saw the Norts as a swarm, as relentless and featureless as the chem roaches they resembled.

Then, almost without him realising it, he was on the train. He leant over to pull Venus up beside him, and she was too tired to protest, her body almost a dead weight in his arms. The Southers must have been waiting for him. The troopers manning the guns at the rear of the train saluted, and then the vast machine roared into life and pulled out of the station – slowly, then faster, faster still, whistling the wind painfully past the abrasions on his face.

After a few minutes, as the wreckage of the coastal base disappeared behind them, Venus turned to smile at him. Her white hair was mussed and stained with the blood of the Nort she'd bayoneted. There were black flecks of it freckling her face. Her body gave off a strong odour of sweat and adrenaline. Rogue thought she looked more beautiful than anything he'd ever seen. He felt his heart rate speed up and his mouth dry and hoped that there was no sensor in Helm that could detect it.

"Well, looks like we made it," Venus said. She began to clean her nails with her knife, taking care not to look at him. "I'd say you and me make a good team."

Rogue thought so too, but didn't say it. "Don't relax too much, Venus," he said. "My gut tells me this ain't over by a long way."

NINE
HELL ON WHEELS

The hovertrain sped on into the stark desert frontier of the continent. Here the chem was thinner, but it didn't bring relief, just allowed the two suns to burn down all the brighter onto the people below, emitting levels of radiation that could be fatal after only a few minutes' unsuited exposure.

Rogue's skin was designed to withstand the suns as well as the air of Nu Earth, but even he found it hot. The air was choked with dust too, thrown up by the hyperfast passage of the train. It seemed crazy that this barren, changeless landscape was something men would kill and die over. But then Nu Earth had never been valuable for what was on it, only for where it was – near the crucial hyperspace gateway that the black hole above it supplied. Everything on the planet's surface was just collateral damage, all the great cities that had been built up here, the hopeful places that colonists had intended as a reminder of home. It was all rubble now. When the war was over, Rogue imagined Nu Earth remaining empty, a prize that no one wanted any longer.

His radio crackled into life, jerking him out of his thoughts. He wasn't very surprised to hear Kovert's voice on the other end. "Rogue, I'm monitoring your progress. You saved a lot of lives today, GI."

"Get to the point, colonel," Rogue snapped.

Again, he heard the smile in the other man's voice, as if Rogue was behaving just the way he expected.

"You're not out of this yet, trooper. Now that Nu Atlanta's fallen, the Norts are massing ahead for their main attack on Harpo's Ferry. It's our last stronghold on the continent and it's crucial for us to keep control of it. If you can get there on time–"

A roar of gunfire cut off the sound of the colonel's voice, seeming to echo endlessly through the dry desert air. Rogue squinted over the high sides of the open-air carriage and saw what looked at first like a regiment of miniature sandstorms heading towards the train. After a moment they resolved themselves into figures, the grotesque two-legged shape of stammels powering through the sand towards the train. The wind carried the sound of their riders towards him, a high uncanny ululation. Then the first pinpricks of fire appeared against the distant figures and Rogue heard a scream as a Souther beside him was taken through the forehead by a high-speed projectile round.

"Sorry, colonel," he said into his radio. "Like you said, we're not out of this yet." He switched off the signal before Kovert could reply and turned to the Souther squad beside him. "Get everyone forward to the front of the train."

The Southers hesitated a moment, then obeyed, confident in Rogue's leadership. He hoped their confidence wasn't misplaced. He could see the sharp spikes of gun turrets on the carriage ahead, along with the bulkier form of an AA gun. "Come on," he shouted at Venus, and leapt over the dividing wall and into the next carriage.

Before his feet had even landed, a ball of Lazooka fire consumed the place where he'd been standing, incinerating the other carriage and all the Southers still on it.

The main thing about stammels, Pietr had discovered, was that they stank. He needed to press his knees tight into the mottle-skinned beast to keep his seat as it lolloped over the desert sand on its two stocky legs, but he hated being that close to it. He imagined its stench seeping greasily from its skin and through his chem suit. It wasn't that fanciful an idea. If the smell was detectable through the chem mask's filters, it must be unbelievably strong.

The beast was closer to the train, galloping in a group of six, the other riders so close that Pietr felt he could have reached out and touched them. But he didn't. He was concentrating on sucking his chest in, trying to make himself seem as small and lithe as possible. It wasn't until after he'd stolen a stammel from the holding pens and ridden off with the legion towards the train that he'd realised that every single one of the other riders was female.

Fortunately, none of them could spare the time to look at him too closely. The train was huge, the largest mechanical thing Pietr had ever seen. The stammels stood a good fifteen feet high, but Pietr still felt like they were fleas trying to suck the blood out of a dinosaur. Beside him, he saw one of the stammel riders raise a rifle to her shoulder and shoot off a round at the train, still a good hundred metres away from them. It seemed entirely futile, but, carrying with startling loudness through the desert air, he heard a scream, and a tiny body fell from the train to the sand below.

The other riders all raised their rifles in the air, letting out an ululating cry of triumph more frightening than the scream. Pietr raised his rifle too. As soon as he did, his precarious balance deserted him and he suddenly felt himself sliding rapidly backwards down the long tail of the stammel.

It was what saved him. The round of return fire from the train passed exactly through where his body had been and took the rider behind him instead. With a desperate scramble, he was able to pull himself back onto the creature. As soon as he had the reins he pulled them sharply left, dragging the creature away from the terrifying hail of machine gun fire churning the sand beneath its double-hooved feet.

The machine gun fire seemed to follow him. He could see where it was coming from now, a central carriage on the train, and inside it what looked like a fleck of blue, a drop of water in a sea of sand. Pietr realised that the fire was going high, aiming for the bulk of the riders behind him. The arc was taking it closer and closer to him. The only way out was under and back, through the curtain of bullets.

Deliberately this time, he repeated his earlier manoeuvre, sliding backwards and down the tail of his stammel. His chem suit scraped against the spines on the creature's back and for one horrible second he thought it was going to tear, but the stammel rider's suit he'd stolen was designed to withstand its mount's skin and the material held.

As soon as he had a firm grip, Pietr twisted his foot forward to kick it as hard as he could against the stammel's flank. For a moment it hesitated, as if not quite believing what he wanted it to do, but the creatures had been trained and bred for combat and it obeyed his command, however reluctantly.

The bullets passed so close over Pietr's head that he heard their high-pitched wine and the miniature thunderclaps of the self-propelled incendiary rounds as they reached supersonic speed. If just one of them pierced the protective shell of his chem suit he would be finished.

None of them did. After an endless stretch of time that probably only lasted two seconds, he was through the hail of fire and out the other side, in the clear, as the bullets hunted bigger prey, the big cluster of stammel riders he'd abandoned.

He heard their battle shrieks turn into cries of pain as the hot metal found soft flesh, but he couldn't make himself care. He had to get to the train. He had to get to the man who was firing those bullets. Then everyone, every death, would be revenged.

Rogue's gut instinct back at base had been right. The Norts weren't letting the hovertrain go easy. In fact, they weren't letting it go at all. The stammel riders were relentless, and no matter how many he mowed down with the train's flak guns, there was always another, and time after time a shot would ring out and a Souther would scream and that would be another one lost.

"How many of them are there?" Venus shouted from the gun beside him as she sprayed fire into a cluster of riders who'd ventured too close to the train. The lead rider fell screaming, dragged along for yards behind her stammel by feet still hooked into its stirrups. The creature's dumb, big-lipped face looked up at them, meeting Rogue's eyes briefly with what looked almost like a quizzical frown, as if to ask him what it had ever done to deserve this.

"You and me both, buddy," he wanted to say to it.

"I'm picking up at least five hundred stammel bio-signs," Helm answered Venus's question. "You'd better be careful, V."

"I can take care of myself!" she snapped at him, and Helm lapsed into wounded silence.

"Err, Rogue," Bagman said. "I think you should look up."

"Can't!" Rogue gritted. The nearest squadron of riders seemed to be carrying a Lazooka slung between their mounts. If they got off a round of that, the train could take some serious damage.

"I *really* think you should look up," Bagman repeated.

Rogue cursed and did as he asked, keeping his finger depressed on the machine gun's trigger as he risked a glance up at the sky. Then he cursed again.

Circling elegantly in the breeze, high above the train but getting lower, were the unmistakable silhouettes of gliders. The suns emerged briefly from their concealing clouds and the underwings of the gliders flashed a vivid scarlet and yellow, like a hornet. Beneath the brightly coloured canopy, the men were barely visible.

Nort Sun Legions. Damn it! Those guys carried bombs, big ones. He couldn't afford to have them start dropping on the train.

"Cover the stammels," he shouted over to Venus. "I'm gonna take care of the flyers."

"Roger that," Venus said.

"There's a Lazooka unit at eleven o'clock," Rogue told her as he scrambled across the carriage to the big AA-gun. "Better take that out first."

"Teach your grandmother," Venus shot back, but she sounded amused rather than irritated. A burst of flack was already raking across the stammels hefting the Lazooka between them. Rogue just had time to see them stumble and fall, their bestial faces looking stupidly surprised, and then all his attention was fixed on the skies.

The sun legionaries should have made nice clear targets with their garish wings and wide silhouettes, but they were coming in with the suns behind them and suddenly the colouring of their gliders made sense, camouflaged and almost invisible against the glaring light. Rogue would have liked to just let loose across the whole sky with A-A fire, but he knew that ammo was short. He couldn't afford to give their position away without taking the enemies out.

By the time his eyes had adjusted to the blinding glare of the sunlight, one bomb had already been let loose. He felt the explosion before he heard it, rocking the train from side to side on its tracks so that for one moment Rogue thought it might come off them altogether. There was another explosion only a second after, a Lazooka round this time. Without him as back-up it looked like Venus was struggling to keep the stammel riders contained. A few more hits like that and the train wouldn't be making it anywhere. He could already hear the engine juddering, a catch in its rhythm as one of its pistons failed to fire.

He shot down one sun trooper, the falling figure twirling and twirling as it fell like a sycamore seed, then another, but there were always more and they were low enough to be deploying their payloads now. It was only a matter of time before the train took a critical hit. Amazingly, he saw salvation ahead. In the distance, but rapidly approaching, was the mouth of a tunnel, a blackness in the mountains ahead, gaping like a mouth to consume the endless desert sand. If he could hold the Norts off that long, they might make it. If.

Right up until the moment he grasped the metal strut of the train and heaved himself from the back of his stammel, Pietr didn't think he was going to make it. Even then, he was left hanging by only one arm, his feet dangling far too near to the ground. At the speed the train was travelling, he knew that any contact with the coarse sand would scrape the chem suit and then the skin and flesh right off him.

Jaze had always told him that he was weak, but as he pulled himself inch by painful inch onto the low-level platform skirting the bottom of the train, he found that strength was something you could find when you needed it.

Once he was on the hard metal surface he lay on his back for a few minutes, gasping for breath, staring up at the sun through the polarised lenses of his chem suit. He was alive. It had seldom felt this good. He breathed in a deep breath of stale air, then heard the footstep just a few feet to the side of him, and kept the air in his lungs, frozen, until the pressure of it was too much and he had to let it out in as soft a hiss as he could manage.

A Souther. His first instinct was to hide, to lay low until the trooper had passed. But he realised that he was going to have to pass through a whole train full of them. In Nort uniform there was no way he was going to make it. He was going to need a Souther uniform. Which meant he was going to have to kill this Souther. More than that, he was going to have to kill him without doing any damage to his chem suit.

The Souther's footsteps came closer. Then they paused, as if he was listening. For a desperate moment, Pietr thought he had heard the soft whisper of the spent air venting from his air tanks. He braced himself, ready to grab the man if he came nearer and fling him from the side of the train.

The man didn't come and Pietr realised that he could hear another sound, louder than the breath of air from his suit. It was the very gentle whine of tiny motors. It was, he realised, the sound of auto-binocs finding their focus.

Which meant the Souther wasn't looking at him. Even better, it meant that the Souther was looking away from the train, through devices which would cut out his peripheral vision entirely.

There would never be a better time than this. Before the fear Pietr felt gripping his gut could paralyse him completely, he eased himself to his knees and then to his feet.

The Souther was close to him, closer than he'd realised, less than two feet away. It seemed impossible

that he wouldn't see him. The green-clad upright figure didn't move. The binocs remained pressed against
the clear plastic at the front of his chem mask.

He was standing very close to the edge. Pietr
would have to be careful that any move he made
didn't send the man tumbling from the train. Clearly,
as if it had only happened yesterday, he remembered
his basic training. Cruel, miserable old Sergeant
Gillash taking the raw recruits through all the ways
one man could kill another man. "You're going to be
Kashans," he'd said to them. "The best of the best.
Other soldiers need a weapon to kill. Kashans can do
it with their bare hands." Then he'd taken the neck
of the Souther prisoner and snapped it with one
clean twist.

Pietr didn't let himself think about it. He kept his
mind in the past, in a time when this was just training, put his hands around the dull metal of the
Souther's helmet – and jerked.

Even through the chem suit, he heard the soft
snap. The body went instantly limp in his arms, far
heavier than he'd guessed it would be. It took a
moment's fierce struggle to heave it away from the
edge of the train. Now all he needed to do was find
an airlocked section where he could change from
one chem suit to the other without exposing himself
to Nu Earth's toxic atmosphere. Grimly, he began to
drag the corpse towards the nearest door.

The tunnel was only a hundred metres ahead of
them. Fifty. Rogue let off a final salvo at a low-flying
squadron of sun troops as Venus sprayed metal into
the nearest stammels, and then they were through.

It got worse. The tunnel had looked tiny in the distance, hardly big enough for the train to fit through.
All wrong. It was huge, larger than the train by far.

Large enough to allow a squadron of Hoppas to fly down after the train. Large enough for them to carry on pursuing it as it rushed at breathtaking speeds round the looping twists and curves of the tunnel's length.

"Give me a break!" Bagman said. "Don't these guys ever give up?"

"Not fair!" Gunnar said. "When am I ever going to see some action?"

Rogue fired into the Hoppas, taking one down, but one of the others had already dropped its payload of Nort troops onto the train behind him. "Right about now," he said to Gunnar. The tunnel twisted sharply to the left, forcing the Hoppas to drop back for a moment, and he used the time to snatch Gunnar from his back and set him up on his tripod on the deck beside him. "Watch my back," said Rogue. "I'm gonna take care of those Hoppas."

"Norts to kill and I even get to decide which ones to take out for myself. Life is good," Gunnar said, already firing into the approaching troops. The hail of fire tore them to shreds, scattering their bright remains over the dull metal of the train. But there were more where they came from, and more Hoppas too.

Even with Venus beside him, Rogue was barely able to keep the Hoppas from blowing the train out from under him. Only the twisting of the tunnel saved him, stopping the Hoppa captains from ever getting a good lock. After a while, it stopped being about reflexes and started being about psychology.

Take that Hoppa: the pilot liked taking risks, liked zooming in just before a tunnel turn, hoping that Rogue's attention would be away, thinking he was already safe. The next time the train flung itself round a bend Rogue was ready. He sent fire ahead of him, to where he knew the Hoppa was going to be, and it flew straight into it, blooming into a ball of fire.

Then there was the pilot of that Hoppa there. He wasn't too brave, liked to hang back behind the others and let them take the damage, then dart in and shoot his missiles when Rogue's attention was elsewhere. Rogue sent a round powering through the two forward Hoppas to take out the one lurking behind.

Hoppa after Hoppa, with Venus meting out death of her own beside him, and still the train dove on through the tunnel, swimming through solid rock.

Then, distantly, Rogue began to see a lighter circle against the grey, as small as a coin. A second later it disappeared, only to reappear again, a fraction bigger this time. The end of the tunnel. They were nearly through.

Then they *were* through, emerging high into the mountains, the air suddenly bitterly cold, a starling contrast to the desert they'd left only minutes ago. The sun legions were back, but far fewer of them. The action below must have taken its toll, and maybe not many of them had the power to make it to this altitude. The Hoppas too were slowing, falling behind the train like runners who had finally given up the race.

Almost unbelievably, they were going to make it.

Secure in the sealed atmosphere of his field dome, Kovert stroked his moustache – a nervous habit he'd never been able to break – and studied the read-out in front of him. He hated surprises, especially the unpleasant kind. Damn his agents for not getting him information about the Nort plans sooner.

"Get me a line through to the Rogue Trooper now!" he shouted at his assistant.

The assistant bent obligingly over the radio, but his expression said he knew it was useless. The machine gave him nothing but static. "No go, sir," he said, straightening up. "Norts must be jamming our signal."

Kovert slammed both palms against the table with a loud crack. Damn it! This was the worst possible news.

At first, Rogue didn't know what the noise was. He thought it must be some other Nort vessel, bigger than any they'd yet met, something huge to let out such a vast roar.

But the noise wasn't coming from above them. It was coming from beneath. He felt it in the metal of the train, a terrible shaking that threatened to break the train apart. Only it wasn't the train that was collapsing, it was the viaduct beneath it.

"Rogue…" Venus said. She looked into his eyes, the emotion in her own unusually naked, and he knew that she'd felt their death in the fall of the viaduct.

"Scan out, Venus," he growled at her. "Just 'cause we're down don't mean we're out. If we stay with the train we've got a chance." Even as he was speaking he grabbed Gunnar, tying him to his chest, using his other hand to check that Helm and Bagman were secure. Then he grasped the handrail behind him, his grip as firm as he could make it but his body as relaxed as possible. Staying tense through a fall was the way to get hurt. Venus watched him, her mouth open as if she wanted to say something. Then she snapped it shut and did as he'd done. Her body curled in on itself, a small blue ball.

The train fell.

It was like the death throes of a huge serpent or an impossibly large beast. Metal shrieked as it twisted and sheared. The engine plunged straight into the ravine, tumbling thousands of feet to its destruction, nuclear engines toiling futilely to drag it along a track that was no longer there. The carriages were luckier. When the arches of the viaduct gave way, falling in graceful almost ballet-like curves, they threw the rest of the train against the side of the mountain.

The impact was loud. The Nort sappers who had placed the mines which led to this destruction were deafened, clasping hands instinctively against ears which were pouring blood. They'd never hear again.

The carriage carrying Rogue and Venus grated down the almost sheer cliff face, tearing out vast gouts of rock and vegetation as it went. Then, slowly, it began to turn. Faster, spinning as it tumbled, over and over, smashing itself against the rocks on each impact as if it had had enough of this torment, as if it wanted to die.

It seemed like a crash nothing could survive.

Far away, the sound of the crash could still be heard as a muted echo. The general – who had surrendered his name when he surrendered his nationality – smiled. Nothing stood in their way. Harpo's Ferry would fall. The last-remaining Souther-held land on this continent would be gone. After that, he thought, Nu Earth will be ours.

He paused a moment as he realised what he was thinking. That by "ours" he meant the Norts. The Rogue Trooper, that filthy mutant, had called him a traitor. Was the freak right? Had he betrayed his cause?

But no, it was the Southers who were traitors, all of them, traitors who sold their own heritage down the river when they allowed the genetic aberrations to be created. He had never wavered. He had always been on the side of the angels.

And the angels had destroyed the last possible hope for the Southers and the man who had taken his face from him along with them. He laughed. Life was good. Unless, of course, you were a Souther.

TEN
WALKING WITH
THE ENEMY

The report came in only ten minutes after the traitor had first heard the explosion. These Norts are nothing if not efficient, he thought, glancing over at General Rushkin to see if he was impressed with his operatives' efficiency, but his face, granite grim, gave nothing away.

The figure reporting in on the giant vid-screen that covered one wall of the room wasn't giving much away either. The black visor which covered his entire head denied anything that might have been human about him. Even his posture was robotic, too rigid, too controlled, as if nothing as irrational as pleasure or emotion could move him. Still, the traitor liked what he had to say.

"Morgan reporting, general. The train has been destroyed."

The traitor allowed himself a small smile. But this wasn't the information he was most interested in. "And the GI?" he said.

Morgan nodded once, curtly. "Dead. Even if he survived the crash, he won't survive the petrified forest."

The traitor nodded back at him, then signalled to the hovering radio operator that the vid-link should be terminated. As soon as he was sure the screen was dead, he looked over at General Rushkin. "This Morgan, is he reliable?"

Rushkin looked surprised that he would even be asked. "That black visor he wears is only awarded to our best snipers, those that have killed more than a thousand Southers."

The traitor realised that he had heard of such operatives, the master snipers, but had always assumed that the stories must be Nort propaganda. It seemed not. He smiled at Rushkin, allowing himself to fully relax for the first time. A flicker of movement on another vid screen caught his attention, and he watched as two Blackmare tanks rumbled forward, their vast bulks dwarfing the small command post where the traitor and Rushkin sat. Around the tank massed the ranks of Nort infantry, an endless stream of them.

"Good," the traitor said. "With the GI dead and the information I have on the Souther defences, nothing can stop us now."

Pietr opened his eyes to darkness, but the darkness wasn't absolute. A spectral glow was coming in from somewhere to his left, a small chink in the gloom. He tried to move towards it, and only then realised that he couldn't move at all, that the reason for the pain he was experiencing was the mound of debris pinning him to the ground.

Suddenly it came back to him: the train had crashed. He was amazed that he'd survived it. He certainly hadn't thought he would, during the long, loud fall into the void. Experimentally, he tried to move his fingers and toes. They moved without difficulty, so it seemed that his paralysis was due to the weight of the wrecked train above him rather than any serious injury.

It was a miracle that his chem suit hadn't torn in the descent. Just one rip, and the toxic atmosphere would have finished him off long ago.

This just meant that he'd die slowly. After all this, to get so close... Well, maybe it proved his brother right about him: he was a born failure, a quitter who never finished a job. Jaze had died a hero. His parents would be sent his remains in a coffin draped in the Nort flag, with a full military guard in recognition of his service.

Pietr would die a deserter. His remains would rot here, forgotten and unfound, and all that his mother would know about him was that he had let her and his brother down. He wondered if he could ease his hand down to the knife that hung at his waist, open a vein in his thigh and at least let it all end quickly.

He was so absorbed in his self-recrimination that for a moment he didn't register the fact that the area of light above him was growing. Bit by bit, the grey-blue moonlit sky was being revealed. There was the sound of someone grunting with effort, and the clank and banging of fragments of metal and rock being cast aside.

Pietr found that he wasn't ready to die after all. "Here! I'm in here!" he shouted.

A few minutes later, he felt the pressure on his legs and chest ease and suddenly there was nothing between him and the open air but chem mist. The figure of his rescuer loomed over him, stark black against the silver moon. It reached a hand out towards him and he gratefully let it pull him to his feet.

Then the figure moved sideways, away from the moon, so that the moonlight shone directly onto its profile. For a moment Pietr thought it was just a trick of the light that it seemed so blue, but then it asked, "You all right, solider?" and he knew that it really was the Rogue Trooper.

"I'm... I'm fine," he stumbled, too numb to do anything else.

Before he could react, the GI shoved a bent metal pylon into his hands. "Then get digging. There are others still trapped under the rubble." He turned away without waiting to see if Pietr was obeying him, utterly confident in his command.

For a brief moment, Pietr had a clear line of sight at the Rogue Trooper's back. All he'd have to do would be to reach down to the energy pistol still strapped to his waist and snap off one shot. There was no way he could miss at this distance.

But his hand stayed stubbornly by his side and then the GI was out of sight, off helping some other trapped Souther, and the moment was lost.

It turned out that only six of them had made it out of the wreckage, along with the Rogue Trooper and another blue-skinned freak, a woman of all things, whom the other GI seemed to call "Venus". Pietr couldn't take his eyes off her though she paid him no more attention than she did to the scumbugs glowing and buzzing around them. She had eyes only for Rogue, eyes that lingered a little too long every time they passed over him. It bothered Pietr to see someone so clearly viewing the Rogue Trooper as a man, and not a monster.

The other Souther troops were looking at the GIs uncomfortably too, as if, even though they supposedly fought on the same side, they were no more at ease with them than Pietr was. Pietr was painfully aware, too that he *wasn't* fighting on the same side as everyone around him. He kept his face turned away, hidden in shadows, and prayed that no one would be able to see just from the cast of his features, or the discomfort in his eyes, that he was one of those who had brought them here in the first place, where so many of their friends lay buried. High above them, silhouetted against the sky, he could see the sagging, broken arches of the viaduct. Closer were the trees, moss the only living thing on them, their great, twisted shapes turned to stone in some long-forgotten natural catastrophe. In the moonlight they looked like the ghosts of trees, restless and haunted spirits which boded ill for everyone beneath them. Pietr didn't think he liked this place at all.

The other Souther troops seemed to share his unease. Unconsciously, they were grouping closer and closer together, as if the presence of another warm human body, even wrapped away inside a chem suit, could keep out the unearthly cold of the forest.

"Bagman, we need a heads-up on where we are. Any structures nearby?" Rogue said, and for a moment Pietr assumed he must be talking to one of the other Southers. The voice that answered seemed to come from Rogue's own equipment, a strange mechanical voice that sounded neither human nor computer.

"Digi-map's showing what looks like an old hydroponics facility nearby," the voice said. "Could be shelter and food there."

One of the other Southers must have seen Pietr's puzzled expression because he leaned over to whisper, "It's a biochip. All the GIs have them, absorbs their personality when they die and then their buddies can store them in their equipment till they get re-gened." He looked at Pietr suspiciously. "I thought everyone knew that."

"Oh, I knew *about* it," Pietr said hastily. "It's just actually seeing it, you know…"

The Souther seemed to relax. "Yeah, I know – freaky isn't it? And he's got three of them, Gunnar, Bagman and Helm they're called, all died at the Quartz Zone along with the rest of the GIs. But I guess a GI's tour of duty never ends, unlike the rest of us. Even when they die they don't get to ship home, 'cause this is the only home they have."

"The facility had better be close," one of the other Southers was saying. Pietr could see beads of sweat standing out on his face, shimmering a pearly white in the moonlight. "I've only got two hours of air reserve left."

At his words, there was a general fumbling with cylinders and gauges. Pietr was horrified to find that he had little over two hours' supply left himself.

"I've got less than thirty minutes left!" another of the troopers said, a note of barely suppressed hysteria in his voice. Running out of clean air would be a worse way to die than in the crash itself. He looked at his companion. "C'mon, let's go find that hydroponics plant." Not even bothering to check that any of the others were following, he set off at a sprint towards a small clearing in the trees ahead of them.

He was almost there when the beam of light hit him, a brief flash of red that was gone as soon as it appeared. The second after the light blinked out, a shot rang out, one single sharp retort. For a moment, Pietr thought it might have missed, but then the Souther toppled slowly to the ground, his hands clutched to his throat as a thick, black liquid pumped out of it, the colour of blood in moonlight.

"Sniper! Everyone get down!" Rogue said.

Pietr was on his face in the moss of the forest floor even before Rogue had finished speaking, his heart thumping so loudly that he thought the enemy snipers – no, his own side's snipers – would be able to track and kill him from the sound alone. Desperately he peered into the trees, trying to locate the source of the shot, but the forest gave nothing away.

"Nothing showing on my sensors, Rogue," a mechanical voice said, one of the other biochips, Pietr guessed. "They must be wearing stealth suits."

"We can still spot 'em from the red flash of the sighting beam," Rogue said. "Any of the rest of you got sniper scopes yourselves?"

"A girl never leaves home without it," Venus said.

Pietr saw Rogue give an involuntary smile and then quickly suppress it. "What about the rest of you?" he asked. No one answered, and after a moment he continued, "All right then, you soldiers better hang back. Me and Venus will clear a path through for you, and you can take care of any ground troops."

Take care of any ground troops: it was such an innocent phrase. But in Pietr's ears he heard it differently: you can kill any of your own men you see.

Before he had time to work out what he was going to do, Rogue and Venus were off, and Pietr found himself running after them despite his doubts, unprepared to find himself alone in the petrified forest with nothing but the smouldering wreck of the train for company.

There weren't any ground troops, though, just the snipers, hidden high in the canopy of the trees, loosing off shot after shot at the Southers below, so that Pietr found himself jumping at the slightest sound, the snap of a brittle stone twig beneath someone's boot, or the tinkling rustle of the wind through the petrified leaves. And though Pietr wasn't asked to kill any of his fellow Norts himself, he found himself silently and helplessly cheering Rogue and Venus on as they did it for him, feeling a leap of joy when one of their shots found its mark and there was the distant scream of a sniper dying.

Despite the other people in the forest, Pietr felt terribly alone with his fear and his uncertainty. At first the Southers had clustered together, but as soon as they realised this made them an easier target, they'd spread apart, trying to make themselves as small and silent and insignificant as they could, hiding in the moon-shadows of the vast dead trees.

Even so, Pietr saw two Southers fall, then another. One was the man who'd complained that he only had two hours of oxygen left. Not a problem for him now,

Pietr thought morbidly as he stepped over the other man's corpse and tried not to look at the expression of pain and fear on the dead man's face.

Rogue and Venus didn't even seem to register the death, never took their eyes from the forest, as if they could see through the darkness to the targets beyond. Maybe they could. Pietr had heard that the Souther freaks had superhuman abilities, bred in the twisted genetic programme which had produced them. Twisted or not, Pietr was glad of them.

Another of Venus's shots found its mark, and Pietr heard her whisper, "Seven-five to me, Rogue," a smile evident in her voice. It amazed him, how easily killing seemed to come to these people, how war seemed to be such a game to them, one whose rules they'd mastered long ago. He couldn't imagine ever feeling that way himself.

But Venus's whisper had been unwise. The snipers might not have superhuman senses, but they had top-of-the-range equipment and something must have picked up on the sound. Two shots rang out from the forest in quick succession and then two more Southers were down, each taken clean through the head.

After that Venus and Rogue were so silent that Pietr often lost track of where they were, following their trail through the forest by blind instinct alone, picking them up again only when they fired, sparingly, hitting their mark nearly every time.

As they crept on and on through the forest, Pietr began to believe that they were going to make it, that these two Southers together really could take on his own side's most elite fighters and win.

He saw the wall of darkness towering ahead of him. It was a gate, closed and far too tall to consider climbing. Wearily, Pietr jogged towards it, not knowing what else he could do. Beside him, the two remaining Souther infantrymen did the same, the expressions through their chem masks as grim as Pietr suspected his own was. Then there was a flash of red, the crack of gunfire, and suddenly there was only one Souther left beside Pietr at the gate.

Quicker than Pietr could follow, Rogue spun and snapped off a shot of his own, taking the sniper out of his tree over two hundred yards away. But the damage had already been done: the Souther troop's eyes stared up at the silver moon, glassy and blank.

"What are we going to do?" the other Souther said, his voice thick with fear. Pietr could see that he was only a boy, no more than eighteen. My own age, Pietr thought, but he'd stopped thinking of himself as a boy the second the shot had taken his brother through the heart.

"Could be a way to the control booth up those cliffs," one of the GI's biochips said.

Pietr looked up, then up again, at the almost sheer rock face. "No way we're going to make it up there," he said.

"Don't worry about it kid," Venus said. "We'll take care of it for you, then come back down when it's open."

"What about...?" the other Souther asked, then trailed off as he seemed to realise that the GIs were offering to risk their lives for him and he had no call to complain that they were leaving him defenceless.

"Seem to have taken care of most of the snipers in the immediate area," Rogue said gruffly. There was no criticism in his voice but no sympathy either, just one soldier to another. "Just keep down, keep quiet and keep your eyes open."

The Souther drew himself up and snapped off a salute. "Sir, yes, sir!"

Rogue almost laughed. "I've got no rank in your army any more, soldier. Don't you know I've gone rogue?" Before the young trooper could stammer a reply, he'd run off into the darkness, Venus like a blue shadow at his heels.

It was only when the GIs were gone that Pietr realised that not once during their entire journey through the forest had it occurred to him to hope that a sniper's bullet would find them. It's because I mean to kill him myself, just as soon as we're clear of this forest, Pietr told himself. I will kill him, I will, I just need time.

"Think they'll be all right?" Venus asked Rogue as they scrambled up the rock face. The other GI was ahead of her and it gave her a chance to admire the clean, tight lines of his body as he scaled the rocks, moving with an effortless grace that had been bred into all their kind but seemed to have reached perfection in Rogue.

"They can look after themselves," Rogue said quietly. "They're soldiers, same as us."

"No soldiers are the same as us," Venus replied. "You know that."

They were silent for the rest of the climb, concentrating all their energy on getting up as quickly and efficiently as possible. Venus liked this, this pure action, utilising every instinct she possessed and every skill she'd learnt. It made her feel whole. Everything else, dealing with people, dealing with Rogue – her feelings for Rogue, whatever they were, and she wasn't quite sure – that was all much harder.

They wanted us to be machines, she thought, but they made us people by mistake. If they hadn't, Rogue wouldn't still be out here, chasing down the man who betrayed his friends, giving everything he has to bring him to justice. He'd have returned to headquarters after the battle like a good little soldier. And I wouldn't be out here either, following after Rogue because... Well, just because.

After about ten minutes they reached a break in the cliffs and suddenly the solid rock opened up into a dark hole ahead of them. Above, the cliffs stretched upward, seeming to lean outward as if they were bending back towards the ground.

"What do you reckon?" Venus said.

"Try the caves, babe," Helm said. "The rock face above ain't solid according to my sensors."

Venus looked at Rogue, ready for him to make the final decision. "Rogue?"

"I say we listen to Helm," Rogue said "We can always turn back if there's no way through."

There was a way through, though, and it seemed to be sloping upwards. The caves themselves were lit by a spectral, unhealthy green light from the glow of plants that had absorbed so much radiation that they'd started to emit it.

The trouble was, they weren't the only mutants in the place. Venus and Rogue had gone no more than twenty paces when Venus spotted the first one, a bony, foot-high scuttling shape in the gloom.

"Chem spiders!" she said, her voice an octave higher than she would have liked it. She fired off a shot but it went wild, the sound echoing round and round in the caves till it sounded like she'd emptied a whole magazine.

Rogue followed with a shot of his own, more controlled, but this one missed too. "Thought you were locked on, Gunnar?" he said.

"Damn things move too fast!" Gunnar snapped back. "You're gonna have to do it on manual."

Things was right. Venus could see more of them, their legs chittering against the stone, mandibles clicking together in anticipation of the meal in front of them.

Then, far quicker than she could have imagined, one of them sprang forward and sank those mandibles into her thigh. She let out a helpless scream of fear and began beating at the thing with her bare hand, crushing two of its legs but still not dislodging its jaws from her flesh. She could feel the slow, paralysing poison beginning to seep out from that grip and through her leg, numbing it, turning it into a dead weight on her body.

"Knife, Venus!" Rogue said, letting off shots into the darkness, taking a couple of spiders down and missing a couple more.

Feeling like an idiot, she groped her other hand down to pull the bowie knife from its sheath on her calf and carefully cut the hideous creature away from her skin. As soon as that one was gone, another one attacked, but she was ready this time and managed to cut it clean across the body, dropping it to the cave floor in two throbbing, faintly glowing halves. A horrible smell seeped from the corpse, the smell of a creature that liked its meat rotten.

A few more shots from Rogue, and a few more close encounters with her blade, and the chamber seemed to be free of spiders.

"You okay, Venus?" Rogue asked. She was warmed by the concern in his voice, but shamed by the cause of it.

"It's just a flesh wound," she muttered. "I don't like spiders is all."

Rogue gave her a long, considering look – then threw back his head and laughed. "And there I was thinking there wasn't anything on Nu Earth that could scare you."

She smiled grudgingly. "Watch it, Rogue. I've still got a knife in my hand."

Rogue sobered again. "Then you'd better get it ready. There are more where those came from."

Even as he spoke, she could see the creatures approaching, tiny eyes glowing toxically in the darkness.

"I'm Hind," the Souther trooper said to Pietr suddenly, his voice a nervous whisper. "Calman Hind." He held his hand out as if to shake it, then seemed to have second thoughts about it and dropped it again. "I just want you to know that, so if I die there'll be somebody who knows who it is who's died. I don't want to die nameless, do you know what I mean? I want it to matter to someone, even if it's someone I've only just met." Behind the chem mask his eyes were so wide with fear that Pietr could see the whites all the way around them. His breath was coming in short, terrified gasps so that his words puffed out in little jerks and gasps.

"I don't want to die at all," Pietr said firmly. "And we're not going to."

"Have you seen a lot of battle, then?" Hind asked, seeming a little reassured by Pietr's words. He dropped to a crouch, his arms clasped over his knees as if he was trying to make himself as small a target as possible.

After a second Pietr crouched down beside him. "A few fights," he said.

"This is my first," Hind told him. "I only shipped out to Nu Earth a week ago. The train was supposed to take me to my posting at Harpo's Ferry. Guess there's no point now. All the rest of my regiment died in the crash." When Pietr didn't respond, he asked, "Have you lost anyone, any, any buddies, in the war?"

"Some," Pietr said, and then, not quite sure why he was revealing this: "My brother."

Hind turned to stare at him. He looked stricken. "Oh, oh that's terrible. Were you close?"

Unexpectedly, the question struck Pietr in the gut like a blow. Without ever having thought of it before, he knew that the answer was no. He and Jaze had never been close, had never understood each other in the slightest. Pietr had a better idea of the thoughts flitting behind this Souther's eyes than he ever had about his brother's. "No," he said, his voice so controlled that it came out flat and cold. "Not very close at all."

After that Hind lapsed into silence. The only company was the click and whirr of the forest animals, invisible in the darkness around them, which seemed to press in on Pietr closer and closer as time went on.

Hind seemed to feel it too because he didn't stay silent long. "Think they're ever coming back?" he asked. His voice sounded raw and shaky.

"Sure," Pietr said, though he was anything but. "They wouldn't leave us, would they?"

"No, of course not," Hind said, as if he was shocked that Pietr had even considered this as an option. "They're GIs! But what if something happens to them? What if they get killed, or hurt, and we just wait and wait until our oxygen runs out?"

Pietr took a glance at the other man's tank gauge. "You don't need to worry, you've still got five hours left."

Hind glanced at Pietr's tank in turn, and Pietr saw his face whiten, more ghostly than ever in the moonlight.

"What is it?" Pietr demanded, hearing his voice quaver.

"You've only got fifteen minutes left," Hind said.

Pietr drew in a deep shuddering breath – wasting precious oxygen, he thought bitterly – then let it out again as a soft hiss. "Then they'll have to come back soon," he said, as firmly as he could.

"No, no, we can't risk it," Hind said. "Here, I'll transfer some from my tank to yours. There's a valve somewhere." He began fiddling with the controls of his tank, detaching a tube from its side.

"You can't do that," Pietr said, shaken by the offer. "You might need it for yourself."

"Of course I can," Hind said. He was filled with a determination he had lacked earlier. "I'm not going to sit here and watch you die beside me, am I?" He reached across and began to attach the tube from his tank to Pietr's.

A second later, his fingers dropped down slackly, and his head nodded forward onto his chest. At first Pietr thought that he had somehow fallen asleep, just dropped off in the middle of talking to him. But then he realised that the sound ringing in his ears was the shot from a sniper rifle and the liquid trickling darkly from the corner of Hind's mouth was blood.

A moment later the gates behind him finally creaked open and the midnight blue figures of Rogue and Venus loped through the darkness towards him. Pietr barely even acknowledged them. He couldn't stop staring at the dead face of the enemy who'd been willing to risk his own life to save Pietr's.

Morgan took a moment to enjoy the startled expression on the dead Souther's face. Little more than a boy really, but Morgan had killed boys younger than him. Then he lowered the rifle and took his eye away from the sight. With his focus broadened, he could see that the two Souther troopers were no longer alone. The darker shapes of the GI freaks had rejoined them, and somehow they'd got the gate open. This was proving to be a more challenging job than he'd imagined.

Good. Kills were so much sweeter when you had to work for them. "Morgan to sniper units," he said into his radio. "The others are yours, but the Rogue Trooper is mine."

It was on the way into the hydroponics plant that Pietr met his first Nort ground troops. The drill probe broke through the surface of the earth with startling suddenness.

Pietr froze, but Venus and Rogue knew what to do. They took cover while the drill's own defences made attack impossible, then used their cover to take out the Norts who emerged with ruthless efficiently. Still, there were a lot of them, and when a second drill probe erupted behind them, there was no way they could take them all out before they'd closed the distance, especially with the beam rifles some of them were carrying.

Pietr raised his gun, but for what felt like an age he just stood there, holding it, his finger slack on the trigger. These were his own men; how could he fire? One Nort came up to him, screaming a battle cry, insect-like and inhuman behind his chem mask, and suddenly it was kill or be killed and it didn't seem like any kind of choice at all.

Pietr's finger squeezed the trigger even before he'd made the conscious decision and the Nort jerked back and down, never to rise again. After that it was easy to shoot two more – he just had to think about Hind's face as the boy had offered him his oxygen – and then the battle was over and they were able to trot into the hydroponics plant itself, a rusty derelict that had some air tanks on offer but not much else. Pietr hurriedly refilled his supply, giving all his concentration to the task, careful not to leave any of it over to think about what he'd just done.

After a while, he became aware that Venus had crouched down beside him. A few feet away, Rogue was fiddling with his radio, trying to pick up a signal through the massive rock baffles around them.

"You're green, aren't you?" Venus said. "This your first action?"

"No," Pietr said uncomfortably. "I've been on Nu Earth a couple of weeks."

"Which unit?" she asked. The question was casual, friendly, but it brought Pietr out in a cold sweat.

"Fifth," he said, taking a wild guess, but Venus just nodded and it occurred to him that the GI's probably didn't have much to do with the regular army, didn't know any more about it than he did. He was careful to keep the relief out of his face.

"Your voice sounds real familiar," Helm said suddenly, and the fear that had disappeared came back with full force.

Pietr had to swallow twice before he could answer. "Guess maybe we saw each other back on Milli-Com," he said eventually. "I would have been shipping out around the same time as you." He had a sudden, vivid flashback of himself kicking a helpless GI prisoner as he lay bound on the floor of their boat, the prisoner that Rogue had risked so much to come back and rescue.

"Yeah, maybe," Helm said doubtfully.

Thankfully, Rogue's radio crackled into life and the conversation ended. "Rogue?" a voice demanded from the radio, in the clipped, confident tones that screamed top brass.

"Still here, colonel," Rogue said. Something in his voice told Pietr that he didn't entirely trust the man he was speaking to. Then Rogue's tone darkened as he added, "Venus made it too, but most of the others weren't so lucky." It surprised Pietr to hear Rogue sounding as if he cared, as if the lives of the other Southers, men he'd never met before that day, really counted to him. Pietr had never heard the same attitude from his own comrades, and certainly not from the officers. Men were just cannon fodder to them.

"I need you at Harpo's Ferry, GI," the voice from the radio continued. "There's a patrol boat waiting to pick you up at the river, a day's fast march from where you are. Sorry we can't get any closer, but those damn Norts have total air domination where you are. I'm beaming the boat's co-ordinates to you now."

Pietr saw a robotic arm extend from the side of Rogue's backpack, holding out some sort of digital map to him. "Here ya go, Rogue," a mechanical voice said, and Pietr jumped before realising that it was just another of the biochips. "I've highlighted the area in red, shouldn't take us too long."

Pietr could see the red dot from where he was standing, travelling across the surface of the digi-map as if the co-ordinate was somehow moving. "I'll be there, Kovert," Rogue said. "Just make sure the rescue craft is too."

As Pietr continued to watch, not really paying attention, the red dot he'd noticed crept right off the edge of the digi-map and began to move steadily up Rogue's body.

Only when it reached Rogue's head did he wake from his half trance to realise that something wasn't quite right about this. The biochip seemed to come to exactly the same realisation at exactly the same time. The robot arm did a perfect double take, then spun to look for the source of the dot, the laser beam, Pietr guessed, which must be projecting it.

"Rogue, look out!" the biochip shouted.

With a speed and fluidity that left Pietr in awe, Rogue rolled to the side then came back up to his feet, his massive gun already cocked and aimed at the source of the laser. The shot missed him by a good two feet.

It passed straight through where he had been standing and buried itself in Venus's thigh with an audible
meaty thump. She let out little more than a tightly controlled gasp of pain, but a gout of blood erupted from
the wound onto the metal floor of the base.

Rogue flinched slightly, as if he felt the wound himself, but he didn't spare a glance for his fallen
comrade. Almost before Venus had finished collapsing
to the ground, clutching her injured leg, Rogue had
sent a return salvo in the direction of the Nort.

A second later, another bullet came back in the opposite direction, almost as if Rogue's own shot had
bounced, missing Rogue's head by little more than an
inch. The GI was already on the move, weaving in and
out of the ruins, snapping off shot after shot, never
pausing long enough to present a steady target.

"Soldier, I need some help here," Venus said, and
Pietr guiltily snapped his attention away from the battle and towards the fallen woman. He knelt down
beside her, but then just stared helplessly, watching the
thick blue blood ooze out between the fingers she had
clawed against the wound.

"Know any field medicine?" she asked, forcing the
words out between teeth gritted in barely contained
pain.

Pietr shook his head. He'd never felt more useless.

"Never mind," Venus said. "Just help me fix a tourni-
quet for now. Got to get this bleeding stopped."

Pietr nodded, then froze again. He had no idea what
he could use to tie off the wound. Despite the obvious
agony she was in, Venus managed a smile. "Don't
worry, I'm not gonna die on you yet," she said. "Spare
air tube on your chem suit could do it."

Blushing, Pietr hurriedly pulled the tube away and
began gingerly fixing it round her thigh.

"Tighter," she grated.

Pietr found he had to grit his own teeth as he pulled the tube tight, and Venus let out a hiss of breath, but she didn't complain so he tied it off in a double knot.

Rogue was nearer now, double rolling over the ground onto his belly, and Pietr saw another of the lethal red beams that preceded a sniper shot crawling towards him.

"Rogue, coming up at you!" he warned, but the other man ignored him, just standing there, looking calmly through the sights of his gun, letting the red light approach ever nearer. The GI drew in a deep breath, held it, and fired.

"We got him, Rogue!" one of the biochips said, its mechanical voice crackly with excitement.

"Not sure, think we might have just winged him," Rogue replied, sighting through his gun again.

"Rogue, I think we have to get out of here now," Pietr said. Rogue snapped one look over at his fellow GI and seemed to reach the same conclusion. He tossed his gun back over his shoulder and ran to Venus's side, dropping to his knees on the ground to examine the wound for himself.

"How you doing, Venus?" he asked.

"I'm just peachy," Venus said, but her voice was husky with pain.

Morgan picked himself up off the ground. He was so angry he was shaking. He thought he might have injured himself a little as he fell from his perch in the petrified tree, but he could feel no physical discomfort; the rage was all-consuming. To have been bested in combat, and by one of those blue-skinned Souther freaks!

He snapped open his radio and opened his channel, though this admission of defeat tasted terribly bitter in his mouth. His comrades would hear of it and he would be shamed in their eyes, a fallen hero. "Base 342, Rogue Trooper is heading in your direction." He continued to glare in the direction of his nemesis as he concluded, "Make sure he dies."

ELEVEN

SISTERS ARE DOING IT FOR THEMSELVES

Venus was too proud to let Rogue carry her, but she had her arm slung over his shoulder as he helped her limp towards the exit of the hydroponics plant. He didn't like how white she looked around the mouth, as if she was using all her strength just to keep from showing him how much she was hurting. The Souther trooper trailed behind, covering their back, though Rogue was glad that he also had Bagman's eyes covering the terrain. The boy had a spine, but he was green.

"What's your name, kid?" he asked him.

The boy seemed to hesitate a moment, perhaps surprised that Rogue had spoken to him. Then he said, "Peter. Peter, sir."

"Just Rogue will do," Rogue said gruffly.

"Though you can call me sir if you want," Bagman quipped.

Peter looked puzzled, clearly not sure whether Bagman was joking.

"Ignore him, kid," Gunnar said. "There are no ranks here. Cover our backs and you'll get our respect."

"Got it," Peter said.

"Rogue," Helm chimed in, and Rogue instantly knew that it wasn't good news. "I just intercepted a Nort transmission – looks like they're sending in reinforcements."

Rogue cursed. He thought they might have bought themselves a little more time than that.

Venus pulled away weakly from his grasp. "You'd better leave me," she said. "I'm only going to get all of you killed."

"No way that's gonna happen, Venus," Rogue said, surprised at the emotion in his own voice. "So you might as well not mention it again."

"What Rogue said," Helm growled.

"Yeah, me too," Bagman added, sounding slightly less certain. "We're gonna need to head to higher ground, though. Kovert's map shows a gully that should lead us out of here."

"I'll project it on your heads-up," Helm said.

Rogue could see instantly where Bagman meant, a narrow ravine leading up into the mountains that would be highly defensible once they got there. But it was on the far side of the hydroponics plant, a good five hundred yard scramble though the derelict hulk of the building, maybe twenty minutes at Venus's crippled pace, if she could even make it that far.

With that ability to read his thoughts, which both amazed and frightened him, she said, "Don't worry about me, Rogue, I'll keep up – all you gotta do is clear a path."

Rogue wanted to say something else to her, though he wasn't quite sure what, but then the first Hoppa came into view and Rogue knew that he'd run out of time. He unwound Venus's arm from around his neck and pushed her gently towards Peter. "Take care of her and follow me."

Even in the time it had taken him to do that, the decapitators were on them, buzzing like a vast mechanical swarm of hornets. It was a bigger cluster than any Rogue had seen before and he knew that he'd have no chance if he tried to take them individually. Worse, the little machines were fitted with enough AI to spot that Venus was the weakest member of the group, and like all hunting packs they would go for the weakest first.

He could use that to his advantage. Veering to one side, he left them a clear path to Venus and they took it gladly, zooming in as if they could smell the blood still oozing from her thigh. Rogue got a brief glimpse of the white, shocked expression on Peter's face at this apparent betrayal. But the boy didn't leave his position at Venus's side, even though that left him in the path of the murderous machines, and Rogue didn't worry about it any further, just waited till they were almost on her, then dived straight at her, knocking both her and the boy to the ground.

The decapitators were going too fast to change course so quickly. He saw the leader spin wildly, as if trying to correct its course, but they were only meters away from the pillar Venus had been heading towards. Then they were on it and a huge chain reaction exploded into a ball of fire. Rogue used his body to shield Venus from the shrapnel of the blast, little blackened pieces of decapitator shredding the dry vegetation all around them.

He could tell that the fall had hurt Venus, but he didn't bother to apologise because he knew that she'd understand.

From then on the battle was a frantic, grim fight for survival against odds he wasn't entirely sure he could survive. Hoppas dropped wave after wave of reinforcements into the derelict shell of the building, and where the Hoppas couldn't reach, the drill probes came.

If it hadn't been for Venus, gamely struggling after him, leaning on the Souther recruit as lightly as possible, too proud to show she was down and very nearly out, Rogue felt that he might just have given up. Blank insect face after blank insect face loomed up in front of him, and one after another he shot them down.

Whenever he could he stooped to gather the wreckage he left behind when he'd killed them, throwing it into Bagman's open maw, ordering him to make Sammie after Sammie, because taking down the Hoppas before they could deliver their deadly payloads was the only way he was going to win this battle.

By the time they were only halfway to their destination, Rogue was so exhausted he felt his vision blurring. All enemies had started to look like the same enemy to him, as if he just kept shooting down the same man who just kept rising from the dead. One time, when he swung to take a shot at the drill-probe-delivered squad behind him, he caught a face in his sights and for a moment it was just another enemy and he was going to fire and take it down and move on. He realised that it was a face, a frightened young face, pale brows pulled up tensely onto its smooth forehead, and he recognised it as Peter. This one's on our side, he told himself, swinging the shot away to take out the Nort whose knife had been about the end the Souther's life.

Miraculously, they were through, and the ravine loomed before them, a black slit in the grey rock of the mountain. There also was a Hoppa, hovering in the air to cut off their escape route, every gun trained on Rogue.

"A Sammie would be damn useful right about now," Rogue growled to Bagman, aiming and firing at the Nort troops he could see ready to drop from the ship, but they were well-shielded behind its thick armour plate.

"Working on it, Rogue," Bagman said.

"Well, work harder!" Gunnar snapped. "I'm gasping for some ammo here!"

Rogue ignored them both, concentrating on slowing the Hoppa's approach any way he could, throwing micro-mines at it that he knew didn't have the power to take it down but might at least confuse the pilot, stop him from homing his missiles on Venus, sheltered behind Rogue's body, the only protection he could offer her. Then he heard another noise. A drill probe, behind them.

"I've got it, Rogue," Peter said. Rogue heard him load and cock his own weapon, then a volley of shotgun fire. The kid hadn't seemed like he was too well acquainted with which end of a gun was which, but Rogue knew the Hoppa was the bigger danger and he had to trust the kid to handle it. Fear for your life either brought out the best in people, or the worst – seemed like it was time to find out which it was for the kid.

The Hoppa was only ten metres away. No way its guns weren't getting a lock now.

Bagman said, "Got it, Rogue." The robot arm reached out to drop the heavy mass of a Sammie missile into his hand along with the launcher.

Rogue fitted and fired it in one smooth motion. Then he swept a protesting Venus up in his arms and ran as fast as he could towards the missile, knowing that if he didn't get past it, then the Hoppa and into the ravine, then the explosion of the huge vehicle wouldn't end just the lives of the troops on board.

He nearly didn't make it. Behind him, farther behind than was safe, he heard Peter give a gasp of fear and pain as the searing heat of the fireball that was suddenly all that was left of the Nort Hoppa took him. Rogue carried on running, outrunning the conflagration, down the ravine, faster than he'd ever run before, as if Venus's weight in his arms was nothing.

Venus had stopped protesting and her face was buried against Rogue's chest, shielding her eyes from the intense light of the explosion. He could feel her moist, warm breath puffing out in ragged gasps against his skin. She sounded bad, maybe going into shock from the injury or blood loss, but he couldn't worry about that.

Even as he heard the explosion suck back in on itself behind him, its oxygen supply exhausted in the chem-heavy air, he kept on running. "Another Sammie, Bagman!" he shouted.

"Why?" Bagman said, then seemed to realise that this wasn't the time for argument.

Rogue could hear the hiss of air out of an oxygen tank and that meant Peter had made it, though he couldn't spare the time to turn round and see what kind of state the boy was in. He knew that as soon as the heat of the explosion had died down, and maybe before, the Norts would be sending every last man left down the ravine after them.

Finally, the long dark tunnel broadened, and ahead of him through the grey rocks he could see the yellow sky coming down to meet the jagged edge of a plateau, the high mountain plain he'd been heading for. Only when he was a good twenty metres out on it did he finally turn around. The boy Peter was staggering towards him, further behind but still clear of the ravine, so Rogue put Venus gently down on the ground and reached out a hand towards Bagman. "Sammie," he said.

Without a word, Bagman deposited the missile in his hand. Rogue fitted it to Gunnar, carefully this time – he couldn't afford to miss with this one. Then he aimed down the ravine and fired.

"Not gonna get many Norts with that," Gunnar grumbled.

"It's not the Norts he's aiming for," Helm said.

Peter looked at him, puzzled, as if he was on Gunnar's side, not quite understanding what Rogue had done. Then the first rumble began, gentle at first, but building and building, the sound of rocks only loosely bound to each other deciding to cut and run. After that came the screams of Norts trapped in the fall, suddenly finding themselves facing not just a lone GI but a whole mountain on the way down.

Then there was just silence and a cloud of dust rising up towards the sky from the avalanche far below.

From the ground, Venus smiled up at him, though he could see the effort it cost her. "Sometimes, Rogue, very occasionally, you impress me."

They set up camp for the remainder of the night not far from the giant rock fall that Rogue had caused. They were still perilously close to the Nort forces, even camouflaged under Rogue's field tent, but nobody argued. You only had to take one look at Venus, or hear her shallow, wheezing breaths, to know that she couldn't make it very much further without a rest. That she might not be making it much further at all.

Once they had the tent set up, Bagman made some med kits for her, but she was so far gone that they could do little more than stabilise the damage. Helm could have asked Bagman exactly how bad Venus was hurt, but he chose not to. He didn't think he could handle that kind of news.

He didn't think he could handle very much more bad luck. The fighting had been so constant from the moment he'd died, so unremitting, that he'd begun to find himself losing the fighting spirit he'd always prided himself on. He'd been bred for war, he'd always known that, but on Milli-Com he hadn't really known what that meant. Now, on the ravaged surface of Nu Earth, he began to grasp it. He was meant for this, day after day, week after week, and then year after year, with no end in sight, not even death – because that had already happened to him.

The moon continued its path across the sky, silhou-etted for a moment perfectly against the vast black hole, the gap in the fabric of space-time which was the one thing which made this hellhole so valuable, which had led his people and their enemies to reduce it to a hellhole in the first place. How appropriate, Helm thought, that we're literally fighting over nothing, over the ultimate void.

He wondered for a moment why he even wanted a body again, when all he could use it for would be more fighting. But then he glanced over at Venus, and saw her smiling up at Rogue as he tended to her wound, the special smile she used to save for Helm, and he knew that he'd give anything at all to be flesh and blood again, to be the man that Venus had fallen in love with. He just needed some goddamn luck for a change. Was that too much to ask?

The sun rose in the morning to sparkle off a very dis-tant ribbon of water which Bagman assured them was the river where their boat was waiting. Helm spotted two life-signs crambling over the grey rocks towards them in the shape of the chem nurse, Sister Sledge.

Rogue squinted at her. "How the hell did you find us?" he asked.

She shrugged. "I got a message there'd been a train crash, and there might be survivors down below, but the way seems to be blocked by most of a mountain."

"There was a train crash," Helm told her. "You're looking at the survivors, and yeah, we were the ones who caused the rock fall."

The chem nurse smiled. He was flattered to see that she looked directly at him as she did, recognising that it was him who was speaking. That Souther recruit Peter, who Helm was convinced he *had* met some time ago, still couldn't seem to figure out which of the biochips was which.

Then Sister Sledge spotted Venus, who was so weak now that Rogue had to hold her canteen of water as she drank, and her expression grew more serious. "Looks like there's some work for me here."

Roughly forty minutes later, Sledge had patched Venus up better than Helm would have believed possible. The GI Doll's face had gone back from pale, icy turquoise to a much healthier sea blue, and her breathing was now regular and even, without that hitch of pain that had been growing more pronounced as the night wore on.

"'Preciate it, Sister," Rogue said, the rough edge of raw feeling in his voice. Helm didn't like that at all. Rogue had no business going all emotional over Venus – that was his job.

"No problem," Sledge said, gracing him with the sunny smile that hinted at feelings of her own, a hint Rogue didn't seem too inclined to pick up on. "Want me to take another look at the guys while I'm at it, see if there's been any further deterioration?"

Rogue shrugged, a little too casually, Helm thought. "Sure. Everything seems to be okay, though."

Sledge shrugged too. "Better safe than sorry."

Rogue went back to looking after Venus as Sledge went to inspect Bagman, flipping his chip carefully out of his casing, so Helm watched Venus too, watched the sly little smile on her face as Rogue fussed around her like he was her damn mother. He was concentrating so hard that he didn't actually see the expression on Sledge's face himself as she examined Bagman, just saw the reflection of it in Rogue's. By the time he'd spun to face the chem nurse she'd schooled her expression to look calm, professional.

"What's wrong?" Rogue demanded.

"It's…" Sister Sledge began, then hesitated, like someone who couldn't bear to break the bad news.

"Just tell me," Bagman's voice said from her hand. "I gotta right to know, don't I?"

"All right," Sledge said. "The deterioration is much worse than I expected. At the rate it's going, I don't think you're going to last more than a day."

A cold silence followed. Venus was the first to break it, swearing colourfully. "Those damn incompetent Milli-Com scum – they can't get anything right!"

"Scan out, Venus," Rogue said flatly. "We can handle this."

"It's… It's okay, Rogue," Bagman said. "I'm fine. I mean, I feel fine. We can still go after the traitor. I know I can keep myself together till then."

"No way, Bagman," Rogue said. "That mobile lab you were talking about?" he said to Venus. "Call it. Arrange a rendezvous as soon as you can. I'll sweep the area, make sure there are no Norts around to mount an ambush, and then we'll get the boys fixed up."

For almost the first time since he'd lost his body, Helm felt himself feeling pure and simple gratitude to Rogue, and he remembered why they'd been friends almost since the day they'd stepped out of the artificial wombs. He was so taken up with the thought that he'd soon have a body again, a body he could use to show Venus that he was every bit the man he'd always been, that he didn't pay much attention to what his scanners were telling him, to the sudden speeding up in Sister Sledge's heart rate as soon as Rogue said the words "call it". He didn't have any thinking space left over to wonder why those simple words should have got the chem nurse so nervous, or so excited.

Pietr knew he couldn't go on like this. Just what the hell did he think he was doing? He'd come here to kill Rogue, and somehow he'd ended up fighting with him, and worse, fighting with him against his own men.

As he trotted after Rogue through the shallow gullies of the high plain, heading for the rendezvous which Sister Sledge had set up for them, he wondered how many Norts had died in that avalanche, the one Rogue had set off so casually to cut off their pursuit. Ten? Twenty? A hundred? A hundred definitely seemed possible. When Pietr had run away from his regiment, he'd been resigned to the fact that they might think him a traitor, but he'd never imagined that he might actually become one.

He looked ahead of him at Rogue, shadowed by the high walls of the gully, and thought that it would be very easy to just squeeze off a shot. Helm might warn him about it, but why would Helm even be checking up on Pietr? Except that he couldn't do it. Rogue had saved his life, several times, and he deserved more than to be shot in the back by a man he thought was a friend.

If Pietr was going to kill him – and Pietr had to kill him, or everything everyone had ever said about him would be true – then he had to do it face to face, with honesty. Which meant that he had to get away from Rogue as soon as possible.

The opportunity presented itself sooner than he'd expected. The ravine they were walking through grew shallower, but soon other ravines branched off it and before long they were walking through a maze-work of grey-brown cliffs which only Helm's sat-linked map function allowed them to navigate through.

Slowly, Pietr allowed Rogue, Venus and Sledge to draw ahead of him. They didn't notice. He was supposed to be covering the rear anyway, and Sledge and Rogue were too wrapped up in taking care of Venus, who was back on her feet and on the mend but still not able to walk without assistance. When the next left-branching corridor of rock approached, he took his chance.

As soon as he was out of sight, he pushed his heels into the ground and ran. For a few minutes, all he could listen for was the sound of pursuit, straining to hear over the hissing of his chem suit's air vents. None came, and ten minutes later, he slowed down.

He found, ridiculously, that he was almost hurt that no one had come after him. He shook his head and started looking around for a way out of the ravine. The rock was jagged, sharp enough to tear through the material of his suit, and he didn't want to risk an attempt to climb the sides, not with the suit itself to weigh him down. Overhead, the sky was only a thin slice of yellow, barely pouring enough light down to brighten the rock's colour from black to grey-brown. Up ahead and to his right he thought that the yellow sliver of sky might be broadening. He ran off in that direction, and found that the ravine was finally sloping back up to meet the surface of the mountain plain.

The territory he came back up into was different from the one he'd left more hilly, as if the mountains were trying to reassert their dominance over the plain. It was impossible to see more than a few hundred yards in any direction, the view blocked by the gently curved mounds of the hills, their surfaces scattered with a sprinkle of hardy high-altitude plants.

Pietr hunkered down and pulled out the Nort radio he'd kept hidden inside the utility pouch of the chem suit he'd stolen from the Souther on train. He discovered that thinking about that dead Souther filled him with more guilt and self-loathing than any memory of the Norts he'd killed, but he ruthlessly suppressed the thought. He'd made a mistake, but now he was going to rectify it.

Very carefully, he began to cycle the radio through all the base transmission frequencies he knew. It only took a few minutes to home in on a signal from a small contingent of Norts, camped no more than a kilometre from where he was sitting.

Pietr set his jaw and pushed himself to his feet. He would find these Norts, rejoin them, put himself back in Nort uniform where he belonged. Then he would come back and face Rogue like a man.

It wasn't until they faced their first minor battle, a group of Norts camped out at the end of the ravine, that Rogue realised Peter was gone. The battle itself was short, brutal and a foregone conclusion, ending with the Norts lying in a steaming heap beside the field radio they hadn't even had time to use. At first, Rogue thought Peter must have been hit in the battle, but there was no sign of his body anywhere in the vicinity.

"Picking up any trace of him, Bagman?" he asked.

"Nothing at all, Rogue," Bagman said. "No life signs nearby except us."

Venus looked around, a frown on her face. "What the hell's happened to him?"

Sister Sledge looked round too, but briefly. "I don't like to say this, but I don't think you've got time to look for him."

"Probably fell down a hole ten kilometres back," Helm suggested.

Rogue didn't like the idea of leaving the boy all on his own, but Helm was right; he was probably lying dead somewhere and if they looked all they'd find would be a corpse. While he'd liked the kid well enough in the brief time he'd known him, Bagman, Gunnar and Helm came first. "Fine," he said, "we go on. How long till we connect with the mobile med-unit, Sledge?"

She looked at the digi-map in her hand. "Shouldn't be more than a kilometre now, Rogue. If there were fewer hills, we'd be able to see it from here."

The landscape was easy going, just scrubby little mounds of dry earth, but the hills left plenty of cover for a potential ambush, so Rogue took it slow, shielding Venus with his body when he thought a possible sniper might have a good line of sight. There was nothing, though, an almost surprising lack of resistance to their progress.

"I don't like this, Rogue," Venus said. "The Norts should be after us in force by now. They've had plenty of time to regroup from the hydroplant."

Rogue shrugged. "Maybe they just don't think we're that much of a threat."

Venus didn't say anything, just raised a sarcastic eyebrow. Rogue might have said more, might even have admitted that she had a point and that despite the urgency maybe they needed to stop and reconsider what they were doing, but just before he could, Sister Sledge shouted out and began to wave her arms.

Ahead of Rogue, he could finally see what sho'd been leading them towards. It didn't look very much like any field hospital he'd seen. The vehicle was big and blocky, and armoured like some kind of hybrid Blackmare tank, but it was playing the Souther national anthem, and the Souther flag was flapping merrily above it in the light breeze.

Sister Sledge ran eagerly towards the vehicle, and two dark figures – one tall, one short – walked out to meet her. When they drew near enough, Rogue saw that they were both, incongruously, wearing bowler hats under their chem suits.

As soon as he saw Rogue and Venus, the taller one turned to the shorter. "Well, Mr Bland," he said. "It appears that our patients have arrived."

As Pietr approached the blip on his digi-map that marked the position of the Nort troop, his steps slowed. He told himself that it was because he had to be careful. He was wearing Souther uniform and if his own side saw him in it they were most likely to shoot first and ask questions afterwards. Or maybe it was because he knew that even if they believed he was one of them, they'd soon find out that he was a deserter too, and then they'd shoot him anyway, or send him to a court-martial and let the court-martial do it for them.

Whatever the reason, Pietr found himself creeping up towards the small field camp as if it belonged to an enemy. He took a moment to learn the sentry's routine, then waited until he was in the other half of his circuit, and dodged inside his perimeter, still keeping hidden in the lee of some rocks. He realised as he did how much broader a field of view the Souther chem suits gave, with their clear face plates. The insectile Nort suits narrowed vision down to two tunnels, keeping the whole world at a distance. Thanks to that, the sentry didn't see him, and he was able to get himself to within five metres of the rest of the troop, gathered unprotected round their small stove unit.

They looked so relaxed and so happy that he decided he really had nothing to lose by throwing himself on their mercy.

Then he saw what it was that had them in such a good mood. They had a prisoner, a Souther, and they'd clearly decided that he wasn't worth taking into headquarters, being too low-ranking to have anything of interest to the brass. So instead they'd decided to have some fun.

As Pietr watched, two of the Norts drew back their feet and kicked them into the prone body of the Souther, bound helplessly on the ground in front of them in a tangle of razor wire. The impact was so hard that the prisoner's body actually flew into the air. Pietr heard his cry of pain and fear at the triple impact, two from the Norts' boots and once from the ground on his way back down. But the loudest noise was the laughter of the other troopers.

Pietr carried on watching as they each took a turn, and when they grew bored of that, one of them casually reached back and pulled off the prisoner's chem suit mask. Pietr watched with them as his face turned first red, then yellow, and finally black, as the toxic atmosphere ate him away from the inside. He screamed the whole time, a helpless high keening that sounded more like an animal than a man.

Once the Souther prisoner had finished dying, Pietr turned on his heel and walked away from the camp.

The inside of the vessel looked a little more like a field hospital, but not much. Rogue took a moment to scan it, eyes taking in everything, the racks of electronic equipment, the cases of guns – slightly out of place, but then you needed to be armed if you were going into a war zone – and most of all the three tanks, filled with a dense blue liquid, in which his three friends would be reborn. The two Souther medics, still wearing their strange chem suits over their strange uniforms, were staring at him impassively.

"Are you satisfied with our arrangements, Mr Rogue?" the taller one, Brass, asked. His voice was soft and cultured, nothing like the harsh, emotionless voices of the Gene Genies.

Rogue shrugged, then looked at Sister Sledge. "Look in order to you?"

She nodded. "This is the most up-to-date equipment there is." She turned to Venus, who was leaning wearily against a wall, her eyes flat with tiredness and pain. "Lie down over there. I can fix you up properly now."

Venus hesitated a moment, glancing at Rogue, but he nodded to her and she let herself sink down onto the slick metal surface behind her. "I'll give you something for the pain first," the chem nurse said to her.

Rogue saw Venus's eyes drift shut as the other woman pressed a med-dispenser against her arm. Rogue watched her for a moment longer, but Sledge seemed to be taking good care of her, gently pulling aside the material of her trousers to expose the still healing edges of her wound. "Guess it all looks fine," he said to Brass.

"You have the... the biochips on you?" Bland, smaller and fatter, asked.

Rogue took off his helmet and kitbag and set them down on a small work surface, pushing aside an assortment of scalpels and las-knives to make room for them. After only a second's hesitation, he put Gunnar down beside them.

"You ready guys?" he said.

"Bring it on," Gunnar said. "I'm lookin' forward to holding a gun again, instead of being one."

"Ready as I'll ever be," Bagman added, sounding a lot less sure. It occurred to Rogue that of all of them, he seemed to mind his disembodied state the least. But then Bagman had always lived his life more inside his head than out of it.

"Where are the bodies?" Helm said. "I thought we were gonna be put into blank-minded force-grown clones, but those vats are empty."

Rogue realised that Helm was right. He turned to Bland and Brass with a frown. "They haven't got much time. No time for you to grow bodies from scratch. I thought Milli-Com would have sent you what you needed."

Bland shook his head. "Alas, there was no time, Mr Rogue. But never fear. We have an alternative solution."

"We have you, Mr Rogue," Brass said.

Rogue looked at them through narrowed eyes. "Me?"

Bland moved aside, and Rogue saw that he had been standing in front of a chair festooned with medical equipment, syringes, read-outs – and restraints. "Indeed," he said. "We can use the template of your body to recreate bodies for your... comrades. All we need to do is extract some information from it, genetic and hormonal, and the re-gening vats will be able to use the amino soup inside them to build your friends' bodies in a matter of minutes." He gestured at the pile of equipment containing the biochips, and then at the chair behind him. "If you would just... release your friends, then take your place in the chair, we can begin."

Rogue looked at him, at the blank expression on his face, and he hesitated. It didn't take a genius to see that Bland and Brass weren't too on the level. Sledge trusted them, but then Sledge wasn't on the run from her own side, she didn't need to be paranoid; Rogue did and he was and he knew a chem rat long before he could smell it.

"What are you waiting for, Rogue?" Gunnar said. "Time's ticking away and we're ticking away with it."

"He's right," Helm said, after a moment's hesitation that told Rogue he was having some doubts of his own. "What choice do we got?"

And he was right, of course. There was no choice to be weighed up, not when the danger of his buddies losing their lives tipped the scales so completely one way. He thought he knew what Bland and Brass's game was. They hadn't mentioned Rogue's desertion, hadn't said anything to him about returning to Milli-Com, and that in itself was suspicious. If he let them tie him down in that chair, he doubted they'd be releasing him again, at least not until the Milli-Fuz had turned up to take him away.

Well, it was a small price to pay. Whatever happened, he wouldn't give up on tracking down the traitor general – Kovert would probably find a way to help him – and his buddies would be alive again, properly alive, to help him do it.

Rogue reached out to the gun, helmet and kitbag beside him and carefully snapped the biochips out of their casings before tossing them to Brass. "Here are my boys," he said. "Make them into men." Then he strode to the chair behind Bland and sat down in it, resting his head delicately against the cold metal of the headpiece.

With startling speed, Bland snapped the restraints into place around Rogue's wrists and ankles, and last of all around his chest and forehead. Only when they were all in place, and he'd checked them twice, did he allow himself to exchange a small, satisfied smile with Brass.

Pietr was lost. Metaphorically, definitely and physically. When he'd walked away from the Nort camp, ghosting out as silent and unnoticed as he'd arrived, he hadn't really had any idea where he was going. Now he realised that even if he did he wouldn't know how to get there. The great plain above the mountains was vast and featureless and without Bagman's digi-map to guide him he knew that he could wander it for days, or more likely hours, because his oxygen was running low again and he knew that after what he'd seen back at the camp he wouldn't allow himself to run so low that he ended up breathing chem. He might not be much of a shot, but even he couldn't miss his own head.

Maybe that's what he should do anyway. Just end it. It wasn't like he'd done anything useful from the moment that he'd landed on Nu Earth, or even before that. He hadn't done one consequential thing in his whole life.

With trembling fingers, he pulled out his energy gun and held it to his head. His finger squeezed gently on the trigger, then a little more.

He had a very clear mental image of his brother laughing at him, his head thrown back and his whole body shaking with it. Laughing with a joy he only seemed to display when he was tormenting Pietr. Then Jaze's face was replaced with that of Schulz, of all the other troops who had laughed at him and mocked him because he couldn't be like them.

Very slowly, he lowered the gun from his temple. Pietr realised that he was wrong, that he had done something, or at least had started to do something. It just hadn't been the thing he'd thought he was doing. Now, he knew what he had to do. He had to finish it.

He re-holstered his gun and pulled out his radio. It had, he'd remembered now that his mind was clearer, a nav-satellite uplink implanted in it. He could find exactly where he wanted to go now that he knew where it was.

As soon as Bland and Brass started laughing, Rogue knew that he'd made a very big mistake. "Venus!" he shouted, but her eyes barely flicked open and he saw that Sister Sledge had strapped her down as securely as him. He caught the chem nurse's eye.

"Going to tell me what's going on?" he asked.

She shrugged, her face so devoid of any human feeling that it didn't look pretty at all. "Just business, GI, sorry. They made me an offer too good to refuse, good enough to get me off this scumhole for life."

"What the hell's she talking about?" Gunnar's voice grated, high-pitched, from the palm of Brass's hand.

"It was a set-up, you moron," Helm answered from right beside him. "Rogue, I'm sorry."

Rogue would have shaken his head, but the restraints wouldn't let him. He kept on talking, delaying, using every second of the time to figure a way out of this. "The guys never were in any danger, were they?" he said to Sledge. "That deterioration you were talking about – you were just playing them."

She laughed nastily. "Pretty easy to do, I've got to say. Your buddies may be loyal, Rogue, but they sure aren't bright."

Rogue knew that her gloating tone was meant to bait him, but he ignored her. Scum like her were for killing, not for getting worked-up about. He turned his attention back to Bland and Brass. "So who are you working for? The Norts?"

Bland shuddered theatrically. "My dear boy, we work only for ourselves. We shall be selling you to the Norts, of course, provided they can muster sufficient funds."

"Which shouldn't prove a problem, Mr Bland," Brass added, "now that we have the rather comely form of this female GI to add to the package on offer."

"You touch a hair of Venus's head and you'll wish you were never born!" Helm snapped from Bland's hand.

Bland just laughed at him. "If we had the inclination, or indeed the ability, to actually re-gene you, perhaps that threat might have some substance. As it is, I'm afraid you'll be going to the Norts exactly as you are – so unless you plan to electrocute me to death, I'm afraid your threat is a little empty." As if he'd suddenly realised something, his face paled, and he dropped the biochips hurriedly onto a table beside him. "They can't electrocute me, can they?" he asked his partner.

"Better safe than sorry," Brass replied, and handed him a pair of delicate metal pincers. Then he turned to their radio. "I suppose I had better contact Nort High Command."

At that point, three things happened at once.

Bland reached forward with the pincers and took the chip which contained the personality of Helm between the small metal clamps. And Helm, who'd realised that he actually *could* reroute the current keeping him alive to deliver at least a mild electric shock, did exactly that. The charge passed up the metal pincers and straight into Bland's hand. He cried out – more in shock than in pain – and dropped Helm to the ground.

Venus – whose systems were far more resistant to drugs than even the chem nurse had realised – woke from the tranquillised sleep Sledge had put her in and found that she was tied up, but not well enough. Her foot lashed out and caught Sledge on the side of her thigh, sending her spinning into a trolley full of surgical equipment – which clattered loudly to the floor.

Masked by the sound of the clatter, Pietr burst through the door of the vessel, his gun clenched in a hand that was white with stress but still managing to point it straight and firmly at the two body looters.

He hesitated, gun wavering between Bland and Brass, and even more uncertainly, the figure of Sister Sledge pulling herself up from where Venus had kicked her to the floor.

In the second when the gun was pointing at Sledge and not at them, Bland and Brass both reached for the escape chute switch and their two hands slapped down on it simultaneously. They had never been attacked in their own base before – they made it a habit to stay well clear of any battle – but they liked to be prepared for any eventuality. The floor beneath them dropped away, and they tumbled out to the dry earth beneath. They were running even before they'd fully regained their feet.

Pietr wasn't following them, though. Still inside their now abandoned base, his attention was all on Sister

Sledge, walking towards him with hands outstretched entreatingly. "You're not going to hurt me, are you?" she asked.

"Who were those men?" he demanded, backing away as far as the confined space would allow him. "Why are Venus and Rogue tied up?"

"She's a traitor, Peter!" Rogue shouted. "Don't let her get close."

But she was a woman, and defenceless, and he still didn't really know what was going on, so his gun dipped slightly, the muzzle pointing towards the floor rather than her chest. Sister Sledge smiled gently. She reached out a hand towards his cheek, as if to touch him affectionately.

At the very last minute, he saw the tiny glint of silver in her fingers and his gun was up again and pointed at her chest and he'd let out an energy bolt into her at point-blank range before he recognised the thing in her hand as a needle.

For a moment, he remained frozen in shock, staring down at her still-smoking corpse.

"You did the right thing, kid," Venus said, her voice sounding groggy.

"Yeah," Bagman's voice added, from somewhere on the floor. "That needle in her hand is coated in chem. Would have killed you instantly."

"Okay," Pietr said shakily.

Before he could add anything else, Helm suddenly said. "I know you! I know your voice, I knew I did."

Pietr, who had been lowering his gun, raised it again – even though the only two other people in the vessel were still bound and immobile.

"I don't think you do," he said.

"Don't try that," Helm said, his voice managing to sound cold and hard even through the mechanical distortion. "Don't trust him, Rogue, he's a Nort. He's one of the scum who captured me right after the Quartz Zone Massacre. Kicked me in the gut when I was lying injured in the bottom of his ship."

Pietr found his eyes caught and held by Rogue's strange, blank gaze. "Is that true, kid? Are you a traitor too?"

Pietr realised that his gun was now trained squarely on the GI's chest. All it would take would be one squeeze of the trigger and he really could finish it, avenge his brother, return as a hero to the Nort ranks. "It's true," he said. "My real name's Pietr Hultz. You killed my brother, back at the Quartz Zone."

"I'm sorry," Rogue said, and sounded like he meant it, "but this is war. And men die."

Pietr stared at Rogue for a long time, but he wasn't really seeing him, he was seeing his brother's face, twisted in the expression of contempt it always seemed to wear around him. "I know," he said eventually. "And you're a better man than my brother could ever have been."

Then he put his gun back into its holster and started working out how to free Rogue from his bonds.

Half an hour later, they paused at the brow of the next hill to watch as the micro-mines Bagman had planted blew Bland and Brass's base into a million red-hot fragments.

"I'm sorry, Rogue," Helm said. "Me and the boys nearly got us all killed, and Venus too."

Rogue shrugged. "Doesn't matter. It's in the past." He looked at Pietr as he said this, and Pietr knew that he was talking about him too. "What matters is what we do from now on."

"And what's that?" Venus said, smiling at him. Tranquillisers out of her system now, she was almost back to normal, though she still favoured her injured leg and it was clear that Sister Sledge hadn't made any genuine attempt to heal it.

"There's still a traitor to be caught," Rogue said.

TWELVE
END OF THE LINE

Kovert was waiting for Rogue at the docks. He was taller than Rogue had expected, but the face beneath his chem mask was every bit as cold and hard, bristling with silver-grey stubble and a ruthlessly trimmed moustache. If he was surprised to see Venus, he didn't show it.

The roar of gunfire from the nearby battle at Harpo's Ferry was almost deafening, but Kovert's voice didn't have any trouble slicing through the din. "So, the famous Rogue Trooper, last of the Genetic Infantrymen." He looked Rogue up and down, then looked away as if he wasn't that impressed with what he'd seen.

"You got us here, Kovert," Rogue said. "Now where's the traitor general?"

"We believe he's directing the attack from somewhere behind the Nort lines. There's some other old friends of yours here, too," Kovert replied.

He held out the remnants of a chem mask towards Rogue, its material a dull blood red. Rogue recognised it instantly and flicked a gaze sideways at Pietr as Gunnar said, "Kashans!"

Pietr stiffened, his face whitening beneath his chem mask, but then his mouth set in a grim line and he held himself straight and firm. Rogue had debated whether to tell Milli-Com who the boy really was, but Pietr had chosen his side, and he'd saved Rogue's life, and that was good enough for Rogue.

"The same scum who wiped us out in the Quartz Zone," Helm said, and this time Pietr didn't even flinch.

"Right," Kovert said, as if pleased by their reaction, "but now the stakes are even higher. We lose Harpo's Ferry, and we lose the whole of Nu Atlanta. After that, we might as well kiss goodbye to holding on to the rest of Nu Earth."

Rogue knew that Kovert was using him, but at the same time he knew that he was right. "You've got a deal, Milli-Com man," he said grudgingly. "Just make sure that you keep your side of it when it's over. I want a full pardon for Helm, Bagman and Gunnar, and when you've patched Venus up she can have a pardon too."

Kovert looked directly at Venus for the first time and seemed to notice her injuries. "Not been taking very good care of my lady, have you, Rogue?" he said. "We'll patch her up, all right, but she's not going to need a pardon. She's been doing exactly what I wanted."

Venus's pale face flushed aquamarine with fury. "What do you mean by that?"

Kovert laughed. "Plausible deniability, my dear. I needed you helping Rogue, but I needed to be able to disown you if anything went wrong. I guessed that I'd be able to depend on your... loyalty, to send you after him, and it appears I was right."

Venus was so furious that she wasn't capable of speech, but Rogue saw her raise and tighten her fist. He caught it before she could do any damage with it. The last thing he wanted was her up on charges for assaulting an officer. "Leave it, Venus. He's military intelligence, what did you expect? Go and get yourself healed up."

She pulled against him for a moment, then seemed to give up and dropped her arm. "Fine, but watch your back, Rogue." Then she pulled him into a sudden and unexpected hug, so fierce it knocked the air out of him, before turning on her heel and heading towards the medical tent without a backward glance.

"She's right, Rogue," Kovert said. "You need to be careful."

"I will," Rogue said, meaning of him as well as the Norts.

Kovert laughed again, clearly understanding both meanings, then headed back towards the command centre, leaving Rogue and Pietr alone.

Rogue looked across at Harpo's Ferry, only a few hundred metres to their left. Once a thriving Souther strategic centre, the town was now little more than a smouldering ruin. Hoppas attacked what remained of the town and its garrison from the air, Kashans swarmed over the ground towards it like a plague of red ants, and from the sea came the constant, deafening crump of Nort submarines firing at the shore.

He turned to Pietr. "The Southside's losing here, and losing badly. Ready to join them in taking a last stand?"

Pietr drew in a deep breath and saluted. "Ready as I'll ever be," he said.

They turned and, side by side, headed towards Harpo's Ferry and the toughest fight either of them had ever faced.

Unnoticed by either of them, hidden in the low scrub of the dunes rising from the chemical shore, a Nort spy pulled out a radio and prepared to report in.

The traitor general turned from viewing the battle below him – so satisfyingly one-sided, so clearly going the Norts' way – to study the man at his side, finding himself as usual trying to make out the outline of human features beneath the blank black mask.

"The GI, he's here?" Morgan asked. The general could hear the venomous hatred in the master sniper's voice, almost a match in intensity for his own.

"Now you have another chance to get him in your sights," he told him. Then he smiled. "Only this time you'll have an extra advantage." He reached down beside him and pulled up a metallic case, handling it as delicately as he would a new born baby. In a way, it was his baby – Milli-Com would never have bothered to develop this toxin if it hadn't been for his prompting, a kill-switch for their little experiment in case it all went wrong.

Morgan eyed the case suspiciously.

"Something I stole from Milli-Com," the traitor told him. "The same place where the GIs were created. Call it insurance." He flipped open the lid to reveal row after row of vials hidden within, each filled with a carefully calculated quantity of a very specific toxin. "The GIs were created to be immune to all known toxins. All except one."

He smiled again, feeling the movement tear and pull at his ravaged face and for once not caring, and handed the vials over to the sniper.

The fighting began as soon as they hit the outskirts of Harpo's Ferry and never let up. At first it wasn't Kashans, and Pietr was grateful for that, but there were plenty of other Norts, EMP regiments, shotgunners, Hoppa crews dropped from the air along with their contingents of decapitators, and he shot them down without hesitation. They were the enemy now, it was his job to kill them – and he'd finally found the courage and enthusiasm for his job that he'd never felt when he was fighting beside them.

Rogue fought with his usual grim efficiency, clearing a path through the Nort ranks that even their numbers couldn't immediately plug, and bringing him and Pietr step by hard-fought step closer to the nerve centre of the Nort operations, the home of the spider that had weaved this entire web.

First, they were going to have to do something about those submarines. The ships, visible as grey humps far out in the yellow-green waters of the sea, were raining a steady hail of fire on the shattered remains of Harpo's Ferry and the shattered garrison guarding it. If they weren't taken out, there was no way that anyone, not even Rogue, would be making his way deeper inside the city.

"Hell Cannons up there don't seem to be manned, Rogue," Pietr said, nodding to his left as he kept his eyes forward, trained on the Nort sergeant he'd just shot through the head.

"I can hack it if you can get there," Helm confirmed.

"On it," Rogue said. "There's a pocket of Southers hemmed in over there," Rogue said, using Gunnar to point ahead and to his left.

"I see them," Pietr said. It didn't look to be more than ten men, sheltering behind a heap of fallen masonry from at least fifty encircling Norts.

"Look like they could use your help," Rogue said. "Clear a path out for them while I take out the submarines with that cannon."

Pietr shot one swift look at his face, but it was as unreadable as ever. Was he really suggesting that Pietr take on fifty Norts on his own – and he could see, even from here, that there were Kashans among them – or was this some kind of test? Then he looked back at the Southers, slowly clustering closer and closer together as the Norts cut off their last escape routes, and he thought that Rogue had probably meant exactly what he said. These men were his comrades and they needed his help, it was as simple as that.

"I'll see what I can do," he told Rogue. "Good luck. And–"

"Save it, kid," Rogue said. "I'll see you back in the city." Before Pietr could say any more he was off, sprinting up the shattered walls of the city as if they were no obstacle at all.

Pietr didn't wait to see if he reached the cannons. He knew that he would, and besides, Pietr didn't have the attention to spare. Rogue's move had drawn a good two-thirds of the Norts away with him – they clearly knew who the primary threat was – but that still left fifteen men harassing the beleaguered Southers. Among them were two soldiers in the dull red chem suits of the Kashan Legion.

Very deliberately, Pietr headed for them first. He was able to squeeze off two shots before they even saw him coming. One of them took down an EMP trooper with a shot through the head more accurate than any he'd ever managed in basic training. But the Kashan was only winged and now the whole group of them was spinning to face this new threat. He knew that if the cornered Southers used the opportunity to run rather than to fight back, he was finished.

But the Southers did stay and fight, and most of the Norts span back round to face them, and Pietr was in a fight for his life, but at least not a hopeless one. He felt a bullet whistle past his leg, so close it brushed the fabric of his chem suit, but miraculously didn't tear it. A second later, he'd sent back a bullet of his own, and this one was more accurate. He saw the Nort collapse, hands clutched helplessly to his stomach, as the corrosive chem poured in through the breach.

The Southers had emerged from hiding now, and Pietr found himself fighting side by side with them, outnumbered and outgunned, letting off round after round at the Norts as they tried to push them back, to clear a path out.

After that, he was too close in to use his gun, close enough to see his own face reflected back from the blank insect eyes of the chem-suited Nort in front of him. As he pulled out his knife, he realised that it was a Kashan, and then, almost without thinking, his eyes dropped to the small nameplate on the man's chest and he read the name "Schulz". For one second as he looked at Pietr, Schulz hesitated, not quite believing his eyes. Then another Souther came at him from the left and Schulz swung his rifle contemptuously around, aiming at the man's head. In another micro-second he would have killed him, except that Pietr's knife had sliced clean through his back and into his heart and he wouldn't be killing anyone ever again.

Pietr let the body slide wetly from his knife and turned back to the battle, not feeling a moment's regret.

Looked after by a proper medic finally, one who wasn't in the pay of those body looter scum Bland and Brass, Venus was back in fighting shape pretty quickly. The injury hadn't been serious: no ligaments damaged, no tendons torn, and when she rose to her feet after the medic finished with her she found that her leg could bear her full weight again. She still felt a little weak from loss of blood, but that was nothing she couldn't cope with.

As if he'd somehow sensed her recovery, or more likely as if he'd set someone to watch her, Kovert walked up as soon as she was on her feet.

She'd been working for the colonel for two weeks now, her first assignment since graduating from the Dolls' covert ops regime on Milli-Com, so she'd come to know the old weasel fairly well. And she knew straight off that the expression of concern and sympathy on his face was entirely false.

"Venus, good to see you on your feet again," he said.

"Scan out, colonel," she cut across him. "What do you want?"

"Now is that any way to talk to your commanding officer?" he said. "Especially when he's merely come to ensure that you're taking the proper time to recuperate from your injuries?"

That threw her. She'd been expecting him to send her back into the thick of the action, hoping that he'd send her back to Rogue again, where she could at least keep a close eye on the knucklehead. "You don't want me to do anything?" she said, sitting back down.

"Absolutely not," he said. "Can't waste one of my best assets on a mission she's not in good enough shape for."

There was absolutely nothing wrong with this sentence. In fact, it made perfect sense, but as Kovert walked away, apparently satisfied that she would obey him, Venus felt a deep unease. Kovert didn't want her in Harpo's Ferry, didn't want her fighting by Rogue's side. She wanted to know why.

Once Rogue had made his way to the Hell Cannon, taking out the Nort submarines was easy. The thing had auto-targeting, and what it couldn't do, Helm could. There was something immensely satisfying about blowing up the vast machines from such a great distance, a feeling that he was finally doing a little something to pay the Norts back for the death of his buddies, inflicting some damage that would really hurt. After the last submarine had gone, he didn't have long to bathe in the afterglow.

A second after the gush of water from the submarine's destruction had splashed back into the sea, the cannon two hundred metres to the left of Rogue blew up in a searing explosion of noise and heat that Rogue could feel singeing his flesh even from his position.

"They're targeting us, Rogue," Helm said. "Better get out and into the city now those submarines are gone."

Rogue didn't hang around to argue with him. He leapt from the high wall housing the cannon onto the street fifty yards below. It was just as well he did because even before he'd hit the ground, the cannon itself had been hit and the shockwave of the explosion knocked Rogue from his feet to tumble fifty yards further into the city, causing even his hardened skin to scrape itself raw over the blasted concrete of the street.

He rolled with it, rose to his feet and kept on running, kept on fighting. Inside the city, the battle was even fiercer. Pockets of Souther resistance remained, but only small ones – the city belonged to the Norts now and unless Rogue could get to the traitor general, cut the heart right out of them, then soon the whole of the continent would be theirs.

On the grey, fragmented streets he met his first Kashans. He felt a flare of rage when he saw them in their blood-red uniforms, but he suppressed it because no one fought at their best when they were angry. Still, every time he shot one down he saw the face of one of his fallen comrades and thought that that death at least had been avenged.

His mind was focussed on one objective, on getting to the traitor as quickly as he could, but when he saw a small remnant of Southers pinned down by a Hoppa there was no question that he would help them.

The biochips seemed to read his mind. "Enough salvage here for a few Sammies," Bagman told him.

"Set me on auto and I'll cover you while you collect it," Gunnar added.

Rogue had already begun assembling Gunnar's tripod, relying on Helm to alert him to any flanking attacks while he did. It took him minutes, too many of them, to pick up enough scraps of equipment and metal to satisfy Bagman, and in that time he saw three of the Souther troops fall to the ground and only one of them managed to stagger to his feet again.

"Time's ticking," Helm said, as Rogue swept the ground for more refuse, the valuable detritus of war. "We're giving the traitor time to get away."

"What do you want me to do, leave them?" Rogue snapped, and Helm didn't have any reply to that. Another Souther fell as they watched, a fountain of blood rising from his mouth to splash out and obscure the mask of his chem suit.

Then, finally, the Sammies were ready, and after that taking the Hoppas down was just a matter of aiming and firing. Rogue left Gunnar where he was for the moment to mop up any Nort stragglers and ran towards the remaining Southers. There were only five of them now, and one of them, he suddenly saw, was Pietr. The boy was favouring his right leg slightly, looking like he'd taken a blow there, but he was alive. Rogue saw the former Nort smile at him behind his chem mask, the wild grin of battle. There was a new confidence to the boy, something Rogue hadn't seen in him during their brief time fighting side by side.

Only when he got to them did Rogue realise the reason the Southers hadn't been able to retreat. Behind them, looming so large it blotted out the sky behind it, was the outline of a Nort Blackmare tank. Rogue looked at it and cursed – there was no way he was getting past that in a hurry, no matter how many Sammies Bagman made for him.

"We'll take care of the Blackmare, Rogue," Pietr told him. "There should be a way in to the centre of the city through the storm drains. Take it and we'll cover your back."

Rogue hesitated a moment, but he knew that his was the most urgent mission so he sketched a quick salute back at Pietr, the same one the young soldier had given him, and then headed into the yawning mouth of the storm drain. When he was still running down it, the bitter rainwater that fled here from the parched surface of Nu Earth sloshing around his feet, he heard an explosion behind him about as loud as you'd expect when a Blackmare tank blew up, and he allowed himself a slight, grim smile. It seemed his faith in the young Nort hadn't been misplaced.

It also seemed like every damn Nort in the town followed him down there as soon as the smoke from the Blackmare's explosion had cleared, and they had enough decapitators and pillboxes with them to take out a whole regiment.

But not a regiment of Genetic Infantrymen. Rogue saw soon enough what the problem was: a hotel the Norts were using as a base of operations, pouring more troops out of its doors to face him than should have been able to fit inside it. He decided that they must have tunnelled beneath the place, connected it up to their network of supply tubes and drill-probe tunnels and deeply buried bunkers that had eaten through the surface of Nu Earth like a cancer. That meant the reinforcements they could pipe in through the hotel were effectively limitless.

Well, that was easily taken care of. "Micro-mines, Bagman, lots of 'em," he snapped.

He enjoyed the expressions on the Norts' faces as they saw the source of their advantage sealed up behind them, leaving them to face the blue-skinned monster in front of them alone. But he didn't enjoy it for long. There were still enough Kashans around to present a real threat. Beam weapons seared at him, brighter than the sunlight fighting its way through the chem clouds above him. There were drill-probes too, churning up the concrete of the street behind him when they found their way into the hotel blocked, and the ubiquitous Hoppas, strafing the street as he ran.

For a moment, he had to fight the urge to stay and kill them all, every single Kashan, to stain every one of their red chem suits with the red of their own blood. But if he wanted revenge, there was a better one to be had at the heart of the city, tantalisingly close now. The Kashans were enemies, they'd been doing what they were supposed to be doing, though with a brutality and a pleasure he'd never forgive, but the traitor was the man behind it all – and he was supposed to be on Rogue's side.

Rogue ran on, only taking out the troops who stood in his way, relying on Bagman to guard his rear and warn him when anyone was getting too close. Finally, he made it to the end of the street, so wired on the souped-up adrenaline with which the Gene Genies had filled his glands that the las beams of the Kashan's rifles had started to seem solid to him, as easy to dodge as the obstacle courses they'd set them back on Milli-Com, when he still hadn't known what real battle was.

One flick of his wrist, and he sealed off the entrance to the street behind him and suddenly there were no more Norts. The street ahead, the wreckage of the city, seemed empty, almost preternaturally quiet.

Rogue drew in a deep breath, pulling his mind back into his body from the strange place it floated when he lost himself in the fight. I'm a fighting machine, he thought. It was a phrase the Gene Genies had used often, but for the first time he fully believed it. He was a machine made to fight, but that didn't mean he didn't have choices. His body was a machine, but his mind was his own, and this revenge he was about to take was for him only, not for Kovert or Milli-Com, but for him, Bagman, Gunnar, Helm, Atlas, Zealot, Jitters and all the other GIs who were real people with real names, whatever the Gene Genies might have taught them.

Rogue could see it up ahead, the building that contained the man who could end this all.

"Nearly there, Rogue," Gunnar said, and Rogue thought he could hear some of his own feelings in his comrade's voice.

But he was a GI, and the fight was never really over.

"Look out!" Helm screamed, a micro-second before the shot struck, just soon enough for Rogue to leap out of the direct path of the bullet. It struck the ground beside him, shattering as no bullet should, and when whatever was inside it splashed out and onto Rogue's leg. It *burned*.

Rogue had never felt pain like it. He didn't think, up till that moment, he'd ever really known what pain was. Until then, he hadn't yet met anything that could really hurt him.

"Rogue, it's the same stuff they used to kill Helm," Bagman shouted, horrified.

The safest thing to do was retreat. The sniper – the master sniper, Rogue was sure, because Rogue had failed to finish him off before – could be hidden anywhere, and the street didn't really offer any cover.

But retreat wasn't an option. The traitor general lay ahead, and therefore so did Rogue's path. He ran, weaving, diving, and the glass bullets fell all around him, their uniquely lethal toxin spraying out, vaporising in the air so that even his lungs were filled with the hideous, tearing, burning sensation. The toxin dragged at his insides, telling him to slow down, fighting against him for control of his muscles and sinews, but he couldn't let it win.

The run down the street was the longest he'd ever taken, and when he made it he still couldn't quite believe he was safe. Though safety, of course, was relative.

"He's got us pinned down," Rogue said to the chips, his voice rough with pain. "Not sure how much longer we can last here." The fire had stopped for the minute – the ammo must be too precious to waste – but Rogue knew it would start again as soon as the sniper had found another perch with a clean shot. And beyond the end of the street, there was nowhere else to run.

"Not going to be a problem, GI," said a voice that wasn't Helm or Bagman or Gunnar, a voice he could hear both from his radio and from closer at hand.

Rogue snapped his head around to see Venus crouching in the street behind him, her leg still in bandages and her expression fierce. Then she gave him that crooked half-grin he knew so well. "I can help you."

"Venus!" Rogue said. "Get back, damn it, you're not well enough for battle."

"I'm well enough to cover your back!" she snapped back. "I've got a fix on his location but I can't get a shot off from here. I'll play decoy, let you get the shot in."

For a moment, Rogue thought about protesting. It was a risky strategy, risky as hell, and if anyone was going to set themselves up for target practice, it should be him.

"Let her do it, Rogue," Helm's voice said softly in his ear. "She's a soldier too."

Rogue wanted to argue, but Helm loved Venus, and Helm was right. She was a GI too, she had her own revenge to take, and he had no right to stop her taking it. He nodded. "C'mon guys, you heard what the lady said. Time to end this."

"And if you miss," Helm said, for Rogue's ears only, "the traitor won't have to kill you, cause I'm gonna do it for him."

Then Venus stepped out of cover, and time seemed to slow to a crawl, as if the black hole above them had suddenly drawn closer, warping and distorting every-thing around it.

Rogue saw Venus walk out, head held high, gun tracking imaginary threats, not a trace of fear in her face, though he could read it in the stiff set of her shoulders and the quick rise and fall of her chest as she breathed. He watched, finger itching on Gunnar's trigger, so tense it felt as if the muscles in his arms had tied themselves in knots.

"Where the hell is he?" Bagman grouched, but Rogue didn't have any attention left over for the words. All of it was on Venus, focussed in as narrow a beam as the energy rifles the Kashans carried.

Then, far from the angle he was expecting, over to his left, it came. There was too little time between the red flash of the sighting laser and the shot that would inevitably follow it, nowhere near enough time for Rogue to locate the source of the laser.

As if a part of his brain that had been sleeping before suddenly woke up, he just knew where the beam was coming from, high up on one of the grand, ruined buildings lining the street.

His own shot rang out before he'd even had time to send the message from his brain to his trigger finger.

For one horrible moment, he thought he'd missed. His body curled in on itself, waiting for the return shot to ring out and for Venus to fall, screaming in agony.

The shot never came. Instead, far above him, he saw the black dot of the sniper's body, growing and spinning as it fell to earth, until finally it smashed down on the rubble only a few metres from Rogue. The mask was entirely shattered, the flat hate-filled face inside fully revealed. Rogue's shot had taken it through the forehead.

"Gotcha," Rogue said, all the tension draining out of him.

Venus smiled over at him, more warmly than he'd ever seen. Then she put her game face back on. "Get going, Rogue. I'll keep you covered from here. And be careful. Kovert's up to something but I don't know what."

"Don't worry, Venus," Rogue told her. "Kovert and me want the same thing here." He picked up his radio and punched in Kovert's frequency. "I'm almost at the traitor's position."

A thousand metres away, safe from any danger, Kovert smiled, but only with his mouth. His eyes remained as cold and hard as pebbles on the toxic shore of the Orange Sea. "Excellent work, Rogue Trooper. You know what to do next."

He was very careful to ensure that the radio was switched off, the connection severed, before he turned to the Souther Hoppa commander behind him, a young man who'd risen fast through the ranks because he obeyed every order that was given to him. "Get your squadron into the air," Kovert told him. "You know what to do next."

THIRTEEN
THE TRAITOR GENERAL

There was no one to stop Rogue getting into the lift that took him to the very top of the vast building, but that was because they were all waiting for him there, rank after rank of them, ready to defend the man who should have been their enemy and had made himself Rogue's instead.

Rogue could see the traitor above him, perched on his balcony, and even from so far below Rogue thought that he could read the triumph in the man's scarred face. Rogue had crossed half a continent to find this monster – and he'd hidden himself behind defences that even Rogue couldn't penetrate.

Wave after wave of Norts came at him, snipers and Hoppas and decapitators and what must have been every last Kashan left on the planet. He took them out almost as an afterthought. There was only one thing he was interested in: the man on the balcony above him, shielding himself behind all these other lives, and behind layers of defensive shielding, too, but still visible and therefore still vulnerable.

"There's too many, Rogue!" Bagman said.

"Scan out, Bagman!" Gunnar snapped. "We can deal with anything the Norts throw at us."

"If I get you some Sammies," Rogue said, "can you take out the barriers the traitor's hiding behind?" Rogue asked.

"Sure thing, Rogue, but you're going to have to get higher to get any salvage."

Getting higher meant getting into the thick of the action, putting himself in a place where he'd be vulnerable from both sides. It didn't matter. If he stayed where he was, he could take out ten Norts, a hundred, a thousand even, but eventually he'd lose concentration for just one second and in that second they'd get him and the traitor would get away.

He had to take the fight forward if he was to win it at all. The air was thick with gunfire and the beams of the Kashans' rifles. Norts must have been dying in the crossfire but they didn't seem to care – the only thing they cared about was taking Rogue down. Rogue felt a bullet brush against his arm, so close it grazed the skin. Another came closer still, in and out of the soft flesh of his calf. It left a sear of white-hot agony behind it, but Rogue cut it out of his mind and kept on running forward.

The Norts' faces were hidden behind the insect-like masks of their chem suits, but he thought he could sense their fear. They'd thought they had him outnumbered, that here at last they'd found odds that even he couldn't beat, and maybe they had, but now they were realising that to take him down was going to cost more lives than they could have possibly imagined.

The ground was littered with the corpses of the Norts he'd killed, shotgun rounds when they grouped too close or came too near, machine gun bursts for the ones who hung back, thinking there was safety in distance.

Rogue felt another bullet pierce him, through the arm this time, then another, and a rifle beam took him through the chest, missing his heart by less than an inch. The thought that he had very nearly died floated somewhere in the periphery of his attention. He kept it there, along with the knowledge that the bodies around him had been people, with hopes and dreams and futures the same as any other human's. They weren't people to him now. They were just obstacles. Enemies.

And the biggest enemy of all was staying hidden behind the impenetrable screens of his defensive barriers, watching other men die for him. That was all about to change.

If he'd had time to think about it, Rogue might not have been able to do it. His body was injured, more seriously injured than it had ever been, despite the med Bagman was mainlining into his veins almost constantly. He shouldn't have been able to stand, let alone make it onto the low balcony running the length of the room. He shouldn't have been able to see straight, not with the blue blood running into his eyes from the gash on his forehead where a beam rifle had come within inches of taking his head clean off. He certainly shouldn't have been able to fire, again and again, with lethal accuracy, taking out the Kashans and the EMP units and the decapitators and the pill boxes which wouldn't stop coming after him.

He shouldn't have been able to make all the Sammies Gunnar needed, but he did. Then everything seemed to disappear from his vision, and all he could see were the great, reinforced sheets of metal above him, and the traitor who'd taken everything he'd ever known from him cowering behind them.

"I'm showing you the weak points," Helm said. "All you gotta do is aim and fire and the whole thing's gonna come down."

The world seemed to freeze into a moment of stillness. Rogue *could* see the weak points, the exact joints in the metal holding up the balcony where one clean Sammie shot would take out the whole structure.

He raised Gunnar to his shoulder and fired.

The world started moving again. The Sammies sheared straight through the metal, tearing it away with a shriek that was almost like a human scream. Behind him, Rogue could hear the Norts who'd been pursuing him so relent-lessly turn tail and flee. The wreckage from above was falling straight towards them, huge ragged chunks that would instantly crush anyone caught beneath them, and shards of steel that could tear through a chem suit in an instant.

Rogue didn't move. He only had a few seconds to take the shot, and there was literally nothing on Nu Earth that could stop him. His own life, even those of Bagman and Gunnar and Helm, were very small prices indeed to pay. It wasn't about revenge, not really. It was about honour, and memory, and all the GIs who'd been bred for war, but who might have lived to know something else, if it hadn't been for this one man.

Rogue raised Gunnar's sight to his eye. The traitor's face leapt into sudden sharp focus, horribly scarred, and now terribly scared. Rogue had never really thought about this man as a person before. He'd been a concept, a mission parameter, but as he stared at that ravaged face in his sights he could see the man beneath it, the man who'd had reasons for betraying the GIs, who probably believed he'd done the right thing.

Rogue saw the person underneath the persona, and he hated him. The shot was as clean as it could be while the ground shook beneath him with the arrival of more drill probes and the debris from the destruction he'd wrought – and he took it.

Through Gunnar's sights, he watched the traitor's expression as the bullet hit. Then the traitor was gone, falling away into the darkness behind him.

Rogue was already running towards him. "Let's go fin-ish this," he said, unable to believe that he might actually be able to, that in a few minutes his long personal quest might actually be over.

. . .

Pietr couldn't believe that the battle was over. His own sweat was rank in his nostrils, and his own breathing was so harsh in his ears that he couldn't hear his fellow Southers' cries of triumph.

Pietr looked around at the town which had been a wreck when they arrived and was now a ruin. He knew that the Norts weren't all beaten. They'd retreated inward, towards the centre of the city – towards Rogue. Pietr only hoped that they'd been able to delay them for long enough to buy Rogue the time he needed.

A Souther, a young boy called Quil, clapped Pietr on the back and smiled. "We made it," he said. "My first real battle. Yours?"

Pietr looked round, at the bodies and the blood and the mess that war left behind. "Yeah, it is," he said. The first battle I was fighting for the right side.

He knew that he'd finally become the soldier his brother had said he could never be. And it had been Rogue who had shown him how.

Pietr was still smiling at the irony of that when the bullet from a lone Nort sniper took him through the throat.

As his body lay cooling on the shattered street, a fleet of Souther Hoppas flew low overhead. The pilot of the lead Hoppa shouted into his radio, "We're locked into the GI's radio signals. Launching missiles!"

If Pietr had been alive to see it, he might have wondered, and worried, that Rogue was still in the line of fire, but there was no one left to care as the missiles streaked from inside the Hoppas, enough missiles to bring down the building ahead of them along with everyone in it.

Rogue found the traitor crawling away down a small side corridor like a wounded animal. Rogue's shot had taken him in the chest, but the chem suit had sealed itself over the wound and the general was still alive, clinging to life as tenaciously as any living thing that sees its final hour approaching and realises that it isn't ready to embrace the darkness quite yet.

The traitor turned his head when he saw Rogue approaching, an expression of fear struggling to make itself known over the tight, stretched skin of his burnt face.

Rogue holstered Gunnar and dropped to his knees behind his fallen enemy. "Traitor scum," he said, enjoying the flinch of fear from the traitor as he spoke. For any other man he might have felt a flash of pity, the hunter's pity for his prey – but not for this man. "Killing you won't bring the rest of the GIs back, but at least you won't be able to sell out any more of your own side."

He reached out, slowly enough to make sure that the general knew exactly what he was planning, and grabbed the air tubes feeding oxygen into the mask of the traitor's chem suit. For this man, he wasn't planning a quick or easy death.

His hand was half curled around the tube when Helm's voice screamed in his ear: "Rogue! Incoming air strike!" Even before Rogue had time to react, the missiles struck.

A giant invisible hand seemed to lift both Rogue and the traitor from the floor and fling them in opposite directions. Rogue made a last desperate grab for the traitor's air pipe as he flew, but though he felt his fingers brush it, he couldn't be sure that he had managed to rip it loose. The world was falling in around him, thousands of tonnes of masonry obeying gravity and coming down, and all Rogue could do was run, away from the collapsing building and the certain death within it.

Half an hour later, Rogue found Kovert exactly where he expected – dismounting from a Hoppa on the safe periphery of the destroyed building. Venus was beside him, looking like the battle she'd fought to come to

Rogue's aid had been more than was good for her. Her leg trailed behind her like a dead thing, but the main expression Rogue saw on her face was worry, not fear. He tried not to wonder whether the concern was more for him or for Helm.

"Spread out," Kovert said to the Souther infantry who dismounted beside him. "I want the bodies of the GI and the traitor found."

"Don't bother, Kovert," Rogue said with a small dry smile at the other man's start of fear. "I'm right here."

Kovert turned to find Rogue's rifle centred right on his chest. Rogue knew, of course, that killing Kovert would mean death for him, but right now he wasn't sure he cared. Another Souther who'd betrayed him. "Any reason I shouldn't pull this trigger?"

Rogue saw Venus frowning at him, her initial expression of relief transforming back to worry again, but he ignored her. Whatever happened to him, Venus would be all right, and he knew that he could safely leave the future of the GIs in her hands.

Kovert recovered quickly, snapping on his usual impassive mask as if his brief expression of panic had been no more than a trick of the light. "I had to make sure the traitor was located and killed," he said briskly, no hint of apology in his tone. "All other considerations were secondary."

"Meaning us," Gunnar said bitterly. "Typical Milli-Com thinking."

"Your mission's over, Rogue," Kovert continued, as if Gunnar hadn't spoken. "The traitor's dead and you've more than proved your worth at these kinds of operations." His tone softened as he saw that his words were showing no signs of cracking Rogue's granite facade. "I can help get the charges of desertion against you dropped, get new clone bodies grown for your three comrades." After a moment, when Rogue still didn't speak, he continued, perhaps more honestly, "It'll be what you deserve, a second chance for all of you."

Rogue knew what he thought about that, but he also knew that this was one decision it wasn't for him to make. The debacle with Sister Sledge had taught him that, if nothing else.

"Come work for you, you mean?" Gunnar grated. For once, his tone was neutral, and Rogue couldn't tell what the other GI was thinking.

"Sorry, Milli-Com man," Bagman said, and his contempt was clear. Rogue felt himself relax just a little.

"We're soldiers," Helm finished. "Not spies and assassins."

Rogue smiled – the kind of smile that made Kovert take a step back and Venus's expression shift into a combination of admiration and regret. "Looks like that's a 'no' then, colonel."

He turned and walked away, over the bodies of the many brave Souther men who'd died to allow him his chance to kill the traitor – a chance Kovert had snatched from him, denying him his final moment of revenge.

"You think you can fight this war on your own?" Kovert asked angrily.

Rogue glanced down, and realised that he recognised the face behind the chem mask beneath him, the gentle features harder now, hardened by a war he'd made the choice to fight with honour. Gently, Rogue reached down and removed the chem mask and brushed Pietr's eyes shut.

He didn't look back at Kovert as he continued to march on. "Why not?" he said, his words floating away on the toxic air of the only home he'd ever known. "It's the job we were created to do."

EPILOGUE

Of course, it wasn't over. On Nu Earth, it never is. As Rogue's figure retreated into the chem mists, behind him the remnants of the Souther forces were clearing through the rubble that Kovert's air strike had left behind.

One of them found something. "There's a body down here," the Souther said into his radio, still continuing to prod and dig through the rubble. He was glad, for once, for his chem suit; without it, the smell of death might have been overpowering. The place was a charnel house.

His commanding officer wasn't so delicate. He jumped down into the pit they'd unearthed and knelt down to turn the body over. As soon as he saw the chem mask and the insignia on the suit, he turned to face the others above him. "It's a Souther," he said excitedly. "Real messed up. You'd better call the medics!"

His men rushed away to obey.

Standing, facing away from the body, the officer didn't see it slowly rise to its feet. He didn't see the gun it drew and pointed at his back. And when the shot rang out, the clamour and ringing of the salvage work masked the sound entirely.

By the time the other Southers realised that something was wrong, the body was long gone.

ABOUT THE AUTHOR

Rebecca Levene was born in Essex, raised in Suffolk and now lives in London. She has worked variously as a researcher for a Labour Shadow Cabinet member, an editor of media tie-in fiction, and the story editor of *Emmerdale*. She is currently a freelance writer, with credits on shows such as *Family Affairs* and *Is Harry on the Boat?* Together with her writing partner, Gareth Roberts, she has a sit-com in development with the BBC and another with Tiger Aspect. She has also contributed to Black Flame with *Stontium Dog: Bad Timing* and *Final Destination: End of the Line*.